Praise for *The Silent*

WINNER OF THE BLOC
CRIME DEBUT PRI

'Heartbreaking and harrowing in equal measure.
Dr Jack Cuthbert is a brilliant, damaged genius you'll
want to follow to hell and back'

Pauline McLean, Arts Correspondent, BBC

'The central character perfectly expresses the damage of both
the period and his environment, and the author's pathology
background was skilfully deployed in this highly original thriller'

Tariq Ashkanani, author and Bloody Scotland judge

'Deliciously dark, vividly visceral, heartbreakingly harrowing'

Sharon Bairden, author

ONLINE REVIEWS

'There's a sense of doom, there's a complex and damaged
main character . . . vivid and well researched life of LGBT
people and the medical procedures'

Scrapping & Playing

'I couldn't put it down . . . Jack is a wonderful character'

Lyndas_bookreviews

'A fascinating yet gritty historical mystery with
complex and compelling characters'

Ljwritesandreviews

'Excellently paced and full of tension'

BooksbyBindu.com

'The true definition of an unputdownable page turner of a read'

ginger book geek

A Note on the Author

Allan Gaw studied medicine at Glasgow and trained as a pathologist. Having worked in the NHS and universities in the UK and the US, he took early retirement and now devotes his time to writing.

His non-fiction publications include textbooks and articles on topics as diverse as the thalidomide story, the medical challenges of space travel and the medico-legal consequences of the Hillsborough disaster. His debut poetry collection, *Love & Other Diseases*, was published in 2023 by Seahorse Publications.

The Silent House of Sleep is his debut novel and is the first in the Dr Jack Cuthbert series. You can read more about Allan and his work at his website: researchet.wordpress.com.

Also by Allan Gaw

THE
SILENT HOUSE
OF SLEEP

A DR JACK CUTHBERT MYSTERY

ALLAN GAW

Polygon

This revised paperback edition first published in Great Britain in 2025
by Polygon, an imprint of Birlinn Ltd. Previously published
by SA Press in 2024.

Birlinn Ltd
West Newington House
10 Newington Road
Edinburgh
EH9 1QS

www.polygonbooks.co.uk

1

ISBN 978 1 84697 720 6
eBook ISBN 978 1 78885 799 4

British Library Cataloguing-in-Publication Data
A catalogue record for this book is available on request
from the British Library.

Typeset by Initial Typesetting Services, Edinburgh

Printed and bound by CPI Group (UK) Ltd, Croydon CR0 4YY

For Ellen

Sunt geminae Somni portae, quarum altera fertur
Cornea, qua veris facilis datur exitus umbris,
Altera candenti perfecta nitens elephanto,
Sed falsa ad caelum mittunt insomnia Manes.

Two gates the silent house of Sleep adorn;
Of polish'd ivory this, that of transparent horn:
True visions thro' transparent horn arise;
Thro' polish'd ivory pass deluding lies.

Virgil, Aeneid VI 893. Trans. John Dryden, 1697

Chapter 1

London: 17 December 1928

The rich, oak-panelled room with its high vaulted ceiling of white stucco was designed both to impress and intimidate. High above the courtroom on the domed roof was the gilded figure of a Greek goddess, Themis. Her golden arms outstretched, she bore her sword in one hand and her scales to balance justice in the other. But, contrary to common belief, she wore no blindfold. Justice in this courtroom was delivered with open eyes, and the judge presiding had his fixed firmly on Cuthbert as he rose from the well of the court to take the stand.

This was the first glimpse the jury had of the expert witness. As he walked past their two enclosed rows of seats, what immediately struck them was his height. Some of the jurors were momentarily distracted from the gravity of the setting by the tall, good-looking man. He was dressed in a black, well-fitted, three-piece suit that showed off his broad chest and slim hips. His boots were polished to a mirror finish and his thick dark hair was oiled back and parted with precision. The only glint of colour was the rose gold of the watch chain on his waistcoat.

The ornate sword of state hung vertically above Mr Justice Avery's high-backed chair on the bench. It reminded everyone present that this man had the power of life and death at his disposal, handed him by authority of the king. Such symbolism was not lost on Cuthbert, but he had little time for the theatricality of the law. However, he did acknowledge the judge and his position with a short, business-like bow of his head, and before taking his oath, Cuthbert also turned to his right and similarly offered his respect to the jury. This was neither conventional nor expected, but Cuthbert was in no doubt as to who held the real authority in this court.

'I swear by Almighty God that the evidence I shall give shall be the truth, the whole truth, and nothing but the truth.'

'Please state your full name and profession.'

'John Archibald Cuthbert. Senior pathologist at St Thomas's Hospital and senior police surgeon with the Metropolitan Police.'

'Dr Cuthbert, please would you tell the court what you found during your examination of the body of Charles Edward Everett on the eighteenth of September this year?'

Cuthbert stood erect in the witness box. When he turned to the jury on his right, they caught their first sight of his gaze. His eyes were intense and deep blue, but they also possessed a warmth that was almost cordial. There were eight men and four women all now leaning slightly forward, waiting to hear what this man was going to say.

He spoke directly to them in a manner that no other witness in the trial had used. He brought them into his world and explained in just enough detail the pathological findings in the case. And he used language that was simple yet precise without ever being condescending.

When Cuthbert first came to work in London, he quickly acquired a reputation as an excellent expert witness. Barristers who called upon him knew that he would be an asset to their case. This was not because he was ever partisan, but because they relied on him completely to educate and inform the jury, and indeed the judge, on any and all medical matters. He never needed to consult his notes and was always fully briefed on every detail of the case. And, most importantly, the juries always trusted him.

When he was cross-examined, his expression never betrayed any annoyance at the often childish tactics of some of the barristers. He spoke in measured tones in his deep but soft Scottish accent. When he was grilled, he would occasionally glance over to the jury before answering the more outrageous questions put to him, as if to say, *We adults do have to put up with a lot from these children, don't we?* But he was always completely courteous and invariably thanked his interrogator before stepping down from the stand.

He was known to be unflappable, immovable from his conclusions and resolute in his considered opinions. He offered the courtroom confidence and assurance, which was especially welcome in complex cases such as this.

The prosecution alleged that Charles Edward Everett had been poisoned by his wife. She was now sitting across the court from Cuthbert, in the dock of the Old Bailey, on trial for her life. Her husband had died, apparently of natural causes, after a lengthy illness, and it was only when suspicions were raised by his younger brother that a call was made to exhume the body and have it re-examined. That post mortem examination had shown he had been the victim of arsenic poisoning. A further re-examination, however, had cast doubt on that conclusion. And it was that second post mortem examination that Cuthbert was now relating to the jury.

'Is it your contention, Dr Cuthbert, that Mr Everett died of natural causes rather than any unnatural poisoning?'

'It is not my contention; it is my conclusion. The body of Mr Everett was not poisoned by anyone other than the very ground in which he was laid to rest. The soil of the grave was rich in naturally occurring arsenic compounds. As may occur with any soil contaminants, these leached into his coffin and then into his body.

'I am not surprised that my distinguished colleagues found significant amounts of arsenic in his exhumed corpse. But assigning the origin of that poison to deliberate administration by the deceased's wife was erroneous. Mr Everett had clear evidence of extensive coronary artery disease, and although the state of the body at the time of my examination was poor, it was still possible to detect evidence of a large coronary thrombosis – a heart attack – that would ultimately have been the cause of his death.'

The judge as well as the jurors made notes as Cuthbert spoke, clearly delivering his expert testimony. When the pathologist had concluded, the judge turned his attention to the counsel for the prosecution.

'Your witness, Mr Carruthers.'

'M'lud. Now, Dr Cuthbert, are you really asking this court to believe that the victim, whose body was full of that vile poison, died a natural death?'

'My findings, sir, are based on the scientific method and have nothing whatsoever to do with belief. I am a scientist and I do not deal in beliefs. I deal in verifiable facts.

'Fact number one: the body of Mr Everett contained a high concentration of arsenic.

'Fact number two: the soil in which Mr Everett's coffin was interred contained even higher concentrations of arsenic.

'Fact number three: Mr Everett's exhumed coffin was heavily contaminated by arsenic absorbed from the soil. This absorption would have been promoted by the water-logged conditions of the grave and the thin, rather cheap wood used to construct his coffin.

'Fact number four: we initially hypothesised that Mr Everett's corpse in turn absorbed this arsenic from the contaminated wood of his coffin. To confirm this hypothesis, my assistant and I conducted a series of carefully controlled experiments in which we studied the rate of absorption of arsenic from soil samples into wood and thence into human flesh. We concluded that quantities sufficient to account for the concentrations of arsenic seen in Mr Everett's corpse could readily have been absorbed in the time period between interment and exhumation.

'Fact Number Five: Mr Everett's post mortem examination revealed conclusive evidence of his true cause of death, which was not consistent with arsenic poisoning.

'Therefore, I do not say I believe Mr Everett died a natural death: I know he did.'

Cuthbert looked again momentarily at the members of the jury. He said nothing except with his gaze – *I know you understand, but I wonder how many more times this little man in the wig will need it explained.*

Marjory Everett was gripping the rail on the raised dock in the centre of the court with both hands as she listened to Cuthbert's evidence. She had been in custody for the last three months and was now thin and weary. Her face was grey, her lips drawn, and there were dark circles under her eyes. She dared not hope that the expert's testimony might free her, but she was grateful that he alone seemed to believe in her innocence.

Cuthbert never once looked at the prisoner in the dock, focusing instead his whole attention on the barrister questioning him opposite and the jury on his right. He waited for the brief's next question and stared at him while he rifled through a sheaf of papers. The judge became irritated by the delay and urged him to proceed or allow the witness to stand down.

'Which is it to be, Mr Carruthers? My patience is short.'

'No more questions, m'lud.'

'Dr Cuthbert, thank you for your testimony. You may stand down.'

With that, the reporters in the courtroom were readying themselves for a swift conclusion to the trial. One or two were already reaching over the rail, trying to pass notes to Mrs Everett's lawyer in order to secure an exclusive interview with her when she was released. The lawyer read these and scrunched them up, scowling at the press benches as he did so.

Cuthbert did not stay in the courtroom to hear the outcome, for that was not what interested him. He regarded his task as one of examining the evidence in order to provide the truth of the matter. This was a truth that would only reveal itself through logical enquiry of the circumstances, careful evaluation of the physical evidence and detailed analysis of the human remains. When he delivered this truth, it was up to others to use it appropriately.

*

He left the Old Bailey, and as it was already almost five o'clock, he chose to walk back to his home in Bloomsbury rather than return to the hospital. The late afternoon air was cold and damp, and the pavements of London were still wet with the melting slush from the previous week's snowfall.

Cuthbert trod carefully to avoid the worst of it, but as he turned onto Fleet Street, there were large, dirty puddles of melting ice everywhere. He cursed his decision to walk. His boots, normally black and polished to the highest of shines, were already wet and dull. He shook his head in irritation, and before their condition affected him any further, he hailed a cab.

It would only be a short journey to Gordon Square and Cuthbert spent it bent over, trying to polish the worst of the slush away. However, the damp, dirty stains on his boots were refusing to yield to his handkerchief. He rubbed all the more, almost scratching the leather as his force became frantic.

Suddenly, he was caught by the bitter cordite burning his throat. He tried to swallow to rid himself of it, but his mouth was dry and his tongue was rough. His heart began to thump in his chest. The colour drained from his face. It was starting again. Taking great gulps of air, he shook his head from side to side, vainly trying to clear his mind of the noise and the gunfire. He flinched and cowered on the seat of the cab at the ear-splitting thuds of the exploding shells all around him. The cab driver was watching him in the rear-view mirror. His fare was sweating and shaking. He had seen it before but never in a gentleman like this.

'All right, guv'nor?'

Cuthbert could not speak to reply. He just gripped his briefcase close to his chest, trying to steady himself and hide the worst of it from the driver. Finally, he managed to nod and was relieved that they had already stopped outside his front door on the square. His hand was still shaking as he handed over the coins, and he did not wait for his change. Cuthbert fumbled his key into the lock before stumbling into his hallway and slamming the street door behind him. With the door at his back, he sank to the ground and waited for the horror to subside. It would pass, for it always did, but not before it had crushed a little bit more of him.

He was grateful at least that his housekeeper had been spared this sight of him. The attacks were now less common than they had been, but when they came, they always caught him unawares. For a man so guarded and always so much in control of his own feelings, that was the worst of it.

His heart was now slowing in his chest, but his hands were still shaking as he wiped the tears of the terror from his eyes. He struggled to his feet and found his way into the sanctuary of his study on the ground floor. It was too late to think about anything else.

Chapter 2

London: 17 December 1928

It was also too late for Detective Inspector Franklin to think about further work that day. He was sitting in a back office on the first floor of the Scotland Yard building on the Thames Embankment. He held the Scotch bottle vertically over his glass. It was all but empty, and he strained, trying to wring out the last drop like sweat from a rag.

The light had drained from the December sky, and he had to switch on his desk lamp to see. It created the only island of light in his shared office. He took the last sip, winced at its bitterness and carefully put the empty bottle and glass back in the bottom drawer of his desk. He slipped them under the heavy case files he kept there for the purpose.

He opened the one remaining file on his desk. It was a thin buff folder containing a handwritten top form and a couple of typewritten pages of report that provided the barest of information. There was also a small, black-and-white photograph clipped to the papers. Franklin had never met the smiling young man in the college scarf who looked up at him from the picture. And at this point in the investigation, he was not sure if he ever would.

Alfred George Dawson – Freddie Dawson as he was known to everyone – was 21 when he failed to come home on Monday 10 December 1928. He was a third-year student at University College London and lived at home with his parents, Alfred and Maud, in a quiet, unremarkable street in Hampstead. They reported him missing that evening, but given his age and the time of year – 'are you sure he won't have gone to some end of term party?' – his disappearance was not taken seriously by the police until almost forty-eight hours later. Only then were his classmates questioned, his last movements logged and his family interviewed.

'Has your son ever done this sort of thing before, Mr Dawson?'

'How many times do I have to tell you? I've been asked all these questions by your sergeant. No, he's never done anything like this before. He works hard at university. He's studying to be a lawyer and he's got some of his final exams in the new year. He didn't go to a party. He didn't go and stay with a friend. If he wasn't in the library, he was here. I'm telling you, that's all the boy did.'

'I know, sir, but he is twenty-one. Could there perhaps be a young lady?'

'Look, he's as normal as the next boy, but there's no one. He's not courting. He was completely focused on his studies. He knew there was plenty of time for all that once he graduated. Something's wrong here, terribly wrong. His mother is going out of her mind with worry now. She knows as well as I do that something has happened to our boy.'

D.I. Franklin, who was leading the missing person's investigation, did not usually take a personal interest in conducting next-of-kin interviews, but this one was different. The chief superintendent himself had been on the phone that morning wanting a progress report on the case. He had said that the father of the missing boy was in his lodge and that meant the brass upstairs wanted everything thrown at the case. The chief superintendent was, however, realistic about the task in hand.

'Look, Franklin, I know as well as you do the boy's probably gone off to get his leg over on a dirty weekend in Brighton, but we need to look as if we're pulling out all the stops on this one.'

The message was loud and clear – get out there and flash the warrant card.

As Franklin left the Dawson house in Hampstead and walked down the garden path, he turned back to take another look. It was very middle class and very ordinary in its own suburban way. The street was lined with houses all as large as the one he had just visited. Each was different in overall design, but all of them had large gardens, red tiled roofs and windows that were trying to evoke a Tudor past. To the casual observer every house on the street would look exactly alike. All apparently the same, except that inside number 18 there was a family that was disintegrating because of the thoughtlessness of a young lad. Franklin got into the front passenger seat of the police car and told his driver to get him back to the Yard.

*

By the fourth day, there was more intervention from upstairs. The phone calls made Franklin increasingly irritated and anxious in equal measure. However, it was unlikely that any real progress would be made.

Long experience in the job had taught him that if a young adult does not want to be found that was the way it was likely to stay. Nevertheless, to satisfy the chief superintendent, Franklin went back to the university to re-interview the boy's teachers and any of his friends he could find.

Dawson had a tutor who, based on uniform's earlier interview, seemed to know the boy better than anyone else they had spoken to. It would be best to start there. Dr Julius Gossett was in the law faculty, and, according to the notes Franklin had, he was a lecturer in criminal law. *Just what I need*, thought the inspector as he rapped on the office door.

However, the lecturer turned out to be quite unlike anything Franklin had imagined. He was young, articulate without being condescending and appeared to be genuinely concerned about the missing student. He was standing by the window when he invited the officer in and was leaning heavily on a cane. As he turned and walked across the room to welcome the inspector, his limp was pronounced.

'I'm sure you're thinking that there might have been some reason for his sudden disappearance. Some problem with his work or such like. But let me assure you, inspector, he was doing well, indeed very well. On track for a good second, perhaps even a first, and they don't get handed out too freely in this place, let me tell you. No, I can't see that it was his work. He certainly wasn't running away from anything here.'

'So you think he ran away, sir?'

'Oh, forgive me, inspector, I don't mean anything of the sort. I realise there are all sorts of possibilities here. Some indeed much more unthinkable than others. But I suppose it is one line of enquiry. No, I don't think it was his work.'

'But what about the other people here? Might Dawson have been running away from any one of them. Friends, say? Young women? A young woman in trouble, perhaps?'

'I know that sort of thing happens, but not in this case. Not here. That just wouldn't happen with Dawson. He wasn't like that at all.'

'It is my experience, Dr Gossett, that all young men are like that. Even those we might least imagine it of.'

'I bow to your greater experience, inspector. I'm just grateful that it's not mine.'

Gossett provided Franklin with a list of all Dawson's year group. He circled the four he thought the boy had been particularly close to. The interviews with each in turn revealed little that the inspector did not already know. As days five and six of the enquiry came and went, Franklin was honest with the chief superintendent that no progress had been made. He also doubted any would, given the nature of the case.

There were so many reasons a young man might want to run away from his family, or his work, or both. Even a young man as apparently unremarkable as Freddie Dawson. Everyone had secrets.

*

The file lay on Franklin's desk awkwardly open and askew. There were other cases that needed his input but this one, despite the futility of it all, kept drawing him back in.

He asked his sergeant to recheck the class listings and members of staff to ensure that all had been interviewed. Perhaps some had been missed in the early investigation. He, himself, decided it was time to revisit the family home in Hampstead and brief the parents on the progress of the case, or the distinct lack of it. The last thing Franklin wanted was a carpeting from the chief superintendent for lack of enthusiasm.

This time Mrs Dawson answered the door. When she saw the inspector, she grasped her hand to her mouth and shrieked. Her husband came rushing to her side, as Franklin tried to make himself heard.

'I'm sorry Mrs Dawson, there's no new development. I just called to ask a few more questions.'

Dawson senior frowned at the inspector as if to say, *You ought to know your job better than this*, but instead managed grudgingly to invite the officer in. The inspector apologised again, and after some tea and more soothing words, he tried to regain the trust of the couple. He outlined in detail everything that was being done to trace their son's whereabouts and to identify a motive, if any, for his disappearance.

Mr Dawson sat blank-faced and unimpressed. 'And you said you had more questions, inspector.'

'Yes, sir. I wanted to check with you if there was anything, anything at all, odd or unusual about Freddie in the days leading up to this. How was his mood? I mean did he do anything or say anything to either of you that when you think about it now seems strange? Sometimes when we cast our minds back at this stage, things that didn't register with us at the time can be significant.'

Mrs Dawson was still wiping tears from her eyes, although she had stopped sobbing. 'I can't think. Can you, Alfred? I mean he was just himself. Always rushing. Always with his nose in his books. He was looking forward to Christmas, I know that. The holidays, you know. He has exams when he goes back, but he said he was allowing himself a few days off his studies over Christmas. He was happy. I thought he was happy. I don't know what else to say. Alfred?'

'It's all right, Maud. The police just have to ask these sorts of questions. Don't fret about it, dear. The inspector's just going now, so we'll have some more tea in a bit. And then you can have a little lie down.'

He rose and fixed Franklin with the coldest of stares. 'Let me show you out, inspector.'

As the door was closed behind him, Franklin mouthed a quiet obscenity to himself and got back in the car. His driver tried to start a conversation about the December weather, but the inspector just shut him down. He needed some time to think about what his next move could possibly be.

Back at the Yard, his sergeant's report on the status of the interviews was on his desk. It appeared that three people who may have seen Dawson the day he disappeared had been missed. These were his dissertation supervisor, a Dr Pemberton, the university lodge porter, George Miller, who would have signed him out, and Clare Haskell, a classmate. The sergeant added that all three had been unavailable for the first round of interviews but were all now back on campus. Franklin, who had been reading the report standing and still wearing his hat and overcoat, turned on his heel and simply called back into the duty room, 'Detective Sergeant Baker, with me.'

*

The porter's lodge at U.C.L. was a small, almost hut-like structure just inside the university gates. It housed a desk, a large array of pigeonholes and an even larger set of hooks all with numbered keys. The lodge porter was seated at the window and was the first and last port of call for anyone entering or leaving the university complex from Gower Street. Franklin showed his warrant card as he asked the small, bald man if he was George Miller.

'Were you on duty here on Monday, tenth December, Mr Miller?'

'I was, right enough, from eight o'clock in the morning until five in the evening. That's when we close the gate, see.'

'And do you keep a record of those entering and leaving?'

'Just visitors. The staff and the students come and go as they please. Wouldn't be easy to keep tabs on all of 'em, would it now?'

'Indeed. We're interested in a particular student. We have

his photograph here, a Freddie Dawson. Would you remember seeing him that day?'

'I wish I could help you, sir. But the thing is they all start to look alike. If he came in, he must have walked past that window. And if he walked out, he must have gone the same way. More than that I couldn't say.'

Franklin did not even attempt to stifle his sigh.

'Thank you, Mr Miller, you've been a great help. Could you do one more thing and direct us to Dr Pemberton's room?'

In the east stairwell of the law faculty, the inspector and his sergeant found Pemberton's door ajar. Franklin knocked, then pushed the door open. Inside, the office was untidy. There were papers on the floor and strewn across two chairs beside the small fireplace. The inspector went in and started to look about, occasionally lifting piles and reading the headings to various papers.

Suddenly, standing in the open doorway was a small man.

'Can I help you, gentlemen?' The voice was sharp and did not sound in the least helpful.

'Detective Inspector Franklin of Scotland Yard, and this is Detective Sergeant Baker. We are looking for Dr Pemberton, Nicholas Pemberton.'

'I am he. What's this about? And what are you doing rifling through my papers?'

'Hardly rifling, sir, merely looking for a place to sit down and wait for you. We are investigating the disappearance of one of your students, Freddie Dawson.'

'Dawson? What do you mean disappearance? When did this happen? I've been in Bristol since last Tuesday, and I'm just back today.'

Embarrassed, Pemberton made a move to tidy away the papers. He invited the officers to sit down while he emptied the books that had been occupying his desk chair on to the floor.

'Please don't trouble yourself, sir, we only want to ask you a few questions. When did you last see Dawson?'

'That's easy. We have a meeting every fortnight on Monday afternoon at half past two. The last meeting was a week ago, here in this office. He was sitting right there where you are now. All the honours students have a dissertation to write as part of their assessment and they are assigned a supervisor. I'm his. What's happened to him?'

'That's what we're trying to find out, sir. Can you tell us about that meeting? Was there anything unusual about Dawson? Anything out of the ordinary? Did he seem like himself?'

Pemberton was starting to look concerned, and he was trying hard to recall that particular meeting, with that particular student, on that particular day.

'I don't think so,' he finally stammered. 'I see so many students, and to be honest it's difficult to remember. He was a good student though. Conscientious. Never missed a deadline and keen, you know. Always eager to do a good job. At least that's how I remember him. I say, you don't think something dreadful's happened to him, do you?'

'As I said, sir, we're trying to find that out. At the moment, we need to keep an open mind. That'll be all for just now, but if you do think of anything else, please give us a call.'

With that, Franklin handed his card to Pemberton, who read it carefully, still looking a little stunned by it all, and put it on top of one of the many piles of papers on his desk.

*

'Another waste of bloody space. Who's next, Baker?'

'The girl, sir. Clare Haskell. She should be in the refectory. She's expecting us.'

'Is she indeed? Well, you better not keep her waiting,

sergeant. I've had enough of this. Report back if you manage to get more than two coherent sentences out of anyone here. I'll see you back at the Yard.'

Franklin strode off across the university forecourt, past Miller at the lodge, who failed to notice him, and out through the gates onto Gower Street. Baker was relieved to be left on his own at last. He found the refectory, which was almost empty at that time of day, and had no trouble identifying the student. The large room was already decked in Christmas streamers, and Clare Haskell was sitting reading alone at a table beside the half-dressed Christmas tree in the corner.

'Thank you for waiting, miss. I'm sorry, it took us longer than expected with the other interviews.'

'Oh, don't apologise, officer, anything for Freddie. But you said "us". Where's the rest of you?'

'My inspector had urgent business back at Scotland Yard, miss. He sends his apologies. I'll be conducting the interview.'

'I am getting a lot of apologies today. Anyway, down to business. How can I help? I expect you want to know all about Freddie and his latest obsession.'

The sergeant looked up from his notepad and was surprised by the girl's eagerness. Most interview statements had to be teased out of witnesses, and apart from the occasional nugget, most were a complete waste of time. This one might be different. The girl looked to be around the same age as the missing person, which was unsurprising as they were classmates. She was alert and leaning forward, peering over her glasses, to check what Baker was writing. She frowned in annoyance when he stopped.

'Well?'

'Obsession, miss?'

'Freddie's dissertation, of course. Pemberton must have told you, surely. But knowing that one, he probably couldn't recall what day of the week it was. I mean, have you seen the state of his rooms? Anyway, Freddie was writing his honours dissertation. We all are, sergeant. And he had been working on domestic criminal cases during the war. You know the kind of thing – suspension of due process in time of conflict, shifting legal paradigms. The usual stuff. But during his research for it, he had come up with some interesting connections, I can tell you. Did Pemberton really not tell you any of this?'

The sergeant was busy taking notes and simply shook his head without looking up.

'Well, the long and the short of it is that Freddie had identified a gentleman who had worked at the Home Office during the war and was now retired. Don't ask me how he found him. He was very cagey about that. They were going to meet that day – the day Freddie went missing. Now, what do you say to that? There must be a link, don't you think?'

'And do you know the name of this gentleman, miss?'

'Oh no, Freddie was keeping that one to himself. Lovely boy, but not really a team player. I mean, a contact like that would have been a godsend to a few of us. They like the dissertation to show evidence of original research, you see. Can't just get it all from books. And an interview with someone like that, with inside legal knowledge and an historical perspective, would have been just the thing. No, Freddie was tight-lipped, but I do know when I saw him leave on Monday afternoon, that he was going to meet the man. I'm sure of it.'

'And what time would that have been, miss?'

'Our last lecture finished at four, and a few of us including Freddie were chatting afterwards. So I suppose it must have been about half-past.'

'And you believe he was heading straight away to this meeting with the contact?'

'Absolutely. We made some jokes about following him just

so we could steal his thunder, and he actually got quite cross. Told us in no uncertain terms to stay out of it. So he definitely had a meeting and that's where he was headed.'

'Can I ask if Dawson had any special attachments at the university?'

'You mean did he have a girl? Not Freddie, and besides there are very few of us around. Do you know how many women are in the third year of law, sergeant? Two. Two out of thirty-four. We're an endangered species in this place. Freddie was nice. Nicer than a lot of the other ones, and I got on well with him, but he was rather single-minded about the course. He did like girls if that's what you're thinking. Had the same look in his eyes as all the rest of them, but I'm pretty sure there was no one he was spending time with. Just his books. And the dreaded dissertation, of course.'

'One final thing, miss. Do you know of any reason why he would want to disappear?'

'Do you think that's what's happened? That he's gone A.W.O.L. and left us all here worried sick about him? Well, if he has, he jolly well better have a good explanation. But, no, I can't think of anything that would make him want to do such a thing. Although when you think about the alternatives, it might be best to believe he just ran away.'

'Did he have any enemies?'

'Freddie! Of course not. Who could possibly want to hurt Freddie? I mean, he was just Freddie, just one of the gang.'

The girl obviously cared a great deal for young Dawson, and the sergeant's questions had forced her to confront some difficult possibilities. She started to look concerned and was beginning to chew on her nails. Baker had to say something soothing, even if it wasn't true.

'Please don't worry yourself, miss. Many of these cases are often due to misunderstandings. There's every likelihood he'll show up next week, right as rain. You've been very helpful, Miss Haskell. If you should remember anything else you think might be important, do please call us.'

'I will. I say, sergeant, have you spoken with Michael Masters? He's another one of the third years and he knew Dawson as well as anyone. He'll be along shortly, in fact. The thing is, we're a bit of an item. Only don't tell him I said that – he'll be mortified. Oh, right on cue, here he is.'

An angular, young man with dark, almost Mediterranean good looks, strode across the refectory and bent down to kiss the girl on her cheek.

'Michael, this is Detective Sergeant Baker. He's asking about Freddie. Can you tell him anything?'

'Dawson? You mean our little stamp collector. He's not really that, sergeant – it's just what we call him. He likes order and completion, and he's ever so slightly dull.'

'Michael! Don't be horrid! Poor Freddie is still missing, and goodness knows what's happened. And he's not dull.'

'Oh, Clare, you know he is. And I'm sure it's nothing very exciting that's keeping him busy. Sorry, sergeant, not much of a help, I'm afraid, but there's really not much to tell.'

Back at the Yard, the sergeant typed up his report of the three supplementary interviews along with Masters' statement and left it on Inspector Franklin's desk. There it would remain along with the other paperwork relating to the case for the next six weeks.

Franklin had finally stopped receiving phone calls from upstairs, and he could afford to move on to other, often equally fruitless missing person cases. But the Dawson file still lay on his desk as a reminder of some very unfinished business.

In his experience, these sorts of cases tended to pan out badly. Even after the first few days of a missing person enquiry, unless there was any substantial lead, it was unlikely that there would be any meaningful developments. Until, that is, the person turned up either alive with some explaining to do or, more often than not, dead.

As he opened the file and absentmindedly turned over some of the pages, he found the small photograph that had been supplied by the boy's parents. Freddie Dawson was ordinary. He wore spectacles, was clean shaven and would have gone unnoticed in any crowd. He was like any one of the thousands of other young men in London. But something was different about him. Something had caused him to disappear that evening in December. Something had happened to him that needed to be explained.

Franklin closed the file as he did at the end of every day and pushed it slightly to the side of his desk. A large map of the city was pinned to the wall beside him. He looked up at it and whispered to himself, 'Where are you, lad?'

Chapter 3

London: 5 February 1929

The dog was barking more than usual. Charles Danvers called her back to heel repeatedly and was becoming irritated by her lack of obedience. Carrying the dog's lead coiled in his hand, he headed across the Common to retrieve her. As he approached, the black labrador was pawing at the ground and barking even more aggressively.

'What is it, Sheba? Come here, girl, and stop that racket at once.'

He reached for the dog's collar to pull her back. As he was attaching her lead, he saw the earth she had disturbed. Danvers was unable to make out what was in the ground, but it looked rough, and something was protruding. Sheba was still barking loudly and straining hard on the lead. He kicked at the confused mass of mud and last year's ferns and the protruding part broke off. It was only then that the smell rose to take hold of him. What he had kicked off was a blackened, rather bloated human hand.

'. . . and then you called the police, sir?'

'What else was I to do, officer? It was horrible. I didn't know what it was at first, but then I knew it had to be a body. There was such a stink. It was Sheba who found it. I don't know how much she disturbed it. I'm sorry about that. I certainly didn't touch it. I didn't have to – I knew there was nothing I could do.'

'Please don't distress yourself, sir. There are just a few more questions to ask, if you don't mind . . .'

Detective Sergeant Baker had switched shifts and found himself on an early that day. He was now sitting with Mr Danvers on the park bench, taking his statement. All the while, the labrador, still scenting what she had unearthed thirty yards away, was straining to get back to it. Baker, who had already seen what the dog had discovered, was pleased he only had a human nose. He was already feeling sorry for the pathologist who would be called out to deal with it.

*

Across the city in Gordon Square, Jack Cuthbert sat suddenly upright. The bedlinen was damp with his sweat, and the stillness in the bedroom was broken by his explosive gasp for air. The throb of his racing pulse bounced back from the walls through the darkness. As he fought to catch the end of his breath, he woke to where he was. His respiration calmed and slowed. There was the outline of the bed and the wardrobes, the chair by the window and the lamp by his side.

He reached over, found the switch and started from the instant glare. The noise in his head was subsiding. The sounds of the wounded disappearing into the fog of morning were fading, and the shells were silenced with the arrival of a winter sunrise. There was the faintest of glows around the edge of his curtains. Without looking at his watch on the nightstand, he knew that it was time to get up, and as always, he was relieved.

When the phone rang, Cuthbert was still shaving. A call that early usually only meant one thing, so he towelled off the last of the soap, folded his razor and put on his dressing gown. His housekeeper would answer the phone but would be calling on him any moment. When he went down, he passed Madame Smith in the hallway. She simply nodded in acknowledgement and handed him the receiver.

'Cuthbert.'

'Good morning, doctor,' said an inappropriately jovial voice from Scotland Yard. 'We have a body for you, sir. Not a pretty sight this one, and whiffy. I'd skip breakfast if I were you.'

'I need the location, constable. What I do not need is your insolence.'

'Sorry, sir. Just trying to find the lighter side.'

'Does a decomposing corpse have a lighter side? Much as I would like to hear your philosophy of death, constable, the location, if you please.'

*

When Cuthbert arrived at the Common, the uniformed officers were gathered across the expanse of grass near a small copse of trees. They were clustered around a hollowed area about twenty yards from the pathway. He strode towards them and was immediately recognised by Sergeant Baker whom he had previously met under similar circumstances.

'Good morning, Dr Cuthbert. The remains are just over here, sir. They were discovered at around half past six this morning by a dog walker. The dog has caused some disturbance, but it looks to be minimal. Otherwise, the scene is untouched in accordance with your standing instructions.'

'Very good. And, of course, good morning to you too, sergeant.'

Cuthbert walked on ahead of the sergeant, towards the find, and Baker was reminded just how tall and broad the man was. Both men were in their early thirties, but that was almost all they had in common.

When anyone at the Yard spoke of Cuthbert, what they usually talked about were his boots. They were always polished to a mirror-like gloss. Baker had also always admired his clothes, which he could see were expensively cut and well pressed. But, more importantly, he was pleased to have this pathologist on the case because he always gave out an air of calm authority. Indeed, he had a reputation at the Yard as the most meticulous of all the police pathologists.

Cuthbert's ideas of crime scene management and his methods were thought by some to be mere affectations. They would even on occasion say as much out loud. Others failed to understand his requirements. Baker was not one of them. He had already worked with Cuthbert on several cases over the last months and had been impressed by the towering Scotsman's approach. Today, he set out to ensure that he had everything he needed to work the case. Baker's own job would be that much easier if he let the doctor do his because Cuthbert also had a reputation for getting it right.

As expected, Cuthbert's first action was to take the attending constables aside and brief them on how he wanted the scene protected. They were to rope off the area and station themselves around the perimeter to prevent any intrusion.

Next, as part of his routine, Cuthbert changed from his overcoat into a white coat. From his bag he took a pair of rubber gloves, two metal probes, a notebook and a pen. Using the probes, he began to separate away the mud and bracken to reveal more of the body. Regularly, he would pause to make notes on the numbered pages of his book, neatly recording every detail of the work in black ink.

Half an hour later, relatively little had been uncovered, such was the slow and painstaking way in which Cuthbert worked, but there were already two pages of notes. Sergeant Baker was expecting Inspector Franklin at any moment, as the news of the discovery on the Common would have reached his desk by now. Right on schedule, a police car drew up at the north gate and Franklin got out.

'Just to let you know, Dr Cuthbert, Inspector Franklin is on his way over.'

Cuthbert did not break his concentration but did register the faint alarm in the sergeant's voice. He was well aware of the inspector, and there was no love lost between them. His work was not fast enough for Franklin, who wanted quick answers, even if they were the wrong ones. As the inspector approached the rope cordon, he hitched it up and was irritated that he still had to stoop to enter.

'So what's the story, doctor?'

'Good morning, inspector. Do watch where you're putting your feet, won't you?'

'I don't have all day, sir.'

'Well, I'm afraid you're going to have to be patient for this one.'

'Is it Dawson?'

'Dawson?'

'Missing person in December, male, early twenties, student, average in just about every way.'

'No, I would say it is unlikely to be your Dawson.'

'How can you be so sure?'

'Well, for one thing this is the body of a much older man, say in his sixties. Also, from a very preliminary assessment, the deceased was short and probably overweight. However, as you can doubtless see, inspector, nothing is that clear, as yet. I need to get the remains out of the ground and back to the slab. And given the state of decomposition, that needs to be done very carefully. Only after a thorough examination in a good light, will I be able to start giving you some answers.'

The inspector said nothing more and just winced at the smell that was beginning to rise more strongly from the body. It was a stench he had endured too often in his career. He turned to go, unsure if he was relieved not to have to pay another visit to the Dawsons in Hampstead, or disappointed that he still had an open missing person case on his desk. Either way, the body would not be his to worry about. If it turned out to be a homicide, it would be the responsibility of Mowbray. He was a 'young Turk' who had recently been promoted to chief inspector, and another one that Franklin despised.

Within the hour, another visitor arrived at the scene, but this one knew better than to barge in unannounced. The young man waited outside the cordon and asked Cuthbert if it was convenient for him to enter. Cuthbert did not need to look up from his work. His assistant's voice was well-known to him.

Simon Morgenthal was almost everything that Jack Cuthbert was not. While Cuthbert rarely smiled at work, the younger doctor found it hard not to beam almost constantly. His disposition was sunny and could occasionally be especially wearing if Cuthbert was not in the mood. Today was one of those days.

'Good morning, Dr Cuthbert. What a lovely day, don't you think? There is a definite hint of spring in the air. Early this year, I would say; after all it is only the beginning of February. Who knows? We might have daffodils in Russell Square before long. I think there may be a chance of a light shower later in the afternoon though, but for the moment we have clear skies to enjoy.'

Cuthbert said nothing because he was used to his assistant's meteorological obsession and his verbosity. He was also acutely aware of Simon's latest cause for happiness as the young man had been unable to keep it to himself for weeks. It might be best to get that out of the way as well, if they were ever to get any work done.

'Thank you for the weather report, Dr Morgenthal. Now, would you like to give me an update on your impending nuptials? I do worry that I might have missed something crucial since yesterday's briefing.'

Simon Morgenthal was, as ever, delighted to talk about his fiancée Sarah and about their forthcoming wedding in all its detail. 'I cannot tell you how excited we both are, sir.'

'That is a pity. I was so much hoping to hear more about the precise level of your excitement and of course that of the delightful Sarah. Maybe tomorrow, eh? But never mind, perhaps we'll just need to do some work instead.'

Morgenthal was still smiling at the thought of his big day. He was artless enough not to notice the sarcasm in Cuthbert's voice, and with the same buoyant lilt, he asked, 'Shall I prep for the soil sampling, sir?'

The young trainee pathologist was only a year out of medical school and had come almost by accident under the tutelage of Jack Cuthbert. There was a family connection that was almost too tenuous to have mattered, but the timing had been right, and despite Cuthbert's initial reservations, he soon discovered that the junior doctor was hard-working and eager to learn. And he also found him very easy to look at.

Morgenthal had raven-black hair and despite still having a boyish glitter in his eyes and a blush on his cheeks, his face wore a rich, dark stubble. He was that perfect combination of youth and maturity that Jack Cuthbert found so attractive. Added to that, he was almost as tall as Cuthbert, which was unusual, and he clearly carried an athletic physique.

Everything about him drew Cuthbert's gaze. But that is as far as it would ever go. In truth, Cuthbert's feelings about men had never advanced beyond the stage of the adolescent crush. He found himself watching, wondering, wishing but always in silence and never saying or doing anything more.

Throughout his life, he had wrestled with such feelings, which, with every passing year, he saw as more and more inappropriate. But if he could not truly accept himself for what he was, how might he ever find the maturity in that part of his life that his peers had long since attained?

His sense of romance, of love, of longing was locked in time, and he looked at Simon Morgenthal and all the others, through the eyes not of a grown man, but of a 14-year-old boy. And while he knew exactly what he was feeling when he watched the young pathologist sitting each day at the laboratory bench in his department, he would never once give it a name, even in the privacy of his own thoughts.

*

As the two doctors worked steadily on the corpse, three unusual features became obvious. First, there were no remnants of clothing associated with the body, suggesting that the deceased was naked when deposited in the ground.

Second, there was also evidence of some form of ligature binding the wrists behind the body, which Cuthbert now ascertained was clearly lying face down in the ground. That fact immediately confirmed that no natural cause might explain this death.

And third, which was the oddest of all, some parts of the body appeared much more decomposed than others. Such differentiation was not in itself unheard of, but here in the uniformly damp earth, it was difficult to explain.

As Cuthbert continued scraping away the soil and debris enveloping the corpse in its shallow grave, he stopped suddenly and surprised his assistant.

'I'll be damned!'

In the six months that Morgenthal had worked with Cuthbert, he had never once heard him swear. What might have prompted it?

'Come here and look at this, Simon.'

Cuthbert stepped back to allow his assistant a closer look and said, 'What do you see?'

Morgenthal wasn't at all sure what he was looking at because the dark mud and the decomposing human flesh were intermingled, making it almost impossible to tell the one from the other.

'It looks like the foot, sir,' he proffered, as much as a stab in the dark as a certainty.

'And how many toes?'

Morgenthal looked at him. Was he playing games? But Cuthbert's expression was anything but playful.

'Five, sir.'

'Count again,' snapped Cuthbert and took up his notebook.

Morgenthal looked carefully at the mess in the ground. Trying not to get too close to the smell that was becoming almost overpowering, he tallied up to five. Then his eyes widened. There were three more poking through the mud.

'Eight, sir, but they don't all seem to be attached to the same foot.' Morgenthal was confused but was trying hard to appear professional even though he was still wondering if this was some sort of strange joke.

'Precisely, and thus what do you conclude from your observations?'

The young man thought hard before he spoke, not wanting to appear foolish. 'That there has been some disturbance of the post mortem remains causing three toes of the other foot to be detached and misplaced in situ.'

'Or?' droned Cuthbert.

Now, Morgenthal was struggling. What else could he say other than that the deceased had eight toes? This would be preposterous and, should he suggest it out loud, might ensure the abrupt end of his apprenticeship.

Finally, he opted to tell the truth. 'I do not know, sir.'

'Or, laddie,' said Cuthbert with an uncommon smile, 'that this is not one corpse. Shall we do a little more digging to find out if I'm right?'

*

Both doctors worked at the site for the next few hours, drawing increasingly mournful looks from the police constables stationed around the cordon. Baker was used to it, but even he thought this was unusual. Finally, he steeled himself and approached Cuthbert.

'Sir, sorry to disturb you. It's just that the men will need a break. Should I arrange for a shift change or do you think . . .?'

'Do I think, sergeant, that I'll ever be done here? A very reasonable enquiry, but I'm afraid this one, or should I say, these ones are going to take longer than usual.'

'There's more than one body, doctor?'

'Indeed, sergeant. And that's what's taking the time. But you're right, the men need a break. Can I suggest you send them off in pairs to eat and whatnot, and leave the others? I estimate we should be ready to move the bodies in another hour. Maybe two. The complication is that they have decomposed into each other, and they can't be separated without damaging them further. I need them intact in order to have the best chance of establishing the facts.'

Sergeant Baker's interest overcame his sense of smell, and he leaned in to look at the corpses. He found it hard to discern what he was looking at, such was the mangled and muddy mess before him. Whatever it was, however, this was going to be a long investigation and rushing it right at the start was unlikely to help.

'Of course, sir. Take all the time you need. I'll organise things to protect the scene.'

Cuthbert was already back at his work and without looking up he said quietly, 'Good man.'

Morgenthal was working at the bottom end of the trench and had unravelled the mystery of the toes, having now cleared away the soil to reveal the second pair of feet beneath the first. From the position, it appeared that the two corpses had been deposited in the ground face-to-face and lying on top of one another. Nothing about this extraction was proving to be straightforward, but the junior pathologist was determined to do the best job he could, if only to redeem himself in the eyes of Cuthbert.

Despite his cheerful exterior, Simon Morgenthal was a worried young man. He was concerned that he was not good enough. He had only been a doctor for a short time and had yet to prove his worth both to himself and his profession.

He had not been able to believe his luck when he landed the job with Dr Jack Cuthbert, but each day that they worked together made him realise just how much he had to learn. The intellectual gulf between the two men also seemed unbridgeable. Cuthbert's mind worked quickly, even if his hands were meticulous and slow. So quickly, that Morgenthal often found that he was still trying to work out what he was looking at while Cuthbert had already taken several steps ahead.

Like all very clever people, Cuthbert failed to understand that others found it difficult to see what to him was obvious. As a result, he would often forget to explain the steps in his logic. Thus, Morgenthal would frequently struggle to see the connection between one thought and another as Cuthbert argued a point. Apparently jumping at random from one idea to the next, Cuthbert was actually following a very clear path through a problem in his mind. However, because of its speed, he was only revealing part of the process to those around him. His assistant misinterpreted this as clear evidence of his own weaknesses rather than as an indicator of Cuthbert's remarkable strengths. And he worried.

It was difficult for him to talk about, even to his new fiancée. Instead, he just kept up the facade, hoping that his proximity to Cuthbert would allow something to rub off.

*

It was almost another three hours before Cuthbert finally gave permission for the remains to be removed to his department at St Thomas's.

It would be years before the pathology department at the hospital would house anything like a forensic laboratory, but Cuthbert had already made great improvements. The laboratory was immediately adjacent to the dissection room and now served a number of purposes. Initially, it had been used solely for the preparation and mounting of tissue specimens before they were examined under the microscope. But, since Cuthbert's arrival, he had arranged for an array of new apparatus to be installed.

The glass-fronted oak cabinets now housed a collection of specialised glassware, tubing and reagents for chemical analyses. The latest comparator microscope took pride of place, allowing Cuthbert to analyse the markings and striations on bullets. And a large array of specialist textbooks filled the shelves.

Increasingly, Cuthbert saw his role as much more than simply a man with a scalpel dissecting a corpse to pinpoint the cause of death. Unfortunately, the mere physical remains he had to deal with were often unforthcoming in that respect, and more detailed investigations were needed. He had thus expanded his remit and was excited by the possibilities that it afforded.

No longer were his only instruments the scalpel, the mortuary scales and the microscope. Now, he studied the chemical composition of his corpses. He analysed their stomach contents, tested for poisons and even typed their blood using the latest ABO system. And beyond that he had already seen even greater possibilities.

The same sort of analyses might be carried out on samples left at the crime scenes. He tested the composition of blood splashes, or perhaps even identified unknown fluids or materials, even individual hairs and fibres that previously would elude all but the sharpest eye. And he was confident that the future would likely bring even better tools for his profession. He would often rhapsodise about that prospect with his assistant.

'Science will ultimately give us the tools we need to solve all the problems that perplex us today. One day, Simon, we'll be able to match a blood stain irrefutably to a victim, or a trace of tissue to an assailant. Our unique identity lies hidden somewhere inside every one of our cells, you know. When we unravel that code, a whole new era of forensic medicine will be upon us. But until that day, I suppose we'd better keep the Bunsens lit and the scalpels sharpened.'

*

Wrapped in a mud-splattered tarpaulin, the human remains were now carried into the dissection room at St Thomas's by four uniformed constables and placed on the slab. The combined weight of the bodies and the associated soil that still adhered to them was considerable, and the oldest of the constables was breathing heavily with the effort.

Cuthbert was completely focused on the work in hand. He often had little time for the living and their temporary problems when he was confronted with such a complex forensic puzzle. And in this instance, he did not even notice the man clutching his left arm. However, his assistant did and could see the man, now pale and sweating, was in considerable pain. Morgenthal went over and sat the constable down on a chair. He instructed one of the others to get him a glass of water, while he loosened the collar of the officer's uniform.

'It's nothing, sir. Happens regular like. It'll pass – it always does. I just need one of me little pills to pop under me tongue. They're in me top pocket.'

'Take your time, constable. Here they are. Just take one, mind.'

Morgenthal had fished the small round box from the constable's uniform pocket. He handed him the glyceryl trinitrate which he had been prescribed for his angina and said, 'You need to take it easy. Just sit there until you get some relief.'

Cuthbert was busy assessing the position of the remains on the slab and was oblivious to the concern his assistant was showing the constable. When he looked up from the corpses, which he had now unwrapped, he was surprised still to see a uniform in his dissection room. Courteously but firmly, Cuthbert said, 'That will be all, constable. If we need you again, we'll call.'

'Dr Cuthbert, a word, if you please.'

Cuthbert was surprised by his assistant's tone and the grave expression he wore.

'This gentleman needs to stay here for a moment, sir. The exertion of carrying the remains has brought on an attack of angina pectoris. I have administered G.T.N. sublingually, and the chest pain is subsiding, but I recommend he is given further time to rest and recover.'

Cuthbert almost smiled, enjoying the earnestness of the young man. However, he checked himself, lest it be misunderstood. Morgenthal was still trying hard to impress him, and Cuthbert did not want to relieve him of that desire. The young man would only advance if he was driven on by it.

'Very good, Dr Morgenthal. I will be in my office if you need me, but you do seem to have it all under control.'

*

At his desk, Cuthbert read over his field notes. He started to make small corrections here and there. He had recovered many bodies from crime scenes, including shallow graves like the one he had just attended, but none had been as complex as this. Never before had he had to deal with two corpses in one grave. And never in such an orientation.

There was a list of questions that his examination of the remains had to answer. He started to write them on the next page of his notebook to help him order and clarify the difficult task ahead.

1. Identify corpse A (superior)
2. Identify corpse B (inferior)
3. Estimate times of death of both corpses A and B
4. Diagnose causes of death of both corpses A and B
5. Explain the anomalous pattern of decomposition observed at crime scene
6. Identify the connection between the two victims

He paused and then completed his list with a final action.

'Yes,' he said, 'that's the point of everything else.'

Just before closing the book and changing into his dissection apron, Cuthbert re-read his list and underlined his last item:

7. Identify who killed these men

He then recalled the words of his most eminent teacher,

Professor Harvey Littlejohn. They were words that had been drilled into him day after day in Edinburgh.

'The specialist in forensic medicine is not a detective. Your job is to gather the evidence afforded you by the crime scene; it is for others to use that evidence to catch the killer.'

Despite having worked in his specialty for the last twelve years, he still found that distinction a difficult one to acknowledge. But it was always dangerous to stray beyond one's area of expertise. 'Let the cobbler stick to his last,' his old professor would say, as the excitement flared in Cuthbert's eyes when he speculated about a murderer's identity, or even their motives. Cuthbert took up his pen again and scored through the last two items on his list.

'Indeed, professor, for someone else to sort out. I'd better stick to my last.'

The three years Cuthbert had spent working in Professor Littlejohn's department at the University of Edinburgh had shaped his career. It was there that he had learned everything he now knew about forensic medicine.

However, he had first encountered the man who would later become his mentor several years earlier. At the time, the world was on the brink of war and Cuthbert was a conflicted young medical student. Littlejohn was Dean of the Medical Faculty, and as it turned out, he was just as troubled as his student.

Chapter 4

Edinburgh: 5 August 1914

Joseph Sebastian Troy was not average. He walked down George IV Bridge from the medical school with great strides, his tousled mop of red hair bobbing high above everyone he passed.

The leather satchel he carried was heavy with books, and under one arm he clutched a sheaf of notes. He turned to see if his companion was keeping up. Cuthbert was almost as tall as him, and they had gravitated towards each other at the start of their first year almost as much because of their shared height as their affinity for each other's smile.

Troy called on his friend to hurry up and Cuthbert ran to his side.

'What an adventure this is going to be, Cuthie. Do you realise how great an opportunity this is? I mean, I can't believe how lucky we are. A war, a bona fide war, just for us.'

Troy was walking faster than usual, but as was his habit, he would never look where he was going. He had come to expect people on the pavement to notice him and give way. Cuthbert listened as Troy talked loudly into his face and became more and more animated.

Although encumbered with his bag and papers, Troy still managed to add flourishes and underline his comments by waving his arms. All this made him an even greater hazard on the street, and Cuthbert was relieved when they arrived at their digs, half-way down the hill of Victoria Street. Their rooms were on the top floor, but the flights never presented any problem to the two young men who took the stairs three at a time.

'So what are you going to do, Troy?'

'It's obvious. We need to enlist as soon as possible. This show's going to be over almost before it's started. If we don't get out there, we'll miss the damned thing. And I'm not going to miss out on this. Not for anything.'

'And our studies? I mean, the new term starts in a few weeks. Surely, that comes first. After all, we'll be going into fourth year. Wouldn't it be better if we finished up here and offered ourselves as doctors?'

'Don't be such a frightful twit, Cuthie. You'll only miss a term. They all say this will be over by Christmas – maybe sooner if we're unlucky. And you think you've got time to swan around in Edinburgh for two years? You're not thinking straight.'

Troy saw the worried expression on his roommate's face; he was becoming irritated by his lack of enthusiasm. Cuthbert sat on his bed staring at the floor while Troy was rummaging through his chest of drawers. He wasn't sure what he was looking for so failed to find it and slammed the drawer closed.

'Look, you're not trying to tell me you don't want to go, are you? You jolly well have to come. I mean, it'll be such an adventure. You can't want to miss out on it. King and Country and all that, old man. And, besides, it's not as if it's going to be bloody. Probably see more of that if you stay here with old Prof. Baxter. Come on, what do you say?'

Cuthbert looked up at his friend, but Troy didn't wait for an answer. He started putting the books and lecture notes that he had been carrying away on the shelf above his bed and pulled out the leather suitcase from under it.

'I wonder what they expect you to take. Never mind, I'm sure I'll find out tomorrow.'

*

The next week was a difficult one for the friends. As the days passed, Troy's excitement grew with the same fervour as Cuthbert's concerns. The latter had worked hard to get into medical school and was now working even harder to stay there. The idea of tossing it all away for the sake of a jolly in France in a uniform for a few months was incomprehensible.

In the dark bar they frequented in the Grassmarket, the table talk had all turned to the war. More and more students were now back in Edinburgh for the coming term, and over his beer, Troy found many more like-minded young men. Although Cuthbert tried to balance the discussions that would almost invariably end in patriotic song, neither Troy nor the others could be dissuaded. He felt himself being swept along with their talk of a once-in-a-lifetime adventure and started to wonder if he was the one at odds with the times.

Before making any final decision, Cuthbert thought it would at least be prudent to discuss the matter with the university. He asked for an interview with Professor Littlejohn, who surprised Cuthbert by agreeing to see him almost immediately.

'Mr Cuthbert, you are not the first to come to my office with this question, and I only wish I had a clearer answer for you. Young men, even educated young men such as yourself, are uncommonly keen to throw away everything for the sake of some excitement. This is regrettable. I do not doubt there are strong feelings of patriotism and honour at play, but what of the honour of your chosen profession? You, sir, will be a physician. There is no higher calling, and if I had my way, we would leave this war for lesser men to wage. You will have much greater battles to fight. You will be crossing swords with disease, and let me assure you that is a war that will not be over by Christmas.

'On a very practical level, I am of the opinion that you and your fellow students would serve the war effort much more effectively if you were to complete your course of studies and enter the fray as medicals. It would be an obscene waste for you simply to join the rank and file.

'Having said all that, if you do decide to take the King's shilling, neither I nor anyone else in the faculty will stand in your way. Should you decide to stay, I would urge you to take advantage of the Officer Training Corps. I myself will be leading this, and I expect a very good showing from the students in the medical faculty. As ever, we must lead the way. These are unprecedented times, young man, and they doubtless call for unprecedented actions.'

The messages were mixed, but there was little opportunity for further discussion, and Cuthbert went out as confused and conflicted as he had come in.

He left the Dean's office and walked across the Meadows to clear his head. By the whalebone arch, a troop of scouts was practising in preparation for the forthcoming parade along Princes Street. The afternoon sun was glinting on the polished brass of their horns, and there were noticeably more flags flying from the buildings in Edinburgh. The stall holder of the tea hut beside the tennis courts was putting up bunting, and even the birds were singing a little louder. All around him there was a heightened sense of the moment, but it was a moment he did not feel any part of.

He walked home past shop windows that were preparing

for victory and honour, and he saw his first young soldier in uniform. The private was younger than Cuthbert and his clean khaki appeared ill-fitting, but he was holding his head up and garnered looks of appreciation from all he passed. That was what Troy and the others wanted, that sense of manly pride, and Cuthbert saw its allure. But he also had to weigh it against the price he might have to pay in the disruption to his studies.

The quad of Old College was still quiet at that hour of the morning out of term, and Cuthbert took himself around the lawn on his way to the Playfair Library. He found a seat by the window without difficulty and spread out his books. He had skins in the first term of the new year and wanted to get a head start. Troy, who would usually be sitting across from him at this library desk, had called off. He had not been to the library at all over the last ten days, and Cuthbert had had to get used to studying alone for the first time since they started medical school.

Troy had already been to the recruitment office in Cockburn Street and signed up. He had been given his instructions and would be joining his battalion for basic training the following week. He would not be starting the new term with Cuthbert, and instead he used the time to pay a visit to his family in Harrogate. Cuthbert expected him back in Edinburgh the next day, where Troy would be spending just twenty-four hours before embarking.

Cuthbert had disappointed his friend more than angered him by his decision to stay on at university. Troy had wanted him to join up and come along 'to share the adventure together'. And now they would both be alone – Cuthbert in the library and Troy on a train to somewhere unspecified. Perhaps he had made a mistake. Perhaps Littlejohn had really been telling him to go and fight. Perhaps he was scared, not of the fight but of the unknown, of how he would acquit himself beside other men, given all that he knew of himself. He found it impossible to lose himself in his studies the way he had always done, and just stared from the dry pages to the view from the window.

The lawn of the quad was being cut by the university greensmen. Two mowers were being pushed from one end to the other in opposite directions and in perfectly straight parallel lines. The smooth, oiled mechanisms made a sound that Cuthbert heard through the open window of the library. It was a sound that reminded him of the satisfying turn of the winding chains on his grandfather's clock. The men were hot with the work and had their shirt sleeves rolled up and their collars off. On such a beautiful summer's day it was difficult to believe that the country was at war. He gave up and packed his things to leave, unsure what it was all for.

*

Troy bounced into their room the next afternoon and threw himself onto the bed without so much as a hello.

'I'm positively pooped, Cuthie. Had a high old time at home. Lots of tears, of course, from mother dearest. Papa is made of much sterner stuff, but he gave me a very military talking to. All very endearing. So what's the fuss in Edinburgh? Have I missed anything?'

Cuthbert was happier to see Troy again than he could have imagined and took a moment to drink in the length of the young man stretched out on the bed with his feet hanging off the end.

'Nothing to report. Edinburgh is always much quieter when you're out of town. And the streets are considerably safer – pedestrian casualties down by thirty per cent. Oh, I hear Deakins and Edwards have both signed up too. I don't know if they'll be with you, but you never know. Looks to be fewer and fewer of us starting the new term. There's even a rumour that the lady medicals will be joining us. Apparently, their school is about to close and they're talking about amalgamation.'

'Really? That should add a little colour to the place. I'm sure they can't all be planning to be old maids. Maybe you'll even find yourself a girl, Cuthie. You certainly don't seem to be putting any effort into finding one anywhere else. And Deakins and Edwards – good show! The more the merrier, I say. Don't suppose you've had a change of heart in my absence. It's not too late, you know.'

Troy was still lying on his back with his eyes closed, so Cuthbert didn't have to hide his discomfort. He wanted time with his friend away from such questions, and that time was running out.

'Troy, what do you say to a climb? We haven't been up a hill in a devil of a time. Come on, while the sun's still shining. You're off tomorrow and it's our last chance.'

Troy was easily persuaded to anything that involved physical exertion coupled with the prospect of competition. He liked to make everything into a race, and Cuthbert was unsurprised when Troy leapt up from the bed and from the other side of the door on the landing was calling, 'Last one at the top of the Seat buys the beers.'

*

On the summit of Arthur's Seat, the rugged outcrop of ancient volcanic rock that overlooked the city, Troy and Cuthbert sat on the grass. Because of the heat, they had allowed themselves the liberty of removing their jackets and the white linen of their shirts was sticking to their backs after the exertion of the climb of some 800 feet or more.

Before them lay a panorama of the city dominated by the castle. They picked out the dome of the university and the turrets of the infirmary, the church spires and the black, smoking chimneys. Behind it all, to the north, was the white ribbon that was the Firth of Forth and, just visible, the red, riveted towers of the rail bridge.

'Now, that's a view, isn't it, Cuthie? First time I came up here I knew this was the place. I mean you Scots already know what a beautiful place you've got, but you do try to keep it a secret. I was just a simple Yorkshire lad dazzled by the bright lights. The Athens of the North, indeed.'

'Dazzled, my foot. And there was nothing simple about you, Yorkie. You've got status and privilege, a five-hundred-acre estate, and your father's a Member of Parliament for crying out loud. So don't play the country mouse card with me.'

'And what about you, Cuthie? You're not exactly a bumpkin yourself. "A man of the world" – wasn't that what Jimmy in anatomy called you?'

'You know very well Dr Jamieson was being his usual sarcastic self when he said that. How was I to know that about the female reproductive system? I was only eighteen, for goodness' sake.'

'Well, now you're nearly twenty, young man. Think what you've learned in those two years.'

Cuthbert blushed and was angry that Troy still had this effect on him. But he had little time to stew before Troy turned and took him by the shoulders.

'Look, Cuthie, we really need to talk about this – man to man. I think you're making a mistake, maybe the biggest mistake of your life. You're going to regret this decision. I know you are, and I don't want you to come running to me afterwards saying I didn't tell you. So I'm telling you.'

Cuthbert dropped his eyes and turned away.

'I know, I know. I just can't leave right now. It's too important to me. I need to finish this. I need to qualify.'

'Damn it, Cuthie. What's more important than this? You're going to miss it and for the rest of your life you'll wonder what if. And you're going to have to explain yourself to the young ladies. I mean, they're already getting quite vocal about those of us who are not rushing to join up. What are you going to say to them, I wonder?'

'I'm not scared to go, if that's what you think.'

'No, I know that. But they don't, and it might get a little grubby. I don't want that for you. When I came to Edinburgh and stepped off that train, I was really quite frightened, you know. I don't think I've ever told you that. I'd always had my brothers at boarding school. I'd never been completely on my own before, you see. Just a boy, really. And I met you that first week. We clicked, didn't we? Even though you're so much shorter than me.'

'Three quarters of an inch.'

'As I said, practically a midget, but I felt sorry for you and said to myself, "Well, no one else is going to take him on, being so deformed." So we clicked, and that was that. I've never thanked you. Maybe friends don't need to. But you have been the best friend of my life. I don't know why I'm saying all this. You must think I'm a dreadful sop.'

Cuthbert was concentrating on his breathing, trying hard to swallow back the emotion that was welling up in him. His friend was saying goodbye and was preparing them both for whatever was to come, and he couldn't bear it.

'The thing is, Cuthie, I don't want to say any kind of big goodbye at the station tomorrow. I just want to leave the digs in the morning, like any other day, and say, "See you later." Could you do that for me?'

Cuthbert nodded as gently as he could, trying not to let the tears filling his eyes spill over on to his cheeks. Troy offered his hand to be shaken, but not to be held. Cuthbert swallowed hard again and simply took his friend's firm grasp for that would be all there would ever be to take.

*

The new term began three weeks later, and Troy had already written excitedly about his training. The letter was long, and with every line Cuthbert saw his friend's arms flailing. He had already met up with other university students who had also joined the ranks and reported that the regiment was 'a very mixed bag'.

'. . . we have had very little spare time since we have been training here. Having been through company drill mixed with route marches, physical drill, semaphore, knot tying and frog and long jumping and the rest, we are all quite pooped. Some of our men were able to go to town on Saturday, but I myself with a few others have been under orders for overseas service and we are now waiting to proceed, so popping up to town seems out of the question for us. We are numbered in alphabetical order, and in that way, we are sent out. We are now fully equipped, and we should be off any day.'

He had certainly learned a lot, some of which would be useful when he got 'out there', and some of which he would blush to share with his mother.

'I've come across curses I've never even heard old Baxter use, and as you and I know, that is saying something!'

His letter was peppered with exclamation marks, and Cuthbert heard Troy's loud laughter with each and every one. Enclosed with the letter was a small cigarette card-sized photograph of Troy in uniform. 'Six of us went along the other day to have our photo taken – all of us in khaki. Quite the conquering hero, don't you think? Thought you might like a little memento.'

He read the letter several times just to feel closer to his friend and then folded it and put it in his inside pocket, but he kept the photo warm in his hand before placing it under his pillow.

*

All that anyone could talk about was the war. It filled every headline, and posters started to appear around the city urging recruitment and decrying the scandal of those who had not enlisted. As he walked to and from the medical school, he imagined the eyes of women on him and the disapproval of their gaze.

At the infirmary itself and during his classes, he was sure of his role and secure in the knowledge that everyone around him understood his decision. But on the streets of Edinburgh, where he had to walk as an able-bodied young man, un-uniformed, he became vulnerable to his feelings of guilt.

The work became harder as the term wore on. Cuthbert had been told that after the rigours of the third-year examinations, he should not expect any respite in fourth year, and now he understood why. The volume of information that he had to acquire, and the diversity of topics, had grown considerably.

In the early years, he and the other students were expected to get to grips with the major medical sciences, especially anatomy, physiology and pathology. These were all difficult, but there was at least a recognised body of knowledge in each. If studied and acquired, that would safely see the student through. In fourth year, however, he had started on the clinical specialities. And that meant much of the teaching was at the bedside and in the clinic.

There, the structure of what they would learn was determined not by any carefully planned syllabus, but only by the haphazard nature of who happened to have been admitted the night before or who attended the outpatient clinic. Of course, examples of many of the common conditions were seen over and over again. But how was he ever to learn about the rarer diseases, which were often what the students were grilled on in examinations? It required even more reading than before. However, this year so much of his time had to be devoted to those rounds in the infirmary that it was often next to impossible to do everything that was needed. The weight of the workload was, nevertheless, in some ways a welcome distraction from the war and everything that entailed.

After the New Year, he started back with just as much enthusiasm as ever. By then, there had been no news from Troy for many weeks, even over Christmas, and although he thought of him every day, he had stopped worrying about him.

Winter, when it came, made Edinburgh look even more magical. The soot-blackened tenements on the High Street now wore white caps and the dark Castle Rock was dusted with just enough snow to show up its jagged lines. After another overnight flurry, the pavements again became one with the roads and the early morning trams would weave their way along Princes Street leaving deep trails behind.

With the thaw came the letter, and when it arrived it looked wrong. Because it was postmarked Harrogate, which was Troy's home town, Cuthbert was suddenly excited that his friend was home on leave. But the writing was unfamiliar, and Troy would never have addressed him as 'Mr John Cuthbert'. Something wasn't right, and he put the letter back in the pigeonhole, thinking that if he pushed it back far enough, it might disappear. He went into breakfast but had no appetite. In silence, he toyed with the boiled egg on the table before him. His landlady, Mrs Green, tried to attract his attention as she laid the toast rack on the table.

'Penny for your thoughts today, young man. I know it's a difficult year the fourth, but you'll get through it. If you've made it through the first three, you'll make it through the last two. All my gentlemen have.'

Cuthbert looked at the middle-aged widow who rented him his room. Could she possibly know what he was thinking? He had spent too long over breakfast and now he would be late for the morning round on the skins ward.

He collected his things, and as he passed the pigeon-holes in the hallway, he reached in and took the letter with him. He ran up the street with great leaping strides, trying to beat the clock. He and Troy had been able to run from their digs to the infirmary's main entrance on Lauriston Place in five minutes when they needed. Today, Cuthbert had to do it in three, and he was glad that morning to have the distraction of physical effort.

He arrived in the entrance way gulping down the air and went as quickly as he could to his locker. There he stored his satchel and donned his white coat. The teaching ward round had just begun, and Cuthbert quietly tried to join the group of five other students, the ward sister, the house physician and Dr Walker, the physician in charge of the skin department. Stealth, however, was never Cuthbert's strong suit, and Walker simply stopped speaking mid-sentence.

'Ah, how good of you to join us, Mr Cuthbert. I do trust that whatever detained you was of sufficient importance to merit the lack of respect you have shown everyone here. Perhaps by way of recompense you can lead on our first case. Front and centre, Mr Cuthbert. Front and centre.'

Cuthbert followed the beckoning finger of Dr Walker and positioned himself on the patient's right side. The lady was in her fifties, and when he examined her, she had obvious soft, round bulbous lumps on her back and above her collar bones. These were non-tender and appeared too numerous to be any form of malignancy.

Cuthbert was puzzled. He carefully weighed the various possible diagnoses. Perhaps these were some form of cyst, or perhaps some benign overgrowth of fatty tissue. They might even be one of the congenital malformations he had read about but never seen, such as Von Recklinghausen's disease. But Cuthbert was making little headway in his deliberation, so Dr Walker interrupted his student's thoughts.

'Come, come, Mr Cuthbert, please don't keep us waiting any more than you have already done. Your diagnosis? Nothing to say. So you have deigned to attend my round but have seen fit to leave your brain still in its bed.'

None of the other students so much as sniggered because they were painfully aware they might be next.

'Could this be Lues disease, Mr Cuthbert, perhaps in its tertiary manifestation?'

Cuthbert joined the other students in looking surprised. Walker had used the standard euphemism for syphilis when discussing the disease in front of patients. Such a diagnosis had not even entered his head.

'It is, after all, the great imitator, Mr Cuthbert. In this ward, you will see many manifestations of that disease, and no two will be alike, but every single one will persuade you that it is something else. Never discount this as a diagnosis, gentlemen. Oh, and I see your sensibilities are somewhat offended by my suggestion that this fine lady of mature years might be exhibiting the consequences of her past. Gentlemen, in considering the origin of this skin condition you must not be unduly influenced by the apparent respectability of your patient. Remember, every bishop was once a divinity student, every admiral a midshipman. Onwards.'

The rest of the teaching round was less memorable, and after his ritual humiliation, Cuthbert lurked at the back of the group largely untroubled for the remaining hour. He had for a while been able to forget the letter still in his trouser pocket, but there was half an hour before Baxter's 10.30 lecture and little chance of him thinking about anything else.

He left his fellow students and went out to find some air. One of the benches in the rose garden was free and he made for that. The beds were dead and empty at this time of year, and he sat on the cold seat huddled in his coat. The letter still looked wrong, and Cuthbert ripped it open to get it over with.

'Fairmont'
Farringdon Lane
Harrogate

February 15th '15

Dear Mr. Cuthbert,

Although we have never met, I presume now to write to you with the saddest of news. Joseph always spoke of you with such warmth and affection in his letters that I felt you needed to know of the news his father and I have recently received. On Wednesday last, we were sent a rather impersonal army form informing us that our darling son was . . .

Cuthbert crumpled the letter hard in his fist and jerked it towards his mouth where he bit the page and tore it with his teeth. It was what he expected, but until he saw the words in that fine copperplate hand of Troy's mother, there was still the possibility that it might have been something else, something simpler. 'Joseph is doing well and sends his best wishes but has asked if you could forward some lecture notes' or 'could you possibly post that dermatology textbook he left behind' or 'he wants you to arrange for his re-entry to the school' or 'yes, it's true, it's really true, he's coming home, safe and sound, if a little the wiser.' But instead, just three words that left no room on the page for the next sentence, the next paragraph or the next chapter of a life: *killed in action*.

Cuthbert did not return for the mid-morning lecture, nor for the clinics that afternoon, nor the round the next morning. He walked first the streets and then climbed the crags behind the city, trying to put some distance between himself and the facts. He looked across to the summit of Arthur's Seat where he and Troy had parted just six months before and found himself talking to a ghost, saying all the things he had wanted to say. He poured out his love for a lost friend but there were no more tears to be shed. It was clear to him now what he had to do.

*

The recruiting sergeant looked him over from head to foot.

'Name?'

'John Archibald Cuthbert, sir.'

'Age?'

'Twenty, sir.'

'Big lad. They'll be happy to see you in the artillery. Any military training or special skills?

'None, sir.'

He was not even clear in his own mind why he lied to the sergeant, but he knew that very little made sense any more. He did know that he needed to go to the front and continue what his friend had started. Troy was a better man than him, and Cuthbert had failed him. His thoughts were now as empty of reason as they were full of the unfilled obligation he felt he owed to the young man he loved.

Chapter 5

London: 7 February 1929

The clattering of the typewriter was distracting, and Cuthbert closed his office door. He had been offered secretarial support but found that he had to spend so much time proofing and correcting the unfamiliar medical terms for the secretaries that it was quicker if Morgenthal did it. His assistant was more than happy to type the examination reports as it brought him closer to the work and to Cuthbert's methods. Unfortunately, however, he had not yet mastered the art of typing quietly.

By the end of the first day of cleaning the bodies with an almost archaeological precision, Cuthbert had still not managed to separate them. However, he did now have a much better picture of their state of decomposition and any external features that remained. The most obvious anomalies, which he had noticed almost from the start, were the inconsistencies in the stages of decomposition of different parts of the corpses. At the scene he had been unable to explain this. Now it was apparent that the two bodies differed by approximately one month.

In itself, this did not mean much because it was notoriously difficult to estimate a time of death from decomposition alone, for that depended on so many factors. The surrounding temperature played an important role, as did the locus of deposition such as in water or soil or dry sand. Also, individual features of the bodies, such as weight and underlying disease could play a part as could the application of any external chemicals, like quicklime.

Despite all this, it was clear that the inferior corpse was in a more advanced stage of putrefaction than the superior one. Had they died at different times but been dumped into a common grave? Had the second corpse been added to the grave later? No answers to these questions were yet forthcoming, but Cuthbert knew they would only be found on the slab in his mortuary.

As he had recorded in his notes at the scene, the superior corpse had his hands tied by the wrists behind his back. Being the uppermost portion, the hands were what first broke the surface of the shallow grave. Cuthbert spent some time examining the ligature, which was still attached to the wrists, even though the right hand had been accidentally detached by the unfortunate gentleman who had stumbled on the bodies. Cuthbert took detailed notes of the type of rope used and had the knot photographed before cutting it free.

Even though the bodies were still firmly glued together, he was able to access the underside of the inferior corpse by turning the bodies over with Morgenthal's help. He was unsurprised to find another ligature and another set of bound wrists.

He noted that the rope was similar if not identical to that of the first body and that a similar knot had been used. Even at this stage, Cuthbert knew he was dealing with a double murder and in all likelihood a single perpetrator.

The police investigation would not make much progress unless the forensic team could supply some idea of the identity of the corpses, so Cuthbert made that his first priority. Normally, in a case such as this, where an unknown body is in an advanced state of decomposition, the usual starting point in identification would be a detailed examination of the clothing. However, here nothing was found either on the bodies or associated with them in the grave. Both bodies were naked. They both appeared to be male from their body shape, but as they were fixed face to face no examination had yet been possible of their external genitalia. Neither were wearing glasses, watches or any form of jewellery.

Although the surface epidermis had sloughed off in several places, the underlying dermis was sufficiently intact on the hands to obtain impressions. These Cuthbert took from both corpses and forwarded them to the fingerprint laboratory at the Yard. Of course, he knew that unless either or both of the men had had previous run-ins with the police, they would be unlikely to find a match. All fingerprints were unique, but that fact was only useful in identification if there was a known example on file with which to compare them.

Further surface inspection of the bodies revealed no obvious physical deformities, birthmarks or tattoos that might have helped with identification. On the head of the upper corpse there were a number of intact tufts of dark brown hair. On close inspection, these tufts were grey closest to the roots suggesting that the hair had been dyed.

Although the faces of the two corpses were confused at their points of contact with each other because of the process of decomposition, Cuthbert was able to insert a probe into the mouth of the upper corpse. As he had hoped, he hit upon a hard surface and with some difficulty extracted a denture. After studying it under the bright examination light, he rinsed it in water and took another look before smiling. Morgenthal rose from the typewriter as he was summoned to Cuthbert's side.

'Look at this, Simon.'

'It's a fairly new-looking denture, sir. I expect it's been made recently, but why does it have that?'

Morgenthal was indicating a conspicuous gold filling in one of the front incisors.

'Vanity in all probability. Some people want us to believe their teeth are all their own. And, ironically, they try to do that by including a gold filling in their false teeth. I'm not sure I'll ever understand people. But it's good news for us.'

'There can't be many dental laboratories that make dentures with gold fillings, and those that do might have records of any that they've made and who they've made them for.'

'Exactly, so let's get this to our colleagues in C.I.D. and see what they can come up with.'

*

The superior corpse would sooner or later reveal himself, but as yet Cuthbert had nothing to go on with the inferior one. That body was taller, and despite the decomposition looked to be younger, but it was impossible to say with any precision. There were certainly no dentures, and he would have to perform some X-ray analysis of the bones to determine the age. However, that would only be practicable once the corpses were free of each other. Cuthbert knew the process of separating them was likely to be disruptive to the remains, and before proceeding he wanted to take a last detailed look at them in their combined state.

Further photographic series were taken, and Cuthbert went over every inch of those surfaces of the bodies that were accessible. In particular, he studied the patterns on the skin left by hypostasis. This discolouration was left after death when blood under the effect of gravity sank to the lowest vessels in the body.

Cuthbert was well used to studying this feature of death because of the invaluable information it could provide. He was beginning to be absorbed in the work, almost forgetting where he was, when something made him pause. Cuthbert often thought of himself as a poor tutor because he would forget to share details of his observations with his assistant. But here, he realised, was an ideal teaching opportunity.

'Dr Morgenthal, your attention, if you please. Remind me what are the classic stages of death?'

The young assistant, who was in the middle of tagging and bagging up the dentures for C.I.D., was jolted by the question. He had of course been reading all the books that Cuthbert had recommended, but as yet it was a rare occurrence for him to be tested on them. He put the bag down on the desk, stood to attention and collected his thoughts before he began to recite.

'The first stage of death is Pallor mortis, paleness of the skin, the second Algor mortis, the cooling of the body, the third Rigor mortis, the stiffening of the musculature and the fourth . . . the fourth is discolouration due to gravity.'

'Called?'

'Is it Livor mortis, sir?'

'Are you asking me or telling me, doctor?'

'Sorry, it *is* Livor mortis.'

'Explain to me the origins of such post mortem staining.'

'As I mentioned, it is due to gravity. Once the heart stops beating the blood collects in the lowest parts of the body and engorges the small blood vessels: the capillaries and venules.'

'Timescale?'

'It begins soon after death, usually within an hour, at first in small patches which gradually fuse together into larger areas, and these become visible to the naked eye usually after a couple of hours. It usually reaches its peak after about twelve hours when it remains fixed, although the colour often changes from reddish pink to deeper shades of purple.'

'Significance?'

'The distribution of the stains depends on the position of the body at death, sir. For example, if it is lying on its back, the whole back will be discoloured except for the parts directly pressing on the surface it is lying on. Any pressure, however slight, will prevent the capillaries from filling and these compressed areas do not become discoloured. Also, the position of any tight band such as a collar or a garter or even the wrinkles in a shirt will be marked by the absence of discolouration. And, of course, that will be true for a ligature too.'

Morgenthal could feel himself sweating the way he used to when, as a student, he would be grilled by the consultant physicians at Guy's. And he was out of practice because Dr Cuthbert rarely put him on the spot like this. His mentor was also inscrutable, and Morgenthal could catch no hint from Cuthbert as to the accuracy of what he was saying. He simply fixed his assistant with an impassive gaze and waited, allowing a silence to develop. Morgenthal struggled to remember anything else he had read that he could say to fill the void.

'And . . . and to the inexperienced eye, this discolouration can be mistaken for bruising. If there is doubt, tissue sections can be taken for examination under the microscope, and that will usually resolve the issue.'

'Usually? What about the rest of the time?'

'I'm sorry, Dr Cuthbert. It *will* resolve the issue.'

Cuthbert simply nodded and Morgenthal knew he was safe. The test over, Cuthbert could again afford to relax his expression and forget about the pretence of standoffishness that he knew was expected as part of his more formal teaching responsibility. And Morgenthal knew he could go back to being an able assistant, at least until the next time.

'Come and look at this, Simon, and let's put some of that theory into practice.'

The ankles of the upper corpse bore a clearly delineated pale band suggesting the presence of a tight ligature, which was no longer present. This was not unexpected given the existence of the wrist ligatures. What was more difficult to explain were the pale stripes running through the purplish discolouration that crossed the upper corpse's back, waist, the back of the thighs and the calves. The deep purple lividity over all these areas suggested that the man had died while lying on his back, but the sharp lines suggested linear pressure points, perhaps even further ligatures.

The body had certainly been moved more than ten to twelve hours after death and had then been buried face down on top of the other corpse. It was the position of the lines that puzzled Cuthbert. Had the man been lying supine on a surface with sharp ridges running from left to right across the body? Or, if indeed they were ligature marks, why was the body trussed up like a turkey? The ankle and wrist ties would surely have been enough to immobilise the victim, so why were others needed? He knew these signs were important and made a careful note of them as he pointed them out to his assistant; he just didn't know yet what they meant.

Morgenthal could see that Cuthbert was perplexed, but he had often seen him before, puzzling over a body, keen to extract the last ounce of information that it could give. This time the problem was literally twice as big, and he knew that they would get no further answers until they had managed to prise the two bodies apart.

They talked for a while about different ways they might do this so that they could preserve as much of the integrity of the corpses as possible. Morgenthal paid close attention for he knew from experience that pulling too roughly on a decomposing corpse could land you on the floor of the mortuary with an arm or a leg in your hands.

Cuthbert's plan involved nothing like that kind of brute force, but rather slow, blunt dissection, with him working on one side and Morgenthal on the other. His assistant relished the opportunity to work so closely together with Cuthbert, even though he knew very little, if anything, would be said during the process.

After almost two hours of careful, silent work, the bodies were still firmly glued together at the chest and abdomen, but their legs were free. Only by the end of the day, were the two pathologists ready to attempt a full separation. Cuthbert stood at the head of the slab and took the shoulders of the upper corpse, while Morgenthal stood on the left at the level of the pelvis and took a firm hold of it in both hands. On Cuthbert's count, they turned the upper corpse over and away from the lower one as gently as they could in a single movement. There was some sound of tearing flesh and the squelch of wet tissue, but the upper corpse was now placed on the adjacent slab, and for the first time the mortuary had two bodies rather than one compound mass.

Morgenthal was sweating, not from the physical effort required but because of the tension. He was, as usual, keen to get it right when Cuthbert was watching. But there was no point in waiting for any approval because Cuthbert was already scrutinising the newly exposed surfaces of the lower corpse's chest and stomach and collecting some dead maggots for examination under the microscope.

He would of course proceed to a full internal examination of the bodies, but there was much to be learned first from surface inspection. Morgenthal knew that would take time and there would be a lot for him to type up before they could move on to the next stage.

He had once mentioned to a friend that he would be busy typing up reports and was met with a blank stare of surprise.

'Five years of medical school and that's what you've become, a typist.'

He had never thought of it like that at all. He viewed it as an essential part of his training to scrutinise the level of detail that Cuthbert went into in his examinations. By having to type the notes, he was forced to read them closely and to absorb them. He learned not only what must be done, but also how it should be described and reported. And, at the same time, it made him feel an invaluable part of the forensic team.

Now that they were separated, Cuthbert ordered the X-rays of the inferior corpse's head, neck, hands, wrists and pelvis. The latter he thought might be the most helpful in determining the age of the victim. Parts of bones ossified at different rates to allow them to grow throughout development. Only when they were fully grown did they turn into complete bones. One late area of ossification of particular interest for this case was the crest of the pelvic bone, which Cuthbert now studied closely on the X-ray he held up to the light.

He was looking for any evidence of fusion between the crest and the main body of the pelvis. If it was fused, then the corpse would be that of a young man aged more than 20. However, if there was still separation, he was dealing with a boy in his teens. There was complete fusion, so this was one more piece of evidence that might point to the body being that of the missing young man whom Inspector Franklin had asked him about at the graveside.

Examination of his dental X-rays showed only partial eruption of the wisdom teeth. As these have almost always fully come through by age 25, this gave Cuthbert an approximate upper limit on the age of the victim. The number of possible males aged 20 to 25 was still too great to contemplate, but it was certainly now worth revisiting the fingerprints as there was at least a reasonable chance that it might be Dawson.

*

As Cuthbert had expected, Dawson had no fingerprints on file, but a visit to his family home secured clear samples. The young man had played the flute and the instrument was still in its case under his bed, undisturbed since he went missing in December. Good left and right thumb prints were retrieved from the metal latches on the case and sundry partial prints were lifted from the flute itself. In addition, a good right palm print was obtained from the finger plate on the inside of his bedroom door. That was mostly likely to be Dawson's as no one else usually pushed a bedroom door closed from the inside other than its occupant.

All the time the technician was collecting the samples, the boy's parents were asking if a body had been found. It had been three months, and they knew as well as anyone else that the chance of Freddie walking back into their lives was now remote. It was all the technician could do to field the questions as sensitively as he could and keep his focus on the job.

*

Now, Cuthbert had the report that the dermal prints obtained from the corpse were a match for those retrieved from the boy's home. That, together with the evidence from the bone studies, gave Cuthbert the confidence to give the inferior body a name. This was Freddie Dawson who had disappeared early last December. As yet, the cause of death was unclear. What was certain was that Dawson had not died a natural death and his body had been dumped unceremoniously in a shallow grave along with the other corpse.

While Cuthbert knew that the precise cause of death and anything else he could glean about the nature of that death and the body's disposal would be of vital importance for the case, he was ready at this stage at least to inform Inspector Franklin that he had found his missing person.

His typed report would be on the detective's desk the next day, but to save any further resources being wasted, Cuthbert lifted the phone to call Scotland Yard.

'Are you sure, doctor?'

'As sure as I can be. We have a positive match from his fingerprints and the bone age and general physical characteristics all match. Yes, inspector, this is Freddie Dawson. And it is certainly murder.'

'But you told me at the scene that it definitely wasn't Dawson. How did you make that mistake?'

'No mistake, inspector. The body I was examining was indeed an older man, but what none of us knew then was that Dawson's body was at the time lying underneath in the same grave.'

Cuthbert didn't appreciate Franklin's tone. There had never been any sense of teamwork between them, and although they had only crossed paths on a few occasions, things had never been smooth.

'When will we be ready for a formal identification by the family?'

'Inspector, you've seen the state of the bodies. Can we not spare them that?'

'You only seem to remember the rules, doctor, when it suits you. We need a formal identification to close this case. I'll expect you to make at least some of him presentable.'

'He's been dead probably three months and in damp ground for who knows how much of that. You are asking the impossible, inspector. If there were clothing or personal effects we could show, that would be different, but the body was naked. And there are no birthmarks or the like that we can show. His face is gone and so has most of his skin. Would you want to look at your son in that state?'

Cuthbert's voice was rising as he spoke. Irrespective of his feelings, he usually managed to maintain the calm exterior he was known for, but this time Franklin was going too far.

'You don't like me, do you, Cuthbert? Well, I'm glad this will be the last one we're working on together. I'm off. Taking my pension – I've had my fill of everything that's turning up at our door these days. World's gone upside down, if you ask me. This is a murder investigation now, and it's off my desk. Somebody else's bag and good for them. No, you don't like coppers. But if you thought I was a pain in your arse, just wait till you meet the next one.'

Franklin hung up before Cuthbert had a chance to ask him what he meant. He expected to have to work with homicide now rather than missing persons, but that could mean dealing with any one of several senior officers. He just shook his head as he had no time to concern himself with Franklin's ill temper, and he returned to the mortuary. He still had another corpse to identify and two causes of death to discern.

*

It was almost a week later that Detective Sergeant Baker brought the news to the forensic laboratory himself as soon as he had received the report. A search of north London dental laboratories had initially turned up a blank, but he had ordered the net to be widened. Sure enough, one A. & H. Dental Technology in Croydon had been found that had done some gold filling work.

One of his detective constables had driven down with the denture from the upper corpse, and they instantly identified it as one of theirs. It had been made eighteen months ago as a replacement for a broken denture, and they had been asked to transfer the gold filling to the new set. The D.C. was impressed with their memory, but less so with their records because it took them over an hour of searching through boxes of index cards to come up with the client.

'Dr Cuthbert, I have a name for you, sir.'

'The denture? Good work, sergeant.'

'A Mr Henry P. Melville. We are running the checks just now, but there are no reports of a missing person by that name, so it might need some more digging.'

'Well, Mr Melville is certainly not going anywhere. Thank you for letting me know, sergeant. We'll keep on working and try to give you a cause of death. Anything you find out, do keep us in the loop though. We often get forgotten about out here in the hospital.'

Cuthbert lifted the sheet covering the upper corpse, which was now lying face up on the second slab after it had been separated from its partner. He looked at the face, now bloated around the edges, distorted in the centre by contact decomposition and tinged with black patches around the orifices.

'Mr Melville, I wish we were meeting under pleasanter circumstances. I am Dr Cuthbert and it's my job to find out your story, sir. And quite a story I expect it is. Whatever your last hours were like, they are difficult to imagine. But, unfortunately, that's part of my job too.'

He returned the sheet and looked over at the other slab with its similarly shrouded mound. There were still so many unanswered questions, but at least the two men had recovered their names – Freddie Dawson and Henry Melville.

His mind raced through the series of further tests that needed to be done, but he looked at the clock and saw that it was after nine. He had sent Morgenthal home hours ago and Madame Smith, his housekeeper, would have already put another wasted supper out for the neighbourhood cats.

He flicked the lights and closed the door.

'Tomorrow.'

Chapter 6

London: 4 March 1929

People in London were remarking on the weather that week. For once, it was not about the enduring wind and rain of winter, but about the unusually dry spell the city was enjoying. There was scaffolding everywhere as new buildings were rising, and the smell of pitch filled the air as new roads and tramlines were being laid.

It had been like this for several years, and people were truly beginning to put the war behind them. The weather was helping for once rather than hindering the progress towards what seemed like a brighter future in a new, modern world.

In his department at St Thomas's Hospital on the South Bank of the Thames, Cuthbert was somewhat oblivious to the tide of modernity sweeping through the streets of London around him. He was absorbed in the methods he had learned a decade before. Littlejohn had taught Cuthbert well. And one thing his professor had always emphasised was just how difficult the dissection of a partially decomposed corpse was compared with the examination of a freshly deceased body.

He had said that so many of the changes that occur in the days and weeks after death blur the picture. The forensic pathologist was therefore forced to slow down and search every indistinct feature for relevance. As a result, Cuthbert refused to be hurried. Rushing things at this stage would only mean the loss of vital evidence.

He had already removed Dawson's internal organs, weighed them and done a preliminary dissection looking for any obvious cause of death. There was no internal bleeding. That coupled with an apparent lack of any puncture wounds, cuts or obvious blunt force trauma and no evidence of fractures on the X-rays, suggested he was dealing with another cause of violent death – perhaps asphyxiation.

There were a number of fairly non-specific signs that might support that diagnosis. He looked closely for the small, sometimes pinpoint, haemorrhages called petechiae. Normally, he would search for these in the conjunctivae of the eyes, the inside of the mouth and on the skin, but all these were in such poor condition that instead he looked for and found them internally, on the surface of the heart and lungs. While examining the heart he also noted the right side was somewhat engorged. Again, this finding was suggestive of asphyxia, but it certainly did not confirm the diagnosis.

When dissecting the mass of decomposing tissue in the area of Dawson's neck, Cuthbert recovered small pieces of bone. These belonged to the hyoid, the small bone at the base of the tongue. This appeared to have been fractured in two places, one on the top of the left horn and the other where the right horn joined the main body of the bone.

In themselves, these fractures meant nothing, for they could easily have occurred as he and his assistant had moved the bodies from the grave or when they had separated them in the mortuary. However, when he examined them more closely, he found tiny traces of adipocere, a solid waxy fat, at the fracture ends.

This substance, he would often tell Morgenthal, looked and felt like mutton suet and was always a very useful finding. After death, when a corpse was left in damp conditions, the normally almost fluid human fat was often converted to this hardened state. This meant that beyond all reasonable doubt the fractures had occurred before the body was buried in the wet soil.

Cuthbert also knew it was very difficult in life to fracture the hyoid in this way other than by grasping the neck very firmly. The obvious conclusion was that the young man had died by strangulation. He looked carefully for any signs of a ligature on the skin of the neck but drew a blank, again because of the condition of the decomposed tissue. Morgenthal was watching closely as Cuthbert re-examined the small almost insignificant bones he had retrieved from Dawson's neck. This time, using his magnifying glass, he carefully studied the remains in the enamel dish.

'Is that the cause of death, sir?'

'It looks like it. Force great enough to do this would certainly be enough to starve the boy of oxygen. In the absence of any other obvious cause, this seems the most likely explanation.

'How would it have been done, Dr Cuthbert?'

'Perhaps like this.'

Cuthbert stood facing Morgenthal and encircled his neck with his large hands. The muscles in the young man's neck tensed, but he did not move to get away. Morgenthal's sharp stubble rubbed under Cuthbert's thumbs as he positioned them over the young man's larynx and pressed gently. Morgenthal coughed, and Cuthbert immediately released his grip.

'It wouldn't be hard to do, as you can see, but of course if I were really trying to throttle you, you would be putting up quite a fight. Dawson wasn't much younger than you, and I'm sure you could both do your best to fight off a frontal attack like that. So that makes me think it might have been like this.'

Cuthbert took Morgenthal's shoulders and quickly spun him around. He took one of his arms and twisted it up his back, both to inflict pain and to immobilise it. From the front he locked his assistant's neck in the vice-like grip of his arm, forcing his head back. Holding him tight from behind, Cuthbert could again feel the young man tense, but this time he began to struggle. As quickly as he had taken him, he released Morgenthal, who was now breathing with effort.

'But even that might not have been enough to do it, not with someone as strong as you, Simon. Although I can find no traces of a ligature, I expect that's what might have been used. All your considerable strength would have been expended in vain trying to free yourself from a rope or a scarf, perhaps tied around your neck from behind. It would have been only a couple of minutes before you weakened and slipped into unconsciousness. Moments later, of course, you would be dead. Now we need to find out what we can of Melville.'

Morgenthal began to tremble as the power of the sudden demonstration started to affect him. He had been completely overwhelmed by Cuthbert, whose physicality he had never appreciated before. The strength in the arm around his throat had doubtless only been a fraction of what Cuthbert could inflict, and even that had been enough to frighten him. He was already overawed by Cuthbert's mind; now he would never quite look at his body in the same way.

What had been the upper corpse was now lying face up on the adjacent slab. This body was clearly not as decomposed as the other, suggesting a different time of death, perhaps by as much as several weeks. Where the two corpses had been in contact – mainly the face, the chest, the abdomen and the genitals – there was some intermingling of tissues. At these points, the more established decay of Dawson had clearly accelerated that of Melville.

Again, Cuthbert took time to scan every detail of the newly exposed surfaces. As with Dawson's body, there were no puncture wounds or lacerations, and the only obvious ligature marks were those around the wrists and ankles. The genitals were bloated, but obviously male, and Cuthbert also noted that Melville was circumcised.

The horizontal pale stripes through the normal post mortem staining that he had noted on Melville's back, thighs and calves when his body was still attached to Dawson were not visible on the front. Cuthbert concluded therefore that they were more likely due to something ridged that Melville had been lying on at the time of his death.

When he commenced the internal examination, he did so with his customary care and lack of hurry. As he was removing the heart and lungs for examination, he noted Morgenthal yawning.

'Am I boring you, Dr Morgenthal? If you would prefer, there are several pages of notes you could be typing up. Don't let me keep you from that.'

'Not at all, sir. Forgive me, I was just hoping I might be able to help a little more.'

'Here, weigh this and perform the preliminary tray inspection.'

Cuthbert handed him Melville's lungs and his assistant scrambled for another enamel tray to collect them. The autopsy continued, and again there were no signs of any internal trauma, only the expected changes in various organs consistent with the deceased's age. However, on the surfaces of the lungs and liver there were multiple petechiae, the same small haemorrhages that had been observed on Dawson's heart and which were suggestive of asphyxia.

'Shall I commence the dissection of the trachea and bronchi, sir?'

'Let's do that together. It might provide the answer.'

Morgenthal carefully sliced through the anterior surface of the trachea down to the point where it divided into the two main bronchi. Immediately, the two men noted the presence of yellowish, semi-solid material in both the trachea and the bronchi. Morgenthal collected a specimen of what he thought might be pus from some respiratory infection, but Cuthbert stopped him and took a probe to separate the material so he could look at it more closely. Intermingled there were some small, more solid pieces, some with ragged edges that Cuthbert took to be partially chewed food. But what surprised them both was when, with his forceps, he extracted a maggot.

'What's that doing there? Surely, sir, we would expect to see that on the surface feeding on the tissues, not in his windpipe.'

Cuthbert extracted several more, all about the same stage of development and all dead.

'Let's look at the mouth and the pharynx.'

After some further dissection, these were exposed, and again there was some yellowish material that Cuthbert was now sure was vomit; and this was mixed with more maggots.

'On the face of it we have a fairly straightforward case of asphyxia due to the aspiration of vomitus, but then again it does not appear quite that simple. I've never seen maggots down as far as the bifurcation of the trachea. This is most unusual, Simon.'

The post mortem staining had suggested that Melville had died while on his back, although he had clearly been moved for burial. Such a position would be consistent with a man choking to death on his own vomit, but it certainly did not account for the other findings. Cuthbert liked a mystery, but he did not like a puzzle to solve where there were missing pieces, and that was what he had before him.

'Let's take another look at those marks on Melville's back and thighs.'

Morgenthal helped him turn the corpse over. The pale stripes running from one side of the body to the other were still clearly visible against the now dark purple, almost blackened, staining. Cuthbert went to the evidence cabinet and retrieved the ligature that had been cut from Melville's wrists and matched the diameter of the cord with the stripes on his back.

It was entirely possible that the same sort of cord had been used to bind Melville's body, but again Cuthbert came back to the question: why? The two pathologists turned the body on its right side so Cuthbert could follow the track of the possible ligature, but the pale area disappeared in the flank even though the dark purple background staining was still obvious. The same was true of the marks on Melville's thighs and calves.

'If these were made by ropes, they didn't encircle the body. He wasn't trussed. It's almost as if he was tied to something. But what? He's already lying on his back; he's immobilised at the ankles and the wrists and now he is bound to something along the length of his body.'

Morgenthal watched Cuthbert blanch as he connected the dots.

'Help me turn over Dawson's corpse.'

Cuthbert took his magnifying glass and studied the skin on Dawson's back, large sections of which had already sloughed off. However, Cuthbert tried to match the positions of the marks on Melville's body and find the corresponding points on Dawson's. As he did so, he found what he was looking for.

'I know what Melville was tied to.'

*

Within the hour, Cuthbert was standing outside the door of the homicide duty room at Scotland Yard. He had only once before been on the second floor of the building, but when he entered the large room, he was reminded of the same air of confusion he had seen on his first visit.

There were ranks of desks peopled by men with rolled-up shirt sleeves, braces and inky fingers. Suit jackets were slung over the back of swivel chairs, and the rattle of typewriters jostled with the hum of loud, smoky conversations. The desk nearest the door had a sign that marked it out as the reception, but there was little by way of welcome on offer.

He stood for a moment surveying the to and fro of the duty room before the officer who should have been manning the desk came back in a hurry. Cuthbert did not smile but looked down at the young man with all the disapproval he could muster.

'May I help you, sir?'

'Dr Cuthbert, duty pathologist. Who is in charge of the Dawson case, laddie?'

The constable straightened and turned to ask his colleagues. There was some confusion as the missing person file had now been reassigned to homicide.

'Must be the Pie,' concluded the constable on the left. The desk constable turned to relay the information to Cuthbert who had been watching and listening.

'That will be Chief Inspector Mowbray, sir. Shall I let him know you're here?'

'The Pie? Is that what you call him?'

The young officer tensed and proceeded apologetically, unsure of how much clout the pathologist had.

'Oh, don't think anything of it, sir. It's just the lads having a little bit of fun, is all.'

'Why the Pie?'

'Mowbray, sir. You know, Melton Mowbray? Pork pies?'

Cuthbert did not smile and simply shook his head ever so slightly.

'Please inform the chief inspector I need to speak with him. At his earliest convenience, if you would.'

The desk constable reached for the phone and said, 'Right away, sir.'

*

The glass door to the office bore the title 'Detective Chief Inspector J. Mowbray' in recently painted gold lettering. Cuthbert knocked and entered. Mowbray was seated behind a neat desk and immediately looked up and frowned, obviously more used to his visitors waiting to be admitted.

'Chief Inspector Mowbray, I'm your pathologist, Jack Cuthbert. Unfortunately, we have not yet had the pleasure. I hope you will forgive this intrusion, but there are a number of features of the case that I think should be brought to your attention.'

Cuthbert took a seat, again without waiting to be asked, and Mowbray had already decided he did not like this new doctor.

'Scotch?'

'A little early in the day for me, chief inspector. But, of course, you're not asking me if I'd like a drink, are you? You are enquiring as to my heritage. I am indeed Scottish, or if you prefer a Scotsman, but let me inform you that "Scotch" is a whisky.'

Nothing Cuthbert said endeared him any further to the chief inspector who disliked anyone correcting him, even in private. For Mowbray, the interview was already over, and he stood to usher the doctor from his office.

'I'm confident that it will all be in your report, doctor. You do write in English, I suppose? Yes, I'm sure you do. Now, if you'll just excuse me, I have work to do.'

Cuthbert did not move. He had many little failings, but lack of nerve was not one of them.

'Do shut the door and sit down, chief inspector. This is important.'

*

James Mowbray had been in the C.I.D. since the end of the war and had dealt with many doctors. He had liked none of them, which was not surprising as he liked no one he worked with, whatever their job. But he had a special loathing for the medical profession.

Now, standing beside his open office door, he knew he had two choices: to stand his ground and throw the pathologist from the room, or to recover some composure and ask what was so important that it had to be delivered in person.

He was more than a head shorter than Cuthbert but had never allowed size to intimidate him. He was strong and stocky, and he had the neck of a wrestler. He knew that what he lacked in height he more than made up for in aggression, and he had proven himself many times against those who had made the mistake of underestimating his strength and completely fearless determination to dominate. But he carried the scars of some of those encounters.

His nose had not been straight since he was 15, and there was a poorly healed scar under his right eye that his colleagues publicly attributed to his war, although quietly they wondered in which London back street it had been acquired. And even more secretly, they pondered how his hapless assailant on that occasion might have fared. In other circumstances, Mowbray might have been nothing more than a street thug, but fortunately for the street he also had a brain.

Despite his lack of any kind of refinement, Mowbray was possessed of a fierce and quick intelligence that had allowed him to climb through the ranks of the Metropolitan Police when his background would normally have been seen as a heavy, dragging chain about his neck.

Born and not so much raised but hauled up in the East End of London, he was orphaned when he was 12. His father had murdered his mother and her sister in what at the time had been a grisly front-page story in the *Gazette*, and the man had subsequently hanged for the double killing. Mowbray had been taken in by a surviving maternal aunt, but with every passing day he acquired more and more of his father's brooding looks. By the time he was 16, his aunt could bear to have him in her house no longer, and only the good fortune of a war prevented him from going hungry in the gutters of Poplar.

In the recruiting office, he used a new surname. He also lied about his age, which was easy because, even then, his muscles were thick, and he was soon shipped along with thousands of others to France. He grew up quickly in the trenches and found friendships there that he had never known in London. More through good fortune than anything else, he made it to the armistice unscathed and returned to England.

One of the older men in his company had been a policeman before the war, and it was his tales of a copper's life that probably set Mowbray on the path he chose. By any standards, he'd had a good war and came home a sergeant with a commendation for bravery. All of that helped with his application to join the force, which the war had sadly depleted, and few other questions were asked at the time. Certainly, no connection was made with the double murder almost a decade before. Needless to say, he kept that part of his life hidden in the background and almost convinced himself that it had all happened to someone else.

At the Yard, he acquired a reputation for getting the job done quickly. Having grown up on the streets and then matured with a bayonet in his hands, he was completely ruthless with suspects. Everyone knew if you wanted someone to talk, you just called for Mowbray. But along with the brutality was the intelligence that allowed him to calculate just how much and how far anything could be pushed.

He knew he was operating in a world that was governed by privilege and patronage and that simply being good at the job would never be enough. He learned to play the game and, as ever, played it very well.

*

Now, standing at the door, he sensed something in this 'Scotch' doctor that might be to his advantage, and he chose the second option. He closed the door and sat back at his desk and held his silence, waiting to find out if his gut was right. Cuthbert pulled a file from the briefcase at his side and opened it on the desk facing the chief inspector. Mowbray looked at the photographs and did not flinch.

'And what am I looking at, Dr Cuthbert?'

'The Dawson case. As you know, we have identified the remains of the young man who went missing in December. He was found in a shallow grave along with that of another man, Henry Melville, about whom as yet you know very little, I understand.'

'Yes, I know all of that, doctor, but my question was, what am I looking at?'

'The post mortem photographs of the two corpses. We had to separate them because they had decomposed into each other. It took a while, but we have learned a great deal. The two men were naked when they were found and there was evidence of ropes.'

'So, a pair of queers is that what you're telling me? Older man meets young lad. Into a bit of bondage. Sex act that somehow goes wrong. Like bloody dogs on heat, the lot of 'em. If I had a shilling for every poofter I've had to untie in this game, I'd be able to afford a better brand of Scotch.'

'I think you're jumping ahead of me a little, chief inspector. I'm not suggesting anything of the sort.'

It was clear from the start that Cuthbert and Mowbray were going to rub each other up the wrong way. Both confident men, arrogant even, but both intelligent and mindful of just what needed to be done to get their own way. Both showed the necessary outward respect for the other's position, but neither felt any kind of inferiority.

'So, what *are* you telling me, doctor?'

'I think it's altogether more complicated than just a sex game, chief inspector. At this stage, I don't really know what it is, but there's something in the back of my mind somewhere that this reminds me of. It'll come to me. You see they weren't killed together. The two men died almost a month apart and were buried together later. Dawson died first. His body has the most advanced decomposition. Melville died, by my best guess, about four to five weeks later.'

'All right, we have a double murder and a single dumping of the bodies. Probably one perpetrator, so we have to find the connection.'

'Connection, chief inspector?'

'The connection between Dawson and Melville. If they're not bumboys, there must be something that connects them. Maybe a university link, family friend, could be anything, but it'll be there, and we'll find it once we sort out Melville's past. There's certain to be something that ties them together.'

'But, chief inspector, that's just it. They were tied together.'

'Yes, you said, and dumped in a grave.'

'No, before they were dumped. Before they were both dead. While he was alive, Melville was bound to the dead and decaying body of Dawson – a corpse that had been decomposing for a month. Whoever killed Dawson then used him to kill the other man. It was Dawson's corpse that killed Melville.'

Mowbray stood up and went towards his window. He had seen a lot in his years with the Yard, and he did not think there were any surprises left. However, as he digested what Cuthbert told him, as the full horror of it sank in, he suddenly needed some air, and he jerked open the window.

'Are you sure?'

'As sure as I can be at this stage.'

'Do you know how they died?'

Cuthbert outlined the evidence he had to support a diagnosis of asphyxia by strangulation in Dawson and asphyxia by aspiration in Melville.

'So the older man choked on his own vomit. Why?'

Cuthbert looked at him and tilted his head quizzically to one side.

'No need to paint me a picture, I get it. But the maggots, where do they come in?'

'Chief inspector, if Dawson had been dead for a month and kept in a warm place, his body would have been writhing with maggots and that includes his face or what would have been left of it. They were tied together face-to-face. Melville wouldn't have been able to breathe without swallowing and aspirating them.'

Mowbray was now leaning forward and taking notes. His demeanour had changed along with his colour. Although Cuthbert knew this was an unusually unpleasant case, he was still surprised that such an experienced officer in homicide would be having such a physical reaction to it.

'I'm sorry if this is all too pungent for you, chief inspector. I just thought that you should be informed as soon as possible of what we might be dealing with. I was certain it would affect your lines of enquiry, especially knowing that both killings appeared to be linked.'

'Yes, you were right to come up, Dr Cuthbert. And like it or not, we are going to have to work together on this one. I'm not sure we got off to the best start, but you look like the kind of man who could rise above such things. And, yes, the irony is I don't like death, even though I work in this department.'

'No one likes death. It just happens to be our business.'

'I've seen too much of it. Even before I got into this line of work. The streets of the East End have always been rough, but you should have seen them twenty years ago. And then there was the war. You know they're calling it the "Great War" now. "Great" – that's a bloody laugh. But I don't imagine the likes of you got your hands dirty in the war.'

Cuthbert thought before he replied. He rarely spoke about his war experiences because that meant having to remember them, and he had resolved to do everything in his power to forget those years. They would still spill over into his consciousness when small, unexpected events would trigger a memory – a word, a piece of music, a smell. But it was when he was asleep that he would have the least power to control them.

In the early years, his dreams became distorted and filled with overlapping images, with places and times mixed together. It was only since he had come to London, really only in the past couple of years, that he had found any quiet at all. At least on most nights the bombardments had finally silenced, and the screams had at last faded.

'On the contrary, chief inspector, I got much more than my hands dirty.'

Chapter 7

Ypres: 12 May 1915

The communication trench was barely two feet wide in places. After the rain, there were at least four inches of standing water on the black, greasy mud that formed the floor where the slatted wooden duck boards had rotted. Cuthbert was bent over almost double as he walked quickly to the dugout.

'Keep that bloody head down, you stupid Jock!'

Cuthbert's sergeant had been appalled from day one at the height of his new private. Although he was by far the easiest of his squad to deal with in every other respect, the sergeant was sure he would be cleaning the tall Scot's brains out of the sandbags before long.

'Sorry, sarge.'

'It's you that'll be sorry, Jock. What's the business from the other end of the street?'

'The C.O. wants us ready by twenty-three hundred hours to receive incoming. He's expecting tonight to be just as bad as the last.'

'Blimey, and there was me planning a quiet one. I was going to wash me hair, and I thought me nails might have finally got done. But, once again me beauty routine has gone up the

Swanee. And, to put the tin lid on it, I've gone and run out of pipe tobacco. Grab a pew, son. No point in standing on ceremony at this end of the street. Have you had something to eat? There's some tinned meat in there that needs eating. Well, it says it's meat on the tin.'

*

When Cuthbert had enlisted, he had all kinds of thoughts about what the front might be like. But none of them matched his experience, which was one of long periods of boredom, hunger and discomfort, interspersed with good humour and of course nights of terrifying noise. And a fear that forever hung in the air along with the smell of cordite.

He had been at the front now for almost six weeks, although no one was there constantly. There were regular rotations with men living, sleeping and doing what fighting they could for stints of about four to six days at a time, before they would fall back behind the lines for some respite.

In the trenches, there was a lot of routine. The afternoons were for sleep, but it was with nightfall that the barrages would start. The thick, smoky darkness ripped apart by shells and the inky blackness turned into day with the blinding flash of the explosions. Suddenly and momentarily, over and over again, it felt as if a searchlight was on you and every detail of your surroundings was picked out by the flash. The pile on the hessian of the sandbags you were leaning on, the dark grey mud-smeared slats of the wooden trench props, the sharp sparkle of the barbed wire and the reflected sky in the stagnant water at your feet.

The trenches were wet, and the smell from the overflowing latrines was everywhere so strong that you could taste it. The men did their best to keep clean, but the stale sweat on clothes worn for days on end did nothing to help.

'I'm supposed to go back, sarge. They want a readiness report.'

'It's all go here, isn't it? Want, want, want. I know what I want. A soft bed, a hot bath and a willing woman, but not necessarily in that order. Tell them we're ready, son. As ready as we'll ever be. And keep that big, daft head of yours down. That's an order.'

Struggling along the unfamiliar trench in the pitch black, Cuthbert stumbled and fell more than once. No lights were allowed lest they should attract enemy sniper fire. He knew the officers' dugout must be no more than another fifty yards or so, but only with the occasional flash in the sky from a shell exploding nearby was he able to navigate.

There was a sudden lull in the bombardment and the darkness closed in around him. He could feel the damp walls of the trench, but he could not see his feet beneath him. With his next step, there was a crunch under him, and his foot was caught. He tugged, thinking the vacuum of the mud had got him, but something sharp was pressing into his puttees. Eventually, he managed to haul his foot free, and he hurried on.

When he reached the dugout, he announced who he was before pulling back the canvas door in case any stray light should escape. He entered when he was told to do so, and immediately the officer screwed up his nose and pointed at Cuthbert's boot. Clinging to his gaiter were the broken ribs and parts of the rotting intestines of one of the Germans who had previously occupied the trench. The smell of the putrid mass sticking to Cuthbert's foot and leg was overpowering. He was ordered out immediately.

Outside, he promptly vomited and started frantically scraping the remains from his boot as he retched again and again. All he managed to do was to coat the remains with even more black mud. He knew he could not survive long in these conditions if he removed his boots, and he tried to find some deeper water in the trench to wash away the filth.

Another bright flash from a shell exploding maybe thirty yards away was enough to light up a shell hole full of water a few yards further on in the trench. He tentatively stepped into it, and the stagnant water came up to his mid-thigh. He did not know what else the water might be concealing, but he was past caring. He had to get clean.

The rain started again, and this time it was even heavier than before. Cuthbert took off his helmet and held up his face to the sky. He opened his mouth to drink in the rain, trying to get rid of the taste and the smell. When the bombardment recommenced, he was already half-way back towards the sergeant's digs, and when he reached them, this time he stayed outside, sitting on an empty petrol can in the rain.

An hour later, when the sarge awoke, Cuthbert asked for permission to go back to the reserve trench and find some way of getting cleaned up. The smell alone was enough to ensure that permission was granted.

*

There were always lulls in the action, and after that evening's bombardment, a near silence fell for two days. There was talk that the Germans had abandoned their trench opposite or had run out of ordnance. No one, however, was too keen to test either theory.

The men still tried to sleep in the afternoons, never knowing when it would all start again, and everyone found plenty to do in patching up the trench. Apart from using the time to ensure that all their supplies of food and ammunition were up to scratch, this was an opportunity to clean. The floor of the trench was always littered with bullet casings, and the general mess created by so many men living cheek by jowl could create very unsanitary conditions. During the fighting there was no time for such niceties, and even when it stopped during the day the men were dog-tired and hardly able to stand, never mind turn their hands to cleaning.

Now, the C.O. had issued orders for the trench to be given a thorough going-over. It was tedious work but distracting, and it even prompted singing from a few of the men. The latest music hall songs were the favourites of the day, and one or two of the men had good voices.

Occasionally, a more bawdy ballad would make it through. While Cuthbert was scrubbing his boots, he would hear the refrain of 'Inky-pinky parlez-vous' strike up. Before long the whole trench would be singing the words. What had started out as 'Mademoiselle from Armentières' had been ingeniously transmuted into a morality tale of sorts entitled, 'Three German Officers Crossed the Rhine' with such colourful verses as:

At last they got her on the bed, parlez-vous
At last they got her on the bed, parlez-vous
At last they got her on the bed,
And shagged her 'til her cheeks were red.

Cuthbert smiled as he polished the toe caps on his boots and always came in loudly with the chorus, '*Inky-pinky parlez-vous!*' The song always brought laughter as well as some censure from the padre who would be invariably present when it was sung. So infrequent were his visits and so well timed were they with the singing of that particular song, that Cuthbert could see that it was no coincidence.

The sarge, not renowned for his respect of the cloth, viewed the churchman with suspicion and regarded him as unlucky. As such, he would always rouse the men into full voice as soon as he spotted him doing his pastoral rounds. It usually did the trick, and the padre would move on, muttering under his breath about the state of modern youth.

Although they were relieved of sentry duty after their rotation back to the support trenches, there was still fatigue work to be done every night. This included carrying food, ammunition and materials down to the firing line for the engineers. All too soon, the relative respite was over, and they were back facing down the enemy.

Over a few weeks of this, Cuthbert had watched the men he was with change. They had become chronically tired, and things that would have made them laugh at the start, no longer stirred even a smile. Occasional scuffles would break out over the slightest of things – a missing deck of cards, a nudge when trying to write a letter home, the sharing of tinned meat.

The sarge, who was from the regular army and older than most of the men, had the teeth he needed to show in such situations to bring it all back under control. He kept order, in part through good humour and every so often with a loud 'bollocking' when nothing else would do. Cuthbert observed him closely and realised that here was a lesson to be learned. How does one man control at least fifty others? How do you exert authority, not for its own sake, but to enable you to get the job done?

He was fond of the sarge, even though he had at times been on the receiving end of his tongue-lashing. Each time he had deserved it, and all the sarge was really doing was trying to keep him alive for one more day.

Many of the men received minor wounds that could be dealt with amongst themselves. They all carried some field dressings in a special pocket sewn into the inside of their tunics, and there were medical kits available. What was increasingly troubling, however, was the number of men coming down with chest conditions that would not shift and, even worse, cases of dysentery.

Cuthbert remembered Littlejohn and his talks on camp hygiene at the O.T.C. Had his professor ever seen the inside of a trench on the Western Front? Many of his pronouncements now seemed to be little more than wishful thinking.

*

The routine of rotation from front line to relief trenches, occasionally further back behind the lines to the villages, and then back again to the front, continued as the weeks turned into months. The lines never seemed to shift, with no meaningful gains or no obvious quarter given, and Cuthbert was doubtless not the only one to wonder what it was all for.

The men did change, not just in their demeanour but also in their composition. The dead and wounded would be replaced, often with new recruits from home, and Cuthbert soon found himself as one of the more experienced in the squad.

He found he could cope with almost everything, but he did grow to dread the regular sentry duty that he and everyone else had to undertake. This was always at night and left you most vulnerable. He was certain that one night he would be hit and that he would most likely die alone from a bullet to the head or shrapnel wounds to the body. But it was the solitude that worried him more than the dying.

One night, no different from all the others, Cuthbert had been assigned sentry duty for two hours from 01:00, and as usual, he was ordered to keep a sharp lookout for any movements from the German trenches approximately sixty yards in front of him. Cuthbert cared little for keeping his head above the trench and scanning across the no-man's-land for any signs of aggression, but he knew he had no choice.

The enemy trench appeared like a winding black wave in

the darkness, and the silence was broken only by the occasional mechanical squeak as the wind caught the coils of barbed wire and rubbed it against itself. Suddenly, there was a flash from a rifle and the air was split by the rapid rattle of their machine guns followed immediately by the report and the nasty thuds on the sandbags he was leaning upon. As a reflex, he folded up and clutched his helmet with his spare hand and then quickly repositioned to fire off about five rounds from his rifle, aiming as best he could at where the flashes had originated.

There was a brief respite, and the only sound left in the night was the ringing in his ears and the sound of his rapid breathing. But suddenly the silence was broken again. A shell was whistling towards him piercing the darkness. When it landed and lodged in the parapet beside him, he was thrown to one side by its impact. It turned out to be a dud, but he knew that had it exploded, he would certainly have died on the spot. Death was commonplace: an average of two men per day were killed in his division. It was a terrible fact, but one that most of the men tried to rationalise by thinking how lucky they were that it was only two.

*

Early August saw Cuthbert and his fellow men relieved by another division, and they were sent a few miles back for a well-earned rest and the first hot bath they had had for several weeks. It was also a chance to have their uniforms washed and deloused.

The so-called rest also consisted of physical drill and runs before breakfast, all in full kit. The division spent a few days like this before being dispatched with all possible speed to Ypres, where they were being sent to support the Canadians.

Another gruelling shift of some eight consecutive days in the trenches awaited them, during which time nearly a hundred men were lost and many more wounded. At the height of it, his division was forced to retreat; fortunately, the enemy did not find this out until two days after they were more or less safely bivouacking in a nearby wood.

They stayed there for five days and then got to work again, digging reserve trenches just behind the front line and building up the parapets which had been demolished by the enemy's high explosive shells. Throughout, the men would work all night and get what sleep they could in the daytime. Before dawn one morning, those who were sleeping were awakened by the sound of thunder. There was confusion and running about in the encampment, and it seemed to them that the hounds of hell had slipped their chains, with shells falling like summer rain.

About half an hour after the bombardment had started, Cuthbert and three others were ordered to start reinforcing the front line. They were ordered up in fours. Their C.O. considered this the safest way to send his men the half-mile over open ground.

While they ran, gripping their rifles and bent low, they zig-zagged to avoid the explosions from falling shells on either side of them. What had been green field just the day before was now pockmarked and scarred by craters, varying in diameter from ten to twelve paces. The men ran with all the energy they could muster, and all made it to the relative safety of the front-line trench. There they were put on immediate sentry watch to relieve others who had either been killed or wounded.

Over the next hour several other reinforcements from the woods arrived including the sergeant and a second lieutenant.

'Lovely day for it, ladies. But the thing is, I've left me parasol back at the tent.'

Despite it all, Cuthbert found himself smiling at the sergeant. A moment later, the officer who was standing just on

Cuthbert's left was hit in the leg by shrapnel from an exploding shell. His scream was piercing as the bones in his lower leg were shattered, and he fell panting into the mud.

Cuthbert reacted without thinking and pulled him up and lifted him on to his shoulder. He ran with him to the nearest dugout, where he ripped off his trouser leg and drenched the wound with drinking water from his canteen to clean it of as much of the mud as possible. He pulled the field dressing pack from inside his tunic and found the phial of iodine, which he opened and poured over the wound. Without warning the officer, he pulled on the leg to straighten the compound fracture as much as he could. The young man screamed again, and Cuthbert held him down as he tried to get up.

'I need you to lie down, sir. Your leg needs splinted, and if we're going to save it, we need to work together.'

The subaltern, who was no older than Cuthbert, looked at the private who was towering over him and yielded. Cuthbert quickly and expertly applied the splints and completely immobilised the leg with dressings and clean bandages.

Once done, he found the medical kit and administered a quarter grain of morphine sulphate by injection to ease the officer's pain. As he was drifting into a sleep, Cuthbert took some ink from the bag and marked the officer's forehead with a clear letter 'M' to ensure anyone treating him later would know what he had received and to avoid any inadvertent overdose.

Cuthbert slumped to the floor as the rush of adrenaline that had prompted his actions subsided. The sergeant found him there and quickly surveyed the scene.

'Right, Jock, we need you up and back out there, and Lord Fauntleroy here needs to be seen to by the M.O. It's slackening off a bit. Just keep your bloody head down for me, all right.'

The wounded officer was collected by the mobile team from the local Advanced Dressing Station, and when they arrived to collect the casualty by stretcher, they alerted the M.O. to his status.

'Who attended this officer, sergeant?'

'That'll be Private Cuthbert, sir. I'm sure he meant to do his best under the circumstances. We were being hammered, sir, and the second lieutenant was in a lot of pain. Sir.'

'Get him in here, sergeant. Soon as you like.'

A few minutes later, the captain looked up from the stretcher that had been laid on two trestles to serve as an examination table. Through the glare of the acetylene lamp, he saw Cuthbert standing to attention in the gloom by the canvas door.

'Well, you're a tall glass of beer, soldier. Where did you learn to splint a leg like that, never mind administer morphine?'

'O.T.C., sir.'

'What were you doing in the Officers' Training Corps? What's your story, private?'

'No story, sir. I was a medical student before I enlisted. The University of Edinburgh, sir.'

'So what the hell are you doing here? What year were you in?'

'I completed half of my fourth year, sir.'

'And why didn't you finish the job, man? What a damned waste. You know you probably saved this man's leg, maybe his life. I'm short-staffed, and this thing is getting thicker. More casualties arriving every day at the A.D.S. Damn it, man, you're coming back with me – I need another dresser. Get your kit. I'll sort out the paperwork with your C.O.'

'Yes, sir.' Cuthbert saluted and about turned. As he returned to the front-line dugout back along the communication trench, he could hear some heavy munitions starting up again over the ridge. His sergeant was sitting on a pile of sandbags cleaning his pipe.

'So, Jock, that's you then, is it?'

'Sarge?'

'You were never meant to be here, son. I knew it wouldn't be long before they caught wind of you. But you never did tell me why. Why did you enlist with the regulars? You could have been an officer, son – had us all saluting you. Some lass I expect. That's the usual reason. Either running away in a hurry or maybe trying to impress her. What was it with you, Jock? A wee bonnie lassie waiting for you back home?'

Cuthbert stood in front of him and said nothing.

'It's all right, son. None of my business anyway. Sooner you get out of this hellhole, the better. And it's hardly goodbye – I'm sure you'll be seeing quite a few of us again before long. Probably on our backs though.'

All the time he had been fiddling with his pipe and had never once looked up at Cuthbert, but as the private walked away to collect his kitbag, the sergeant automatically shouted after him, 'And keep your bloody head down!'

*

As Cuthbert went to collect his kit, he was filled with a confusion of thoughts and memories, especially of his last days at medical school. At the Wednesday afternoon sessions of the O.T.C. only a few months before in Edinburgh, he had listened with the others to Major Littlejohn, as they were expected to call him, when he was not wearing his professorial hat. His lectures on medical military matters had seemed somewhat theoretical at the time, but now they were painfully real.

'Gentlemen, the management of casualties in conditions of war depends on a thorough understanding of the evacuation chain.'

Harvey Littlejohn was almost as famous as his father, whom he had succeeded in the prestigious Regius Chair of Forensic

Medicine at the University of Edinburgh less than ten years previously. He was now Dean of the Medical Faculty and the senior officer of the University Officers' Training Corps.

He doubtless felt he had much to prove, but by all accounts he was a much more congenial man than his father, deeply concerned not just with his subject but also with his students. He was known to be an engaging lecturer with a flair for the dramatic, and although Cuthbert had not yet studied under him at university, his reputation turned out to be well-founded during those sessions at the O.T.C.

'First, if a combatant is unlucky enough to be injured in the front line, he must receive immediate attention and be retrieved by the Field Ambulance. Please note, gentlemen, this is not a reference to any kind of contraption incorporating an internal combustion engine, nor does it sport a large painted Red Cross. No, the Field Ambulance is a mobile medical unit and not a vehicle. It will provide stretcher bearers and dressers and those skilled in first aid. All of these are of the utmost importance for our next stage; that is, the safe transport of the casualty immediately behind the front line to the Advanced Dressing Station.

'I do hope you're making notes, gentlemen. The next time you hear these terms you're very likely to be in one of them. It is unlikely that the A.D.S. will be able to offer much more than temporary relief, and more importantly may be thought of as a staging post, where the medical status of the casualty can be assessed and an appropriate decision made.

'If the casualty is fit enough to be moved, he will next be transferred to the Casualty Clearing Station. This is usually a static rather than a mobile facility, but nothing at all like the hospitals you have been used to, gentlemen. Even though they may accommodate a thousand souls, many will be under canvas and often they will be overflowing with the wounded.

Their role is to offer treatment and respite and to enable as many men as possible to return to duty. Some casualties will be repatriated, and others regrettably will die.'

Littlejohn would often stray from the facts and figures he chalked on his board, so that he could paint vivid pictures of medical care on the front lines. He held his small audience in thrall, and there was always complete silence when he spoke.

'In these weekly seminars, we will cover more than mere theory, gentlemen. We will also be rolling up our sleeves and getting our hands dirty. In addition to the customary rudiments of military life – drill and field operations, marching and signalling – we will learn all the necessary skills you will need to prepare and equip an Advanced Dressing Station. You will learn how to be a stretcher bearer, how to operate and manage a Field Ambulance, how to erect tents and shelters for the wounded and, very importantly, how to prepare a field dispensary and issue drugs. All this you will need as newly qualified doctors operating in a theatre of war. All this, in addition to everything else you have learned and experienced while undertaking your studies of medicine and surgery. Questions?'

A forest of hands shot up in a way they never did during the usual course lectures. Perhaps as Littlejohn was speaking there had been a slow and startling realisation that what they were being taught in this course was real and important. Lives were going to depend on all this, young lives like their own, in a way that all their other studies had failed to impress.

'Will we be covering the principles of first aid in a practical way, professor?'

'In this room, I am not your professor, Mr Evans, I am your commanding officer. Please try to remember that and address me accordingly. It might seem a small point, but as you will quickly discover when you put on the King's uniform, such things matter a great deal in the field.

'In answer to your question, yes, Mr Evans, you and your colleagues will be taught to perform minor surgery, bandaging, the splinting of fractures and the principles of treatment of burns, haemorrhage and shock. All of which will, of course, be more than necessary when dealing with war casualties. Although you are from different stages of the medical curriculum, and will have different levels of knowledge and experience, I and my fellow officers will ensure that everyone leaves here with a complete set of basic skills. Please look upon this tuition as a valuable addendum to your formal education. I firmly believe that as a result you will have a firmer grasp of the management of trauma than your predecessors.'

'Major Littlejohn, sir. It is my understanding that hygiene is a major cause of non-traumatic disease in battlefield settings. Is that true and, if so, will that be a topic of our studies?'

'Excellent point, Mr Gibson, and I thank you for raising it. Yes, indeed, in many previous conflicts the number of soldiers succumbing to infectious fevers was almost as great as those dying at the end of a bayonet or a sword. The administration of field hospitals with particular reference to sanitation, field hygiene and especially water purification will be one of your essential, if less glamorous, roles as a medical officer.'

'Sir, but will we have time to learn all this before it's over?'

'Mr Grant, please have absolutely no fears on that account. Do not believe what you read in the daily newspapers about the duration of this conflict. I am confident that every one of you will have the opportunity to put these skills into practice. And, Mr Grant, I say that with no joy whatsoever. I would not wish this upon any of you, but I am determined that every student from this university will be as equipped for the task ahead as I can make them. So to work.'

*

The A.D.S. was reached by going back along the rear communication trench to the relief trench and then further back over open ground to an encampment at the edge of the woods. The station had been built around the remains of a Belgian farm.

The farmhouse building itself was shelled out. Part of its roof was missing and the white plaster on the roadside wall was pockmarked by lines of machine-gun fire. In the farmyard, there was a mix of smaller outhouse buildings which were being used as either offices or dressing stations, as well as army tents, pitched and sandbagged close to the remaining walls of the house. There were also two vehicles, modified Fords, painted khaki and emblazoned with the Red Cross symbol.

One of these Cuthbert recognised as the mobile X-ray unit. The other he presumed was for transporting wounded men up the line to the Casualty Clearing Station. The Dressing Station was only about a mile behind the front line, but when Cuthbert arrived, it was as if he had come to another country.

On the march back to the station, he was bearing the stretcher carrying the wounded second lieutenant who had by now received a further dose of morphine. The officer was drowsy and looked comfortable despite the bumpy ride. When they had transferred him into the care of the surgeons, the captain told Cuthbert to report to the quartermaster sergeant and then back to him at 16:00.

Cuthbert watched them take the officer into the surgical tent and found himself standing alone on the grass beside one of the old farm gates. He looked down at the fresh green blades around his feet. His boots were clean save for some streaks of mud he had picked up on the way along the relief trench, but he would soon have them polished. He polished his boots now every day despite the ribbing he received from the other men.

He looked up from the ground to the sky and had to shield his eyes from the sunlight that was breaking through the trees. They were just beginning to lose their leaves, and the glare caught him by surprise. Then he heard the birdsong.

There were no birds at the front except for the black carrion crows that scoured no-man's-land, and all he heard there was the hungry cawing of those scavengers. Here, perhaps frightened back by the noise of the shells and the machine guns, or perhaps just finding shelter in the branches, were the songbirds.

He had arrived on a quiet afternoon, and the quartermaster who issued him with fresh underwear and socks told him to enjoy it while he could.

'Come nightfall, it'll be bloody murder here, lad. It's only quiet right now because they just shipped everyone out in readiness for what they're expecting. Poor sods, some of them. They're sending them back up to the front when some of 'em can hardly walk. These last weeks, you need to be at death's door here to get a ticket down the line to the Clearing Station. So make hay while the sun shines, lad, and if I were you, I'd get some kip.'

Cuthbert didn't want to sleep. He knew he should, to be fresh for the work that evening, but although he could still hear occasional rumbling in the distance, it sounded as far away as summer thunder.

The last days had been the worst of the war for him, and he realised that at no time since he had been shipped to the Western Front had he ever been truly alone. But here he was in an empty farmyard without another soul in sight. He wandered across to the nearest tree and sat down with his back against the bark.

Just to sit under that tree in the late summer, with no one shouting or laughing or screaming in his ears, with no one pushing past him through the crush of the trench or jostling him in the queue for rations or mail was something he wanted more than anything. He closed his eyes and felt the sun on his face, and he tuned in to the sound of the birds on the branches overhead.

At 16:00 he broke off his idyll, straightened his uniform and reported to the captain, as ordered.

'I feel compelled to say I'm disappointed, private. Not in you – let me make that clear – but in the circumstances. I did not expect to have to order a fellow medical man to empty the chamber pots and wash the wounds of those we have to deal with. But that is what you will have to do. Oh, we'll make use of your other skills too, but please do not be under any illusion that this is a cushier number than your front-line trench. You're just as likely to be shelled here, and if anything, there is less cover than you're used to.'

Cuthbert stood tall and straight to attention as Captain Oliver spoke from behind his makeshift desk. He was probably only about five years older than Cuthbert but looked and acted ten.

'There is, however, one thing I can sort out immediately.' He held up a paper for Cuthbert to see, and then laid it on his blotter and signed it. 'That's my recommendation to the colonel for your immediate promotion on grounds of specialist proficiency. That was a bloody fine splint. A stripe won't make much difference, but it's a start. I'll continue to do my best for you, lance corporal. Dismissed.'

Chapter 8

London: 7 March 1929

Chief Inspector Mowbray had gathered his team around the end wall of the duty room and was standing in front of a large pinboard.

'Dr Cuthbert here has a theory. I'll let him explain it. If I say it out loud, it will only sound even more far-fetched.'

Sergeant Baker had already summarised the main findings in the case to date, which largely revolved around the discovery of two bodies in an unusual set of circumstances. He had described the disappearance of Freddie Dawson and his subsequent identification as one of the victims and the discovery of the identity of the second victim, Henry Melville.

Now Cuthbert, whom Mowbray had invited along to observe the discussion, found himself on his feet addressing the team for the first time. He took them through a summary of the pathological findings and concluded with the story that he had presented to Mowbray only the day before. The constable in the front row screwed up his face and whispered, 'Jesus.'

'I realise I am proposing a particularly troubling manner of death for our victim, but the evidence strongly suggests that it happened the way I am describing.'

'But why?' The same constable was shaking his head. 'Why go to all that bother to kill someone, sir? Why not just throttle him like he did the boy? Why did he change his tune like that?'

Chief Inspector Mowbray nodded to Cuthbert, indicating that he should take a seat, and he again took centre stage.

'That, my lad, is what you're going to find out. First, I want to know everything there is to know about Freddie Dawson and Henry Melville.' As he spoke, he jabbed Dawson's university photograph and Melville's post mortem photograph, which had been pinned to the board.

'I want to know how they knew each other, what they got up to together and their movements. And, Baker, I want you to lead on Melville. All we've got so far is a name. I want the whole shooting gallery. Whatever the story turns out to be, and it might be rather more mundane than Dr Cuthbert would have us believe, we're still dealing with a double murder, so let's get cracking.'

The chief inspector was stern in his dealings with his team, and they were left under no illusion that he was serious about this case. He demanded a lot of the men under his command, but they watched him put in the hours and work equally as hard as them. He very much led from the front and expected everyone else to keep up.

As the meeting broke up and the men went back to their various desks, Cuthbert asked, 'Have you spoken again to the family yet, chief inspector?'

Mowbray looked at him as if to say, *you are here today at my invitation, but please don't think you're part of this investigation.* However, he kept it civil and said, 'Not yet, but we will be re-interviewing them in due course. Thank you for your contribution today, doctor. I must get on now. You can see yourself out, can't you?'

'Indeed. Oh, by the way, I've remembered what it was I was trying to tell you yesterday.'

Mowbray looked puzzled and just a little irritated.

'You know, chief inspector, where I thought I had come across all this before. Well, I remembered last night when I was reading. It's ancient. In Virgil's *Aeneid* of all places. I'll dig it out for you.'

'I really don't know what you're talking about, Dr Cuthbert, but I'm pleased you've got time to read. Good day.'

As Mowbray closed his office door on the pathologist, Cuthbert said, 'And a good day to you too, chief inspector. Do let me know if we lowly pathologists can make your day any brighter. We live only to serve.'

The constable whose desk he was standing beside as he spoke, looked up at the tall Scotsman, who in turned looked down at him and snapped, 'And what are you looking at, laddie?'

'Nothing, sir. Nothing at all.'

*

Over the following week, there was no communication between Mowbray and his team on the second floor and Cuthbert in the pathology department at St Thomas's. The pathologist had completed his autopsies, and Morgenthal had typed up the extensive reports and delivered them to the Yard.

Their role in the case was officially over, at least until their evidence might be required at any trial, and already another body, that of a young woman who had been the victim of a street attack, was awaiting their attention on the slab. Over the lunch hour, Morgenthal was away in the hospital canteen while Cuthbert sat at his desk. The phone rang, and from its tone, he knew it was an external call.

'Cuthbert.'

'It's Mowbray here. I think we should have another chat.'

'Was there any problem with the forensic reports, chief inspector?'

Mowbray's tone was less formal than in the past and perhaps a little less condescending.

'No, everything was very clear. I'll be straight with you, Cuthbert: we're getting nowhere fast with this. I think we need to look at your ideas again about the murder.'

'Again, chief inspector? I was unaware you had given them any credence, never mind consideration, the first time. But I would be happy to discuss this further. And I should show you that passage in Virgil. Shall I come over tomorrow?'

'No, I want to see you today, but I'm just about to go back to U.C.L. We need to redo Franklin's interviews. They're full of holes.'

'As it happens, I'm teaching there this afternoon. I have a two o'clock lecture to give to the law students on modern forensic techniques. We can meet afterwards, or, if you like, you can come to my house, and I'll give you the book. I'm only around the corner from the university.'

'Give me your address, Cuthbert, and I'll see you at four.'

*

Mowbray disliked having to admit any kind of failure, but he was forced by necessity to reconsider the approach he had taken on the case. The more they had uncovered about Freddie Dawson, the less interesting he had become.

He was just a young student who lived at home, with barely any social life to speak of and certainly no obvious sexual goings-on, with either sex. He appeared to work hard and was a solid student, even if he wasn't an exceptional one. He didn't seem to stand out in any area of his life. People knew him, but knew very little about him, perhaps because there was so little to know. Why he would find himself involved in such a thing was beyond Mowbray.

As for the circumstances of the murders, Cuthbert's reconstruction had appeared fanciful, overly complex. In Mowbray's experience, such ideas were best left in popular fiction, where they belonged. Real murders were often bungled, half-thought-through affairs committed by stupid people.

However, the more Mowbray had dug into Cuthbert's record, the more he had learned that he was far from a fanciful man. In fact, if anything, he was one of the most meticulous and objective of all the pathologists working with the Yard. He was renowned for being remarkably astute, perhaps one of the cleverest of the lot. Right now, Mowbray needed all the cleverness he could muster, even if it meant eating a little humble pie.

He now stood outside Cuthbert's door and studied it. Number 44 Gordon Square was a London townhouse. Five narrow storeys of finery built into a brick terrace around the edge of a large leafy square. There was no front garden and the door up two stone steps opened directly on to the street. A low black railing at the front separated off the servants' stairs down to the basement. Mowbray chose the front door and knocked loudly. Cuthbert himself opened the door.

'I'm just this minute home, chief inspector. Do come in.'

He led Mowbray along the hallway and into his study on the ground floor. Without explanation, Cuthbert rang for his housekeeper and started to leaf through the papers on his desk, looking for the book. While he was unlocking his desk drawer, the study door opened.

'Monsieur?'

The chief inspector was caught off guard by the freshness and attractiveness of the young housekeeper, having expected a distinctly different vintage of staff. He looked her up and down, and Madame Smith knew that she was being inspected. It had been a long time since she had blushed for any man, and the chief inspector would have to try much harder if he expected that kind of response.

'Madame Smith, would you be so good as to prepare some tea for us?'

Unsmiling, she nodded and said, 'Right away, monsieur. It will be served in the parlour.'

As she turned to go, she scanned the chief inspector in return from head to toe and made it plain she found him wanting.

'So what is madame's story? I'm sure she must have one, Cuthbert. Or do you just keep her to be decorative?'

Cuthbert bristled at the insinuation and continued rummaging in the desk drawer. He had almost grown accustomed to the assumption that there must be something going on between his housekeeper and himself but had not expected to hear it repeated by the chief inspector.

*

He had first encountered the slim, young Belgian woman on his doorstep four years previously. She had replied to an advertisement he had placed in the tobacconist's window for a live-in housekeeper. He had expected a queue of ageing matrons, but here was this exotic young woman.

Marie Délanger had been born in Liège and at the age of 15 had found herself one night on a boat crossing the Channel with her fellow countrymen and women to seek refuge in England as the Germans advanced through Belgium.

In the confusion of war, she had lost touch with those of her family who had survived but had made her own way in her new home. She already knew English from school but had learned fluency in the language through necessity and found employment and then marriage in quick succession. She knew she had married beneath her, but refugees are viewed by everyone but themselves as being on the lowest rung of society's ladder, irrespective of their origins. Growing up in Liège, she had enjoyed a comfortable life, with a family that loved music and the theatre. Here in England, she was alive and, for a time, safe, but nothing else.

The Smith whom she wed, treated her as well as he had been taught by his own father, which meant he was a brute. The marriage was never a happy one, but having endured the agony of one escape, Marie was in no hurry to consider another.

Smith never served in uniform. Being a shipyard worker, he had a reserved occupation. But almost as soon as the war was over, he laid down his life as so many of his schoolmates had done. Not, in his case, to any human enemy but to the influenza. Marie caught it too; she survived, but her husband took only twenty-four hours to die. He left her nothing, and she knew that as a young widow, who despite her good English still sounded foreign, she would struggle.

Nonetheless, she never once considered going back to Belgium. It was almost as if she had never forgiven her home-land for abandoning her and her family. Although she had been the one to leave, she blamed her actions on the capitulation of her own country.

After a series of lowly positions in service, she took a chance and applied for something she thought might help restore her feeling of self-worth. 'Housekeeper to a Doctor' was a role she knew she could play, even although she had nothing like the years of experience necessary for the post.

*

'Can I help you?' asked a stern-faced Cuthbert that morning when she arrived at his front door.

'I have come to offer my services, sir. For the advertised position.'

'I think there has been some misunderstanding, miss.'

'Madame.'

'My apologies, madame. The position is for a housekeeper who will be in residence.'

'And you have decided with one look that I am unsuitable? You have neither asked about my circumstances, nor my experience. You have simply dismissed me.'

She stood looking at Cuthbert, unwilling to yield her gaze and forcing him either to shut the door in her face or explain himself. Cuthbert was unused to being spoken to like this, especially by a woman, and he was even less able to reply than usual.

'Not at all, madame . . .?'

'Madame William Smith, sir.'

'Would you like to come in, so that we might discuss the matter without further alarming my neighbours?'

Marie Délanger Smith walked over the threshold and into Cuthbert's hall. She immediately noted the dust and clumsiness of the layout. All things she would be correcting presently.

Cuthbert gestured open-palmed to the door on the right. 'Do come into the parlour, and please take a seat.'

He opened the door for the woman and ushered her into the bright room that received most of the morning light. Marie looked about, surveying the damage and making a mental note of just how much work there was to be done in this house. Cuthbert directed her to a chair and stood on the other side of the room, putting as much distance between them as might be considered decent. He opened his mouth to speak but was overtaken by her.

'I know what you are thinking, sir. You are concerned that I am too young for the position. That a woman my age living in the same house as a single man – you are single, I take it, sir

– that it may seem inappropriate. I can assure you I am more than capable of taking this house and making it run for you like clockwork. I came to England at the age of fifteen and have worked every day for the last ten years, cleaning, cooking and keeping home for one man or another. I am very good at what I do, and you will find no one better for the position. As for the circumstances, I would be disappointed to think that a man of your position and education would be so affected by what others may think.'

Cuthbert was aware of what she was doing but found himself taking a liking to the young woman's spirit. He was studying her as she spoke and had noted the frayed cuff on her blouse and the pallor of her skin. She was not just slim, but underneath her bulky coat he guessed that she was seriously underweight and quite possibly anaemic. She badly needed a job, and despite her somewhat haughty demeanour, he suspected he could work with this one.

Since his arrival in London, he had had a series of very short-term housekeepers, all of whom had left without being asked to leave. He was told that he was difficult to please but that he rarely gave specific enough instructions for any housekeeper to understand his wants. Cuthbert had a feeling, admittedly unsupported by any hard evidence, that the young woman now sitting in his parlour might be the one who would be calling the domestic shots if he gave her the job.

'And Mr Smith, madame?'

'Deceased, sir. I have been a widow for the last seven years.'

Cuthbert frowned and did not enquire further, but simply offered the obvious follow-up question: 'Children?'

'Of course, I have none, sir.'

'Why of course?'

'What mother would leave her children and go to live and work in a stranger's house?'

Cuthbert caught the sharpness of her tone and knew that she considered herself too good for the job, but at the same time he was confident she would do it better than anyone. Trying not to seem too eager, he walked to the fireplace and adjusted the position of a small ornament before saying, 'Well, obviously I will be looking at the other applicants, but if you leave your name and address–'

'Have there been other applicants?'

Again, Cuthbert was taken aback by her rudeness, but he was forced to admit the truth that there had not. However, he refused to give in to her. He bid her a polite good day and asked her to leave her details.

As he closed the door behind her, he thought he would wait until the next day before offering her the job.

*

Now, standing in the study, the chief inspector was apparently still waiting on an answer to his question. The question had not been as rhetorical as Cuthbert had supposed. Without interrupting his search for the book, Cuthbert just shook his head and said, 'No story really. Belgian refugee during the war. Widow. And she runs a very tight ship. Lucky to have her. Very much keeps me on the straight and narrow, Chief Inspector Mowbray.'

'Indeed, I expect she does.'

The chief inspector's interest was not fully satisfied, but he had more pressing concerns so filed his line of enquiry, not under cancelled, but merely postponed.

'Ah, here's the blighter. Virgil's *Aeneid*. You do read Latin, chief inspector?'

Cuthbert realised the question was beneath him as soon as he had asked it and was disappointed in himself. He quickly recovered and pulled another book from the same shelf.

'This is the Dryden translation. Not so accurate as some but certainly more poetic than most, and it's my personal favourite. Let me find the passage . . . yes, here it is in Book Eight.

The living and the dead at his command,
Were coupled, face to face, and hand to hand,
Till, chok'd with stench, in loath'd embraces tied,
The ling'ring wretches pin'd away and died.

'Quite a gruesome picture. Virgil puts the words into the mouth of a character called Evander, who in the book is a king and ally of Aeneas, and he's talking about another king – the Etruscan despot Mezentius – and the atrocious punishments he has thought up for his subjects.'

'And you think that's what we're dealing with? Some fanciful re-enactment of a two-thousand-year-old bit of mythology?'

'Unfortunately, it was probably more than a myth, chief inspector. The ancients could teach even our generation a lesson or two on brutality. But, yes, I think the killer or killers is doing exactly that.'

Chief Inspector Mowbray opened the Latin text Cuthbert had handed him and allowed the dry, yellowed pages to flick through his fingers. He shook his head, unable to find words to express his disgust, when Madame Smith came in to say that the tea was ready.

'Shall we, chief inspector?'

'Four lines of poetry and that's it. Case closed? Not by a long chalk. I'll have that sick fucker.'

'Chief inspector, please! There is a lady present.'

'Begging your pardon, madame. I'm just a policeman that doesn't read Latin. I've no stomach for tea, Cuthbert. I'll see you back at the Yard at your convenience. I need to see those files again.'

Mowbray quickly went back along the hallway and took

his hat from where he had left it on the table and let himself out. The chill in the air was welcome, and he filled his lungs. He waved his driver on because he needed the long walk back to the Yard. The next day would be one of redoubled efforts.

*

Mowbray briefed his sergeant and arranged for the re-deployment of additional manpower. He was working a double murder, and he could argue with his superiors upstairs that the nature of it was going to attract considerable press attention.

The Yard had to be seen to be doing everything it could, and it had to be seen to be doing it right. There would be scrutiny from both inside and out, and there would inevitably be recriminations. There always were in cases like this. Why has it taken so long? When did they first realise? What exactly happened? These and more were the questions that he would have to answer in the weeks and months ahead, and he was not about to leave himself open to criticism. He was looking ahead and preparing his defence because he had played this game for too long to get caught out.

On the flip side, he also knew that this was the kind of case that could be a golden ticket. Although he had only recently been promoted to chief inspector, he already had his eyes on the next rung of the ladder. Cracking a high-profile case like this could make your name, and he had learned that names were the ones who got the superintendent desks here at Scotland Yard.

Mowbray had other cases, but he was quite prepared to shift them onto the back burner to allow this double homicide to take centre stage. However, he knew that might be a high-risk strategy. If he solved it quickly, all well and good, but if he failed, then his failure would be very much in the spotlight.

One of those other cases that Mowbray had downgraded was nevertheless occupying the pathologists at St Thomas's.

Cuthbert had already reviewed what he regarded as a relatively straightforward rape and murder of a young woman from south London, and he had decided that this would be an excellent case for his assistant to cut his forensic teeth on. Morgenthal had been asking to be more involved for some weeks and Cuthbert had surprised him by handing him the reins.

He told his assistant that he would be taking a back seat on this one, but of course he was available if Morgenthal should need any help. His assistant was now aware that you should be careful what you wish for, or at least what you badger your boss for. He knew what needed to be done and in what order, but until now Cuthbert had always been standing beside him, metaphorically, and occasionally literally, holding his hand.

He had laid out his strategy for the examination, which Cuthbert had approved, and now he was collecting surface samples of hair and nails as well as fingerprints from the corpse. In the laboratory, he had the young woman's clothing and effects bagged. He planned to tackle those before performing the post mortem examination in case any evidence from that preliminary investigation might suggest a particular approach with the dissection.

Cuthbert was in his office most of the time and Morgenthal was unsure if he was even watching what he was doing. However, such uncertainty on the part of his assistant betrayed a lack of understanding of Cuthbert's methods. This was still his laboratory and his mortuary, and everything that happened in it was his responsibility, no matter who was doing it. Cuthbert was keeping a very close, if discreet, eye on his junior colleague.

In the middle of the morning, Cuthbert walked casually from his office to the filing cabinet in the laboratory. As he passed Morgenthal examining the underclothes of the victim under a strong light, he asked, 'How is it progressing?'

'Very well, Dr Cuthbert. I am just looking for any signs of a struggle and any physical evidence of sexual assault.'

'Good. And, of course, we must never forget Locard's Exchange Principle.'

'Sir?'

'Please don't look at me like that, Simon, and please do not tell me that you have never heard of Locard – Monsieur Edmond Locard of France, the foremost forensic scientist in Europe?'

Morgenthal looked sheepish and was less upset that he had never heard of the Frenchman than that he had disappointed Cuthbert, who simply rolled his eyes.

'What are you reading if not Locard? "Every contact leaves a trace." That is his maxim, and it needs to be ours here in this laboratory. It is the very foundation stone of our work. It means that it is impossible for criminals to escape the scene of a crime without leaving behind trace evidence that can be used to identify them and link them to the crime. That evidence is here before us, probably in the stains on this unfortunate woman's petticoat, if only we know how to read it. Do make sure you write everything down. I look forward to reading your report.'

Morgenthal made a discreet note of the name 'Locard' and determined to get up to speed with his reading. Lately, he had found that Cuthbert would often go for days without asking him anything, and then quite unexpectedly he would be grilled on some obscure point of an investigation. The only way to impress his mentor was to be as prepared as possible. Only then might luck be on the young man's side.

At the end of a long afternoon at the bench, Cuthbert had been watching his assistant all day struggling with the evidence bags. He finally decided that Morgenthal needed to stop and come back fresh in the morning. Taking care not to include a hint of criticism, Cuthbert told him to pack up his things for the day and take himself off home.

'I expect that fiancée of yours has plans for you bright young things tonight. It is Friday evening after all.'

'Oh, it is our Sabbath, Dr Cuthbert. It's always dinner at home with the family on a Friday night. I will be back in early tomorrow to finish this. Good night.'

Cuthbert had forgotten that his assistant was Jewish and realised he had rarely heard him talk about his faith, if indeed he had any. He had always thought that it was as much a culture as a religious faith. Any Jews he had known at university and afterwards seemed to him to have such a strong, ingrained sense of family. He had always been a little envious of that.

He tidied his own desk of the lectures he had been preparing for next term and took the corridor to the main exit. Cuthbert stepped out and immediately turned up his collar against the rain and put up his umbrella. He brightened as a taxi for hire turned into the street, and raised his hand to hail it, only to find himself being hailed. He turned to see who had called his name and did not recognise the elegant man in his thirties with the walking cane.

'Please forgive the unorthodox approach, Dr Cuthbert, and please do just give me a moment of your time. My name is Gossett, Dr Gossett from the law faculty at U.C.L. I am, or rather I was, tutor to Freddie Dawson.'

Cuthbert was suspicious and immediately on his guard, but his expression revealed nothing. He kept his silence and waited to hear more before bidding the stranger a curt good day.

'I telephoned Inspector Franklin who had interviewed me at the time of Freddie's disappearance. He told me he was no longer attached to the case, given the developments. You see, being Freddie's tutor, I have a pastoral responsibility to the family. He died while he was a student of ours and there are certain obligations. I wasn't sure who to ask. I know you can tell me nothing by way of specifics, but I have to tell the family something, even if it's just that I have been in contact with the police.'

'I am not the police, sir.'

'Ah, and I see you are from north of the border, doctor.'

'With my accent, I have little chance of fooling anyone here on that account.'

'It isn't just your accent, it's your whole bearing. I can tell you are a Celt through and through. A great Scot indeed.'

Cuthbert explained that there was really nothing he could say about the case. It was a tragedy, the boy's body had been recovered – that much was already in the papers – but nothing more could be released, even to the family at this stage. Gossett nodded, quietly acknowledging the position he had put Cuthbert in.

'*Infandum, regina, iubes renovare dolorem.*'

'Yes, indeed, truly "a sorrow too deep to tell". You are a Latin scholar? That's the *Aeneid*, is it not?'

'An occupational hazard, I'm afraid. Lots of Latin in my line of work – the law. But I still take some time to read the rather more beautiful verses of the poets. So economical, so precise, yet so full of feeling. Makes a welcome change from the turgid prose with which I have to spend most of my time. I do apologise for troubling you. It was really rather silly of me. I just suppose I'm clutching at straws. I will bother you no more.'

'Let me assure you, as soon as we've got to the bottom of it, as soon as we have the cause of death, the family will be fully informed.'

'*Felix qui potuit rerum cognoscenti causas.*'

'"Happy is he who has been able to learn the causes of things." You *are* fond of your Virgil, Dr Gossett.'

'No more, I think, than yourself. But isn't it true that a man like you, whose job it is to unravel the causes of the often-dreadful things that are brought to you, must find happiness in that work?'

'Happiness is not the word I would use.'

'Fulfilment, then. Surely that? I will bid you good evening, Dr Cuthbert.' He shook his umbrella and sighed at the sky. 'I was expecting a fair day, but the gods, I see, thought otherwise.'

Cuthbert watched him go, limping and leaning heavily on his cane, as he disappeared into the throng of black umbrellas making their way towards Westminster Bridge.

Chapter 9

London: 8 April 1929

The file on Henry Melville was still on Sergeant Baker's desk, and it remained disappointingly thin. There had been a team working on it for almost a fortnight, but they now knew no more about the man than when they started.

They ran the usual initial checks. They found no Henry P. Melville on any voters' rolls. Nor, they discovered, did anyone by that name have a British passport. They already knew that he was unlikely to have a criminal record because the fingerprints taken from the corpse had not matched any on file. Baker asked for this to be double-checked, but again there was no record of a Henry Melville of that approximate age in the police files.

The closest they came was a 16-year-old delinquent with the same name who had been nicked for house-breaking. They tried birth certificates, although that always took a little longer, and they did find a number of possibles. Given that they did not know Melville's age for certain, they looked for anyone with that or a similar name who had been born between 1861 and 1871. That would have given them anyone aged between

58 and 68, which, according to Cuthbert, should have been a reasonable range to check.

They retrieved nine named Henry Melville, three registered as Henry P. Melville and four as Henry D. Melville. Of these sixteen, nine had died in infancy, two had died in the war and there was no trace of the other five in any census after 1901. Of course, Melville might not have been born in England, but trying to find a foreign birth certificate was next to impossible without more details like an exact date of birth and his parents' names.

The next obvious line of enquiry to be followed was his address, which had been provided by the dental laboratory where he had his dentures made. This turned out to be a fairly down-at-heel boarding house in east London. Baker himself had undertaken the interviews, but he found everyone in the place to be on their guard as soon as he showed his warrant card. The landlady, a Mrs Edna Bryce, was a little more forthcoming.

'I runs a very respectable house here, sergeant, and make no mistake. There's some in this area who have all sorts of comings and goings in their establishments, but not here. My gentlemen and lady guests are all of the professional class. I don't have riff-raff, no, I don't.'

'What can you tell me about Mr Melville, madam?'

'I can tell you he owes me six weeks rent for starters. He came about a year ago – no, make that eighteen months. Good references. Retired – widower, I think – but to tell you the truth, dear, he was always on the go. Don't know what he did with himself, but he would disappear for weeks at a time, without a by your leave, and then you'd see him on the stairs one morning. When he was here, he kept himself to himself. And, to be honest, that's the way I like it, dear. Too much familiarity between the proprietress and the guests never works out well in my experience. Always paid his rent on time, which is why I started to worry. At first, I thought he must just be off on one of his jaunts, but this one was too long. I do hope you find him.'

'What about your other guests? Did any of them have any particular dealings with Mr Melville?'

'Ooh, you'd have to ask them, dear. I'm not a mind reader.'

The tenants in the three other rooms proved to know even less about Melville than his landlady. There was a middle-aged woman who claimed to work in publishing although she was vague about her employer, and a rather well-spoken gentleman who did not seem to work at all, but did appear to be comfortable, if a little inebriated. The last of the three occupied the room directly below Melville. He was an elderly Russian woodwind teacher, who was having the greatest of difficulty understanding Baker's questions.

'Mr Leonid Goncharov?'

'What you want?'

'I'm with the police, sir. I just need to ask you a few questions.'

'Eh?'

'The police. Some questions, sir.'

'I not call the police.'

'No, I know, sir. We're trying to find out about Mr Melville. You know, the gentleman on the second floor, upstairs?'

'He not here. He away.'

'I know, sir. That's why we're here – he's gone missing.'

'He not musical. Always complain, complain, complain. Good that he is gone. He not all here.'

'Not unlike yourself, sir.'

'Eh?'

'You teach music, sir?'

'I teach flute. Do you want to learn to play flute? You want lessons?'

'No, sir. I'm a police officer. I'm asking about Mr Melville.'

'I not call the police.'

'Yes, sir. Thank you for your time. I'll leave you to your music.'

Baker recorded in his notebook that he had spoken to Leonid Goncharov but simply added, 'Possibly deaf, possibly mad, but more likely both.'

After the fruitless interviews, he went back downstairs to see the landlady.

'And one more thing, Mrs Bryce. I would like to search Mr Melville's room, if I may.'

'I don't know what you're hoping to find. I mean he's hardly going to be in there, is he? But please yourself. Just don't break anything. If he doesn't come back, I'll be within my right to sell whatever he's got. I know the law, you know.'

The room was nothing more than a sparsely furnished bedroom. There was a damp patch on the ceiling by the window and the rug by the bed was torn and frayed. It was hard to believe that this was a man's life.

A single shirt was hanging on a rail behind a curtain that served as a wardrobe. There was a dressing gown on the back of the door with nothing in the pockets, a drawer with two odd socks and a vest, and a small shaving kit on the table.

Beside the single bed there was a small cabinet on top of which was a pile of books. Baker squinted to read their titles and made a note of the words he couldn't pronounce.

There was a fairly battered suitcase under the bed, with some more items of clothing, but nowhere in the room was there a single letter or photograph that might have helped explain who or what Melville was.

Baker closed his notebook and scratched his head, but he had one last idea. If Melville had paid for his new dentures with a cheque, he might be able to track down his bank account, but a phone call to the laboratory in Croydon put paid to that; they only dealt in cash.

Now, Baker had precisely nothing to present to Mowbray at the case conference the following day.

As expected, the chief inspector was less than happy with the progress his sergeant was making. 'Nobody knows anything about him? They live under the same roof as him for over a year and they know nothing?'

'Nothing they're telling, sir.'

'Did you get a look at the references Melville gave the old bird?'

'I did, sir, and as you might expect, they didn't look real to me.'

'So we have a man probably in his sixties who takes a room in an East End dive eighteen months ago, and before that it's as if he didn't exist.'

'That's about the size of it, chief inspector.'

'Well, Baker, if you want to stay on this team, it'd better get considerably bigger and fast. Have you considered the possibility that Henry Melville didn't exist eighteen months ago? That you're looking for a man who didn't want to be found, who changed his name? Now, get out there and find him.'

The chief inspector walked off to his office, and Baker stood looking at the pinboard.

Cuthbert came up to him and said quietly, 'It's not my place to interfere, sergeant. That's been made very clear to me by the chief inspector, but I was wondering about the books.'

'The books, doctor?'

'The ones you found in Melville's room. You mentioned in your report that you had trouble reading the titles. Do you have a note of them that I could see?'

Baker first checked to make sure the Pie's door was closed and then got out his notebook.

'*A Latin Grammar* by Charles E. Bennett, Caesar's *Bellum Gallicum*, whatever that is when it's at home, Kennedy's *Latin Primer* and Virgil's *Aeneid*. They were all pretty tatty.'

'Interesting. Did it strike you as odd, sergeant, that such a spartan room would have books like that? I mean he obviously wasn't living the life of luxury, so where did he get the money to buy Latin books, and books about studying Latin at that? Did you look inside them?'

'Just a flick through to check there weren't any letters or the like. People sometimes use the strangest things as bookmarks.'

'What about the fly leaves? Any names?'

'Can't say I paid any attention, sir. Do you think I should have?'

'Well, they're expensive books, and they were obviously important to Melville since they were the only ones there. Maybe he might have written his name in them. His real name, sergeant.'

*

The next afternoon, after a return visit to Mrs Bryce's boarding house, Baker came to Cuthbert's office at the hospital.

'You were right, sir. "W.A. Galton" in every one. I've checked and there was a William Albert Galton born 1864. We have an open missing person file on that one from about eighteen months ago. It might be him. Galton disappears and then reappears as Melville.'

'Could be. What else do we know about this Galton?'

'A sixty-three-year-old man was reported missing on the sixteenth of October 1927 by his wife, Mrs Elizabeth Galton of 128 Kensington Terrace. It's up west and rather a different sort of gaff to where he ended up. He was a schoolteacher but seemed to have just taken early retirement. There was something funny about the statement though. I've checked and the desk sergeant says he didn't believe what she said about that – thought it sounded fishy.'

'What did he teach?'

'Latin, sir.'

'What is the chief inspector saying to all this?'

'I haven't told him yet, sir. I thought you should know first. It was your idea.'

'Well, for both our sakes, sergeant, shall we just forget I've had this little preview. I suggest you report to him right away. If the chief inspector chooses to share it with me, I'll be sure to look surprised. And, if he asks, it was your idea to check the books, all right?'

*

Mowbray was surprised by the speed with which Baker had turned things around and said as much. Now, they could get properly started on the case, and the more they could learn about this William Galton, the better. He ordered Baker to pay Mrs Galton a visit.

'Go gently and don't tell her we think we've got her husband in the cold storage at the morgue. Just try and find out everything you can and cross-check if the Galtons had any connection, any at all, with the Dawsons. And get a proper photograph of him. That one on the board of him on Cuthbert's slab is starting to annoy me.'

*

Baker arrived in Kensington Terrace at three o'clock as arranged with Mrs Galton. On the phone he had been careful to say that this was just a routine follow-up. The house was one of those large white affairs in a crescent near Regent's Park. There was clearly money, but it didn't fit with the rooms he had visited the previous week in the East End. Baker was puzzled why anyone would leave this for that.

Mrs Galton was a stout lady, who obviously didn't enjoy living in the 1920s. She wore clothes from another generation and had the manners to match.

'Detective Sergeant Baker, I do not believe we have met. I am Mrs William Galton. Won't you come through to the library? It gets the afternoon sun and is so pleasant at this time of year. Kitty will bring us tea.'

The interior did the outside justice and was just as opulent as Baker had expected. The library was large and book-lined. On the desk, he noted a pile of slim volumes with gold-lettered titles somewhat similar to those he had seen at Mrs Bryce's.

'Are you a Latin scholar, sergeant? I couldn't help noticing that you took an interest in my husband's books. He was a particular fan of lyric poetry, you know.'

'No, madam. You have quite a collection, I see.'

He turned and looked around the walls as he said this and Mrs Galton simply smiled and said, 'All William's, I'm afraid. Nothing to do with me. I only come into this room for that.'

She pointed to a large arched window that overlooked the park and which filled the room with light.

'I do hope this is not going to be too tedious. I have, after all, given a number of statements to your colleagues, and I really have nothing new to say. I have not seen or heard from Mr Galton for many months. Ah, tea. Just put it there, Kitty. Now, sergeant, milk or lemon?'

Baker had to gently tease out the whole story of Galton's initial disappearance, on the pretext that a new team was taking over all the long-term missing person cases, and he was required to confirm the details. He discovered that Galton had indeed taken early retirement from his post of head of classics at St Peter's, a public school in the city.

Only a week or so later, Mrs Galton had come home one afternoon from shopping and found the house empty. There was nothing missing, no signs of burglary, but her husband was gone. His clothes were all still in his room and no luggage was missing. His passport was still in his drawer as was his watch. The latter was particularly odd, as he never went anywhere without it. It was gold and had been a twenty-first birthday present from his father, and 'it had the dearest little inscription on it'.

'Were there any books missing, madam?'

'I don't think so, sergeant, but, as you can see, if one or two were taken it would be hard to know.'

'Can you tell me why your husband took early retirement?'

Mrs Galton rose and went to the window. She pulled back the fine net curtains just enough to see the couple who were walking through the park below. She looked distracted and, to Baker's mind, also a little irritated.

'Do you think this will take much longer, sergeant. I really do have to get ready. My bridge group, you know. We meet here every Tuesday evening.'

'I'm sorry if I'm keeping you, Mrs Galton, but we are still working on your husband's case, and anything you can tell us would be most helpful. His early retirement?'

'Ah yes, that. I'm sure I don't know why. I thought he enjoyed the job. He certainly didn't do it for the money. A teacher's salary, for goodness' sake! No, I had the money. My father was in mining. Mr Galton liked to play at being the breadwinner, but it was just a little pathetic at times. I think perhaps he wasn't giving it his full attention towards the end. I suspect they let him go. Early retirement is what they call it, isn't it?'

Baker was beginning to think he would have done a bunk too, if he'd been married to this one, but he smiled and nodded and took notes. She was on a roll now and he didn't want to derail her.

'It seemed to start with the letters. He wouldn't show them to me, of course, but they were obviously troubling him. He must have received, what, eight or ten over a period of a few months, and every time one would arrive, he would disappear in here for hours. I really didn't have time for his little neuroses. It wasn't long afterwards that he announced he was giving up his teaching. I think he was expecting me to care. Anyway, as I said, it was soon afterwards that he vanished. And I have not heard from him since.'

'Would you have a photograph of your husband that I could take away, madam? For the new files, you understand.'

She went into the next room and Baker could hear a drawer being opened. She came back with a framed head and shoulders portrait of Mr Galton.

'I think that's probably the best likeness, but who knows what he might look like now.'

Baker said nothing. He asked Mrs Galton about Alfred and Maud Dawson, but she claimed never to have heard of them. Similarly, she said that she and her husband had no connections with U.C.L., where Freddie had been a student.

'There are just a few other names I would like to ask you about. They are people who have come up in our investigations, and it would be useful to know if you recognised any of them.'

Mrs Galton put on the small reading glasses that were hanging from a gold chain about her neck. She perched them on the end of her nose and scanned the list that Baker had handed her.

'No ... no. Oh, I don't think we know any one of that name. No ... no, oh, we do know the Haskells. Charming couple and their two girls. The son, Robert I think, was in William's sixth form. But we knew them socially before that. Why are they on your list?'

Baker sidestepped the question and made his last request.

'What kind of home do you think I run here, sergeant? Do you really think that after a year and a half there will be surfaces or indeed any object in this house that he would have touched that would not have been thoroughly cleaned? Look around you, young man. Do you see any dirt?'

Baker realised he needed to apologise to which he added his thanks for all her help, before making his exit.

'We'll be in touch if there are any developments, madam.'

The chance of retrieving Galton's fingerprints was a long shot after all these months, but at least he now had the connection with the girl. The sergeant himself had interviewed Clare Haskell at the university, and although it was a tenuous link, it was at least something he could report to the Pie. He hoped to add to that after speaking with the headmaster at Galton's school. From what his wife had said, there was obviously a story there.

*

St Peter's was one of the most exclusive boys' schools in the City. Closely associated with the adjacent church of the same name, it had a reputation for its excellent choir and for the number of its alumni who had made it into the Cabinet.

Baker would once have been intimidated by the grand architecture and the even grander people inside, but his years at the Yard had taught him that even the brightest gloss can conceal the most ingrained dirt. The headmaster, Charles Houghton, had agreed to see him. Indeed, he was eager to speak with the sergeant.

'It's a bizarre business and no mistake. Completely un-accountable. Mr Galton was one of our longest-serving and most senior masters. The classics department is such an important part of our school, you understand, and he was the pillar of it.'

'Was Mr Galton dismissed from the school, sir?'

'Dismissed? Of course not. What happened was so out of character that we thought he must be unwell. He came to my office – it was during the autumn term – and announced that he would be leaving. I was taken aback, and of course I asked what had prompted the decision, but he was tight-lipped. Just said he needed a change, and that he would be leaving immediately. Now, that really was not on, and I said so. It is customary for any departing master to see the term out, for the continuity of teaching, you understand. It was most inconvenient, not to say unprofessional, simply to up sticks in the middle of things. But he couldn't be swayed, and he left us the next day.

'He explained his actions to no one, and we simply didn't hear from him again. He even left most of his belongings, books and suchlike. He was in a hurry to leave, that much was clear. But why? Thirty-four years he had been at the school. He was even here before me.'

'And you say he didn't contact you or any of the staff after he left, or after he went missing?'

'Well, that was even odder. No sooner had he left us, than he disappeared completely. I spoke to another policeman at the time, but I got the distinct impression that they weren't looking that hard. I remember him saying that Mr Galton was an adult and thus was free to do as he pleased. If he wished to leave his life, who were we to call him out on it. But I mean to say, what about his poor wife? It really was most irregular.'

Baker showed the headmaster the same list of names and addresses he had shown Mrs Galton, but he recognised no one. When Baker pointed out Clare Haskell's name, the headmaster simply shrugged.

'This is a boys' school, sergeant.'

'Her brother, Robert Haskell, I believe attended St Peter's.'

'That may be so, and I can check for you, but I certainly don't remember the name.'

After half an hour of searching by the school secretary, Baker left the headmaster's office with Robert Haskell's dates at the school and the information that he had gone on to Trinity to read Greats.

*

Back at the Yard, Baker was now able to replace the post mortem photograph of Melville on the pinboard with the portrait photograph of Galton. He also linked the photograph with a length of red string to the details of Robert Haskell. A further string linked Dawson's photograph to Haskell's name besides which had been appended the note, 'via sister, Clare'. As he completed the additions, Mowbray was pacing in front of the board and looking far from pleased.

'It's still very thin. We need to speak to this Haskell chap, and make sure we interview his sister again. Perhaps she knows more than she's telling. Have we found any other links with the school? Some of those posh boys at the university might have been there too. Have we checked that?'

Baker shook his head and immediately made a note in his book.

'And what was Galton up to? Leaving a cushy life with a rich wife and a job he apparently enjoyed, to fly off to a room that's one step up from a doss house. Changes his name, makes no contact with anyone in his previous life and then gets himself murdered. Ideas?'

He turned from the board and fixed his gaze on the two constables and Baker seated before him, but carefully avoided Cuthbert's eyes, who was sitting at the back where he had now become a regular attendee at these meetings.

'Come on,' he said, tapping the nearest constable's head with his finger. 'There must be something in there.'

'Money worries, chief inspector? Or maybe a woman? Perhaps he was having an affair and his wife found out and chucked him out without a pot to piss in.'

'And what's your evidence to support that, constable?'

'None, sir.'

'None, sir. So, next time, think it through before you open your gob, sir. What about the rest of you?'

This time he included Cuthbert in his sweep and the doctor did not disappoint.

'Sergeant Baker mentioned in his statement that Mrs Galton attributed the changes she saw in the victim to a series of letters he had received. That suggests he may have been coerced into his actions in some way, perhaps even through blackmail. Have any such letters been recovered either from the home or the digs?'

Baker answered that they had not. Mrs Galton had never seen their contents and the letters themselves were not in the study after he left. Nor were they anywhere in Galton's digs.

'But if those letters were connected to his actions, they may also be connected to his murder. The sender may even have been his killer. I suggest that finding out more about them and, if possible, recovering the letters themselves should be a priority.'

Mowbray was only half-listening. He started pacing again, and almost under his breath said, 'There has to be a more direct link between them. This wasn't random. This had to be planned to the last detail. These men were selected because they had something in common.'

Mowbray now gave his entire attention to the blackboard and chalked three points in a triangular formation.

'This is Dawson,' he said circling one of the chalk points. 'This is Galton, and this,' he said, adding a question mark above the third point, 'is our killer.' He then drew lines between the points completing the triangle. 'And these are the connections.' He emphasised the line between the points representing the victims. 'That's the one we have to find, and we're nowhere near it.'

Mowbray was almost ignoring the team at his back. Was it the moment for Cuthbert to speak? His contributions were generally discouraged unless they were explicitly sought, but this time Cuthbert was sure the chief inspector was chasing the wrong rabbit.

'May I say something, chief inspector?'

At first Mowbray didn't seem to hear the pathologist, and only once Baker had coughed to attract his attention, did he turn. Cuthbert didn't wait for permission.

'You're still looking for a connection between Dawson and Galton, a clear link. But there is a connection: it's the killer. Maybe he knew them both even though they did not know each other. We can think of the three of them as a triangle, as you say, but if we do that, they are not the points, they are the sides, and the killer is the third side.'

Mowbray frowned and pointed at the board. 'But that analogy doesn't work. It can't be a triangle then, Cuthbert. You're proposing that the two victims were unconnected, but surely any two sides of a triangle are connected?'

'Indeed they are, chief inspector, so perhaps it would be better if we thought of them like this.'

He stood and took the duster and erased the line between Dawson and Galton, leaving the other two lines of Mowbray's triangle joined at the top.

'Now these points are Dawson and Galton, as you said before, chief inspector. But now nothing joins them. They have separate lives and are apart, even divergent, for most of their lives until they meet in death, where they are connected.

Quite literally. But I'm not sure they ever even met when they were both alive. All your investigations haven't been wasted. What you have conclusively shown, after weeks of enquiry, is that these two men's paths never crossed. Until the end, that is.'

'What about Haskell? His sister is Dawson's classmate, and he's a former pupil of Galton. That's a line that would link them.'

'A tenuous one at best. By all means speak with Haskell, but it's a link that you don't need. Whoever killed Dawson probably knew him. That same killer probably also knew Galton. The nature of the crimes, as you say yourself, suggests premeditation and careful planning. There was probably some deep personal attachment between the killer and his victims. But there is no necessity in all this that Dawson and Galton were associated in any way before their deaths. The common ground between them is the murderer. Find someone who knew them both, and you might find their killer.'

The chief inspector ended the meeting without saying anything more. He simply gestured everyone away and, after staring at the blackboard a little longer, eventually left and returned to his office. In the stairwell, Baker called after Cuthbert who was making his way back down to the entrance. He caught up with the pathologist who, standing two steps below him, was able to look Baker in the eyes.

'Sergeant, was there something else?'

'I never really thanked you for that tip about the books. Saved my bacon, sir.'

'It's teamwork, sergeant. We're all pulling on the same oars. No need for thanks. Was there anything else?'

'Well, there is something that's troubling me, sir. It's about the identification. I think something's got lost in all the excitement about uncovering Galton. The thing is, we know because of the denture that the body on your slab is Henry

Melville. And we know that in Henry Melville's room we found books belonging to William Galton. We now have a picture of Mr Galton, and we're starting to learn about his life, but where in all that can we be sure that the body we know is Melville is also really Galton? We don't have Galton's fingerprints and it's all very circumstantial. Unless we have a positive identification, we can't proceed. And we can hardly ask the wife to view the body. It hasn't got a face.'

'But it does have a skull, sergeant. I have an idea. Come with me.'

Cuthbert took Baker to the first-floor photographic laboratory to discuss the possibility of overlaying a copy of Galton's photograph that had been supplied by his wife on an X-ray image of the corpse's skull.

'Not sure we've ever done that before, Dr Cuthbert, but that doesn't mean we can't try. Of course, the orientation will be everything. Do you have the photograph? We can check the scale and the angle of the head and give precise instructions to the radiographer to reproduce the same angle for a new X-ray. We'll have to play around with the scale of the two images and print a copy of the photograph on a transparent base, but theoretically it should be possible.'

Baker retrieved Galton's photograph from the duty-room pinboard, and Cuthbert personally took it down to the photographic laboratory technicians. He stayed longer than he needed in order to watch what they were doing and exactly how they were doing it, such was his fascination with any new and unfamiliar technology.

Once they had studied the picture, they provided a working copy and a set of angles for the radiographer. He then spent over an hour in the mortuary at St Thomas's with the corpse, translating these into settings for his X-ray equipment in order to take an exact replica of the head position in the photograph.

The next day, when the photographic laboratory had both the photograph and the X-ray in their possession, they then started to manipulate the scale. Cuthbert had asked to be called back at this stage as he was keen to see the final outcome.

With the X-ray and the now semi-transparent version of the resized photograph on the light box before him, all Cuthbert had to do was slide one on top of the other and it would be immediately obvious if the skull belonged to the man in the photograph. He superimposed them, aligned the main features, and everything fitted exactly into place. The angle of the nose, the distance between the eye sockets, the line of the jaw and the slope of the forehead – all were a perfect match.

'I think we can say with some confidence, gentlemen, that our corpse is that of William Galton.'

*

When Cuthbert got back to the hospital laboratory, he met Morgenthal just coming out.

'I'm going up to the canteen. May I bring you anything, Dr Cuthbert?'

Morgenthal had asked this question every day they were together in the laboratory, and every day he received the same silent shake of Cuthbert's head. His assistant had been told that Cuthbert did not eat lunch, but he was never sure if that was completely true and thought it best to err on the side of discretion.

When he had gone, Cuthbert half closed his office door, which normally stood open. He unknotted his laces and slipped off his black boots. From his bottom desk drawer, he took out a wooden box containing a soft cloth and a tin of boot polish. He held the cloth tight over his index finger and dipped it into the tin of black wax. With small, slow circular movements, he worked the polish into the leather of his toe caps.

He repeated the process over and over again, eventually adding some lubricant by dabbing the cloth and the polish on to his tongue. Building up layer after layer of polish, the swirls he created on his boots would slowly resolve into the mirror-like shine he was looking for. Only when he could see his reflection clearly in each toe cap was he satisfied.

The process to achieve this high gloss would take him almost an hour every lunchtime. And, more often than not, another hour when he repeated the process every evening. He told himself that he tended to his boots as a form of meditation, but he really knew it was an unhealthy compulsion which he was unable to break.

Occasionally, Morgenthal would slip back into the laboratory, unobserved, and would watch him through the half-open office door. Cuthbert would be sitting at his desk with the bottom drawer out, the tin of polish open, working at his boots. And Morgenthal knew not to disturb him when he was polishing as he seemed lost in his thoughts. He assumed he was thinking hard about a case or trying to get the sequence of cause and effect aligned in his head. But what Morgenthal did not know was that these were the only times when Cuthbert could think about nothing at all. No memories could broach the silent routine he had developed; no thoughts of blood or mire or the squalor of war could find their way into this cleansing ritual.

Chapter 10

North of Ypres: 15 June 1916

Cuthbert heard the first stretcher bearers shouting before he saw them. Although there was a moon and it caught the wet outlines of the men as they trudged across the yard in front of the Dressing Station, it was only as they approached that he could make out there were around fifteen casualties arriving. Some of the stretchers were being carried by pairs of bearers, while others had been placed on two-wheeled carts. The bearers were all in khaki, only distinguishable from the men they were carrying by the Red Cross arm bands they were wearing.

All the wounded had been picked up from the nearest field. Already the yard was filled with activity and the painful cries of several of those they carried. It was nearly midnight, and another busy night was expected. These were the first to arrive and were carefully laid on straw next to the Operations Tent. Their bearers then collected new stretchers and returned to the front-line trenches to retrieve the next group of casualties.

The Operations Tent had been erected and equipped earlier in the day to supplement the dressing bays in the old stables. The large acetylene lamp inside the tent was now lit. By its light through the canvas, Cuthbert was able to undertake the preliminary assessment of the men outside. Tied to each was a buff card – the Field Medical Card – that carried the bare minimum of information. The soldier's name, rank, unit and his wound. If any treatment had already been given by either his comrades or the R.M.O., or even the stretcher bearers, this was pencilled on the reverse. The ones Cuthbert had to look out for were those with red-edged cards. They were the men with the most serious and potentially life-threatening injuries. Cuthbert's job was to work out the order for the men to be seen, to alert the surgeon if there were any critical cases and to assist with their care in any way he could.

Inside the tent, an operating table was fixed in the centre and along each side were the instruments, basins and dressings laid out on the lids of panniers, which served as makeshift sidetables. One surgeon stood on one side of the table, another stood opposite him, and a third at the head was ready to assist or to give an anaesthetic, if necessary.

Quietly and methodically, one wounded man after another was lifted onto the table. His wounds were assessed and speedily dressed, and he was again carried out and laid on the straw. Cuthbert would make each man comfortable by placing one blanket under him and another over him. Morphine was given to all those with the most painful wounds, and any who were able to take nourishment were given tea, bread and jam, and even hot soup when it was available.

In this first group, the wounds, as expected, were mostly from shrapnel, and only one case required an anaesthetic. That man had a bad compound fracture of the thigh and was in terrible pain. Cuthbert watched the surgeons splint and immobilise the limb, leaving it comfortable and in a good position.

One private with a red-edged card tied to his tunic button had a serious abdominal wound for which Cuthbert knew they could do nothing. He arrived on the stretcher, gripping his stomach through his blood-sodden tunic, and Cuthbert could see he was holding in his intestines that were spilling out under his ripped uniform. He was given a fourfold dose of morphine and slept quietly outside until dawn when mercifully his breathing stopped.

Two hours after the first batch, the wounded were still arriving, and the medical officers, bearers and dressers worked on through the night. By dawn, the stretcher parties were finished at last and had come back to report that all wounded had been recovered. By six o'clock in the morning, the large group of wounded, some 112 men who needed to be moved up the line to the Casualty Clearing Station, were sent off to the railhead on returning-empty supply wagons and under the charge of a medical officer.

The thirty-seven men with minor injuries who were considered in need of no further treatment other than a good breakfast would be returned to the front later that day. The eighteen who had died at the Clearing Station during the night were washed and laid out for transport to the cemetery, and their C.O.s were informed.

At the end of the shift, the Operations Tent had to be cleaned, restocked and made ready for the next night, while a number of walking wounded would arrive throughout the day to be dressed and treated along with many cases of trench foot, dysentery and fevers of various types. And somewhere in this, Cuthbert had to find some time to sleep.

After the first few days, he settled into a new rhythm at the A.D.S. and saw more men die than he had ever done in the trenches. He also saw more bravery than he imagined could be possible. Night after night, the medical teams worked to clear the wounded, offering the best that they could in the cramped, ill-equipped and often unsanitary conditions. And night after night, the wounded kept coming. Men were ripped apart by razor-sharp shrapnel or punched through by sniper bullets, and they were losing arms and feet, eyes and even faces. And those whom the shells and bullets were sparing were weakened by infections and falling in their hundreds.

By the light of that acetylene lamp, Cuthbert would occasionally recognise a face or a name on the Field Medical Card that he knew from his own squad. He held their hands just a little tighter than the rest as they were lifted on the table. However, it was when the most familiar face of all appeared that he felt it all most acutely.

'Told you we'd be meeting again, Jock. How's the new billet? I'm just here to recce, you understand. Thought I might spend my bank holiday weekend here. Tell me, what's the brothel like?'

The sergeant was smiling, and Cuthbert smiled back, but he noticed the red-edged card tied to his battle dress.

'I knew you'd be checking up on me, sarge. I can't speak for the brothel, but there is a very good cup of tea waiting with your name on it. Now, let me just take a look at this card.'

'Tea! I ask about the brothel and you offer me tea. Typical bloody medic. But tea would be nice. See if you can get me any sugar, will you? We've run out back on the street.'

Cuthbert read the back of the card and noted that the sergeant had sustained a shrapnel injury to his left side and the R.M.O. had suspected a ruptured kidney. He had bled profusely, and tight dressings were all that were holding him together. There was a good chance that as soon as they unwrapped the bandages he would bleed out.

Cuthbert alerted Captain Oliver who was on duty in the Operations Tent, and he called for the man to be brought in immediately. Cuthbert helped one of the other dressers lift him on to the table, where Oliver started looking at the dressings heavily soaked in blood. The sergeant was pale and sweating, and when Oliver felt for his pulse, it was rapid but weak. Oliver just shook his head and ordered the man to be taken outside and given morphine to make him comfortable. Cuthbert sat with him outside the tent while he received the injection and watched him drift off. The sergeant suddenly opened his eyes and looked at him and gripped his arm tightly.

'What about me tea, Jock?'

'Oh, it's coming, I'm just going to fetch it. Two sugars, wasn't it?'

'Dandy. But remember to keep that bloody great head of yours down, son.'

With that, he fell asleep, and Cuthbert knew it wouldn't be long before he would have to prepare his sergeant's body for the last transport up the line.

*

At the start of August, almost twelve months after he had arrived at the A.D.S., Captain Oliver summoned Cuthbert to the orderly room. This was unusual, and Cuthbert was immediately worried that he had done something wrong or failed to follow some regulation. Since he had arrived, he had had to relearn just about everything he thought he knew about field dressings and the management of casualties.

'Every time I see you, lance corporal, the shine on those toe caps is even brighter. Quite how you manage it in this filth escapes me. Stand easy.'

The captain lit a cigarette and took a long draw on it as Cuthbert nervously rearranged himself.

'Bit of good news for a change. I've just received this morning an intimation from the colonel that leave can now be started. I've chosen four of you to go back to Blighty, starting with those who've been here the longest. And you're one of them. Ten days in England. Can I ask that you let Owen, Mitchell and Pryde know? They'll be going with you. You leave on the mail truck tonight for the nine o'clock boat from Boulogne tomorrow morning.'

Cuthbert felt himself tingling. He did not know whether his reaction was one of surprise, elation or even fear.

'Nothing to say, Cuthbert?'

'No, sir. I mean, yes, sir. Thank you, sir.'

'Where will you go? Home to your folks?'

'I have no family, sir. I'll go back to Edinburgh. That's as much home as anywhere.'

'Very good. Dismissed. Oh, and, Cuthbert, make sure you don't take any of our mud home with you. You know how fond we are of it here. I'd hate for any of it to go astray.'

'Very good, sir.'

Cuthbert left the officer's room feeling lightheaded and rushed over to the outhouses on the opposite side of the yard to find the others. They received the news in much the same way as he had, but Owen at least managed to find some choice words to express his approval.

'Well, fuck my tits and stick a ribbon on them. That's the best news I've had all year. Pardon my French.'

Mitchell, who was attending a casualty in the dressing station beside him, just went quiet and turned away. It was obvious from the shuddering of his shoulders that he was crying, but none of the men said anything. Pryde, who was in one of the outside tents, had an even stranger reaction.

'Right,' he said, 'where's my hat?'

He strode over to the bank of the stream well away from the tents and laid his army cap on the grass. He then took his rifle and at close range fired a bullet through it. On his way back as he was passing a bemused Cuthbert, he said, 'I'm going to wear that walking along Piccadilly and say, "That was a near one!"'

*

The mail truck was cramped, but no one complained. They drove the whole night and arrived at the quayside in Boulogne just after sunrise. The leave boat was docked and preparing to receive its complement of soldiers. First up the gangplanks were the wounded. These were mostly stretcher cases, and among them Cuthbert could see a fair number of amputees. There were also many casualties with head wounds, heavily bandaged. All of them had what the ranks called Blighty wounds – injuries severe enough to send you back home.

On the dock, there must have been several hundred men in uniform patiently waiting embarkation. Their spirits were high, and a few songs even broke out. Cigarettes were passed round, and bottles of army-issue brandy were being surreptitiously drunk.

The passage to Folkestone was smooth and bright. The ship was bursting at the seams with passengers, and a few senior officers were sitting on deck on the only chairs available. The rest leant on the rails and watched the waters of the Channel churn beneath them, knowing that every wave brought them closer to England.

Next, they boarded the boat train to London which was an equally crowded affair but no less good-humoured. Cuthbert would have stood the entire way, if it meant getting home sooner, but he eventually found a corner in one of the compartments and settled in. It was after lunchtime when they rolled into the terminus and found the great glass and cast-iron cavern filled with smog.

French Money Exchanged Here for Officers & Soldiers in Uniform.

The signs were prominently displayed above small makeshift huts spaced along the platform at Victoria Station. Cuthbert joined the others and waited to turn everything he had in his wallet back into sterling. At the window he was welcomed home by a cheery young woman, who handed him the notes and drew his attention to the sign above her counter. *Prevent Being Robbed. Put Your Money in Your Trousers.* Cuthbert nodded and smiled and thought, at least they're not trying to shoot me in the head.

On a set of trestle tables at the platform end, the Red Cross volunteers were serving tea, sandwiches and large wedges of cake. Cuthbert made use of his height and leaned over those in front to help himself and passed mugs to several of the men behind him.

He shared a taxi with one of the other Scots he had met on the boat and made directly for King's Cross Station. As they travelled across the city, from what he could see through the side window, it looked as if nothing had changed. There were certainly more people in uniform on the streets, but everything was still standing. The trees were all wearing their summer foliage in the park, and there were still dogs being walked and prams being pushed.

Only 150 miles or so away, they were getting ready to receive that night's wounded and some of his comrades would no doubt not see another sunrise. He looked down at his rifle and his army trousers which were streaked with Flanders mud, but he was pleased to note that his boots were as clean as they would always be from now on.

They managed to catch the early train to Edinburgh and congratulated themselves, while they caught their breath, that they would not have to waste one of their night's leave in the smog of London. Almost as soon as they took their seats in the compartment, they both fell asleep.

When Cuthbert woke it was night and he could barely see outside. The engine was pulsing and the smoke from the stack would occasionally be blown past their window, obscuring everything. He was unsure if it was the sea he was looking out on when the train curved on the track ahead. He could see the sparks flying from the engine and beyond, far in the distance, the unmistakable lights of Edinburgh.

The train emptied at Waverley, and he found himself back where he had stood in the same uniform almost eighteen months before. It was the first time on his journey that he realised he had nowhere to go. In his rush back to Edinburgh, he had made no arrangements. He saw that there was a kiosk still open near the ticket office and that it appeared to be offering hot drinks. It was so late it was almost early, and as there were only a few soldiers in line, he joined the queue. The girl serving was in a dark blue uniform bearing a Red Cross badge, like those back at Victoria Station.

'Tea, lance corporal? And there are sandwiches. We also have seed cake.'

There was still a warmth in her smile even though she had been using it all day to welcome soldiers back from the front. Cuthbert took the enamel mug from her and sipped the hot drink. He hadn't eaten anything since leaving Victoria and took one of the sandwiches from the plate and bit into it. He fumbled in his pocket, unsure if he had any British coins, when she stopped him.

'No charge. It's the very least we can do to welcome home our heroes. Please help yourself to anything on the buffet – it's all completely free.'

It wasn't the fact that the food and drink were free that caught Cuthbert off guard and made him gawp at the girl. It was being described as a hero. Nothing, he thought, could be further from the truth, at least as he understood heroes. He knew she was just being kind, and he smiled in thanks before finding a seat in the waiting room to eat the second sandwich he had picked up.

It was too late to go looking for digs, and in his fatigue, he could only summon one thought. What about Mrs Green's on Victoria Street? He had left his books and other belongings there, but he knew she would probably have let his room to some other student. Maybe it was worth a try, but he would have to wait until a more respectable hour before knocking on her door.

He must have fallen asleep again on the bench, wrapped in his greatcoat, and when he woke up, he realised he had been lying awkwardly on his rifle which was still strung across his chest. He stood up and stretched and saw that the station was starting to come to life.

Papers in tied bales were being delivered to the newsagents and milk churns were being rattled off the early trains from the Borders. There was no one else in uniform around him. All the others had doubtless gone straight home to their families, and there had been no further trains from London through the night.

He went to the lavatory and did what he could to freshen up, but there was no hot water for him to shave. He hauled himself up the Mound and along George IV Bridge before turning back down the hill to number 32 Victoria Street, where he had shared digs with Troy. It was still very early, but he rang the bell.

*

The bath was the best. And to find some fresh linen in his trunk was a bonus. Mrs Green had opened the door and simply gasped as she took him in her arms. He knew he was dirty not just from the journey but from the war, and to protect her he tried to shrink from her embrace. She, however, was having none of it. Since Troy had been killed, she had lost two more of her gentlemen students to the war and her sense of relief at finding Cuthbert on her doorstep was overwhelming.

'Good morning, Mrs Green. I know this is a dreadful imposition, but I really wasn't sure where I could go. Might I come in, even for a short while?'

She wiped her eyes on her apron and pulled Cuthbert into the hallway by his leather rifle strap and started unbuckling his canteen and mess bag.

'A short while indeed. I will not be having my gentlemen walking the streets of Edinburgh when there is a warm bed waiting for you upstairs. Now, you'll be having a bath immediately, young man, and I want everything you're wearing – and I mean everything – for the wash. Get upstairs to the bathroom. I'll bring you towels and a dressing gown. And then we'll see about getting some meat back on those bones. What on earth do they feed you in that army? There's not a pick on you.'

Cuthbert fell onto her shoulder and wept. Great breathless sobs that he had been holding in for months poured from him. She simply held him and allowed him to cry. His broad shoulders heaved, and the small woman felt the weight of him, and said, 'You're hame now, son. You're back hame.'

Mrs Green later took a tray up to Cuthbert's room and left it outside his door. He was not her first serviceman on leave from the front, and she had learned to take things gently and not to ask too many questions. She just knocked softly and said, 'Some breakfast for you, Mr Cuthbert. Don't let it get cold now,' and went back downstairs.

Later that morning, she delivered Cuthbert's uniform back to him brushed and pressed and was pleased to see the tray had been taken in. This time she had asked if she might come in.

'Mrs Green, that really is too much trouble I've put you to.'

'Nonsense. Did you enjoy your breakfast? I think I did the eggs the way you like them.'

'Of course you did. It was delicious. I had forgotten what fresh food tasted like. About earlier, Mrs Green – I just want to apologise. It was terribly, terribly wrong of me. I hope you do not think the worse of me. It's just I've been so very tired of late.'

'I've forgotten all about that and you should too. Now, I want you dressed and out in that fresh air. There's a whole day waiting for you, so get yourself ready. I gave your uniform a little spruce up, but I didn't have to touch those boots of yours. Never seen such a shiny pair. It must be a terrible job keeping them that clean out there. Why do you bother?'

'It's rather a long story, Mrs Green.'

'And one that you don't need to tell me, Mr Cuthbert. Now, get a move on, or the day will be wasted.'

Cuthbert found himself walking automatically in the direction of the medical school. There were far fewer men in uniform on the streets of Edinburgh compared with London, and he attracted a lot of attention as he strolled up George IV Bridge. One mother pointed him out to her small son who could have been no more than five or six years old. The child stood stock still and smiled at Cuthbert before saluting him. Cuthbert returned the smile and saluted back, to which he heard the woman say, 'God bless you, sir.'

Everything at the top of the road was as he had left it. The medical school building on Teviot Place and the Royal Infirmary straddling the Meadows, the students hurrying between classes and the elderly quad porter checking his watch and shaking his head. Cuthbert went over and leaned down to say hello to the man. He looked up at the imposing soldier towering over him and puzzled for a moment before breaking into the broadest of smiles.

'Why, if it's not Mr Cuthbert. I'm sorry, do excuse me, Lance Corporal Cuthbert. What a pleasure, what a pleasure to see you again, sir. Place hasn't been the same without you, I can tell you.'

'How are things, Mackay? Still chasing the late ones to their classes?'

'I never had to chase you, sir. Not once. How long has it been? A year?'

'Seventeen months, not that I'm counting, but it's good to be back albeit briefly.'

'Well, we need you back, sir. We need the likes of you.'

'How's Professor Littlejohn? Do you know if he's in Edinburgh? I thought I might pay him a visit. You know, just to let him know how things are going.'

'You're in luck. He was up examining the students in Aberdeen last week, but he came back the day before yesterday. Up in his rooms now, I expect. Shall I check for you, sir?'

'Oh no, don't bother yourself, Mackay. The stairs will do me good.'

The Dean's office was on the third floor, and Cuthbert took the stairs one at a time to give himself some time to think about why he was there. Everything that he had done since leaving the front had been automatic. No conscious thought had gone into any of the decisions, first to come back to Edinburgh, then to go back to Mrs Green's and now to be climbing these stairs. But what was he here for? Just to show off his uniform to his old O.T.C. Major? Surely not that. He decided to let providence dictate what happened next, and he knocked on the outer office door of the Dean's rooms.

His rather formidable secretary, Miss Plunkett, looked up and said the expected, 'And do you have an appointment?'

Cuthbert began to explain with all the charm he could rally that he was simply passing and thought he would look in. Miss Plunkett, however, was not the sort to be charmed, even by a man in uniform.

She was about to show Cuthbert from the premises, when Littlejohn's door opened, and he came out with a sheaf of papers for his secretary's attention. When he noticed the soldier in the outer office, he immediately stopped and greeted him with all the grace that he was renowned for. It was clear at first that he didn't recognise Cuthbert, and indeed why should he? But as he looked over the tall lance corporal and studied his face, the penny dropped.

'My word, it's Cuthbert. How are you doing, man? Miss Plunkett, why on earth has this gentleman been kept waiting? Have you offered him tea? You will stay for some tea, Cuthbert? I need to know all about your exploits. Come in, come in.'

Miss Plunkett smiled that smile she kept for moments of defeat, and Cuthbert was ushered into the inner office.

Littlejohn was in his late fifties and sported an Edwardian moustache that had grown increasingly white since the onset of the war. He was self-assured and bore the refined features of a patrician. His wit was as celebrated as his manners, and although he excelled at almost everything he did, he was said to possess the delusion that he was a good bridge player. In fact, at the University Club, they drew lots to see who would be unlucky enough to partner him. When the tea tray arrived, he poured for Cuthbert and took the cup over to him.

'It really is quite splendid to see you, Cuthbert. Tell me, are you well?'

Cuthbert dropped his eyes and paused to consider how best to answer such a complex question. He opted for silence and the slightest of shrugs.

'I can only imagine what you are feeling, but I have been receiving reports from a number of colleagues and students posted at the front. It looks very bloody, very bloody indeed. We have lost thirty-six medical students already. And I fear there may be more as there seems to be no end in sight for this.'

Cuthbert sipped the tea and listened to Littlejohn as he paced the room.

'I have simply dozens of letters from medical students and from their fathers asking for my counsel. Should they stay on at university or should they enlist? What do I say to them?'

Cuthbert was silent. He looked down at his hands clasped in his lap.

'No, I am really asking you, Cuthbert. You've been in that position, and you made a choice, which puts you in a better place than anyone to offer guidance. What do I say to them?'

Cuthbert took a deep breath to steady himself and then raised his eyes to look directly at his mentor. 'Those who choose to go do so for different reasons, sir. For some it's adventure. There is none. For some it is duty and honour. There is no honour in what they will be asked to do or in what they will be asked to endure. For some it is to seek glory. But there is no glory in the trenches, sir. There is mud and excrement, pain and suffering, and there is death, more death than they will ever be able to cope with. What very little the medical men can do is overwhelmed by the number and severity of the casualties they have to deal with. Men are dying and being mutilated in their thousands, their tens of thousands. And all for what? A few yards of Belgian or French soil. That's what it amounts to, sir.'

Now it was Littlejohn's turn to be quiet.

'I'm sorry if I shock you, sir. I do not mean to bring it all back here, but you have to know where you may be sending your students. Do everything you can to keep them here. I implore you: make them study and survive for as long as they can. And if they have to go, at least they go out as officers in the R.A.M.C.'

'And what is it I can do for you, Cuthbert? How can I help you? Because, young man, I can see that you need help.'

'There's nothing to be done there, I'm afraid. I made a

choice. I now know it was the wrong one, but I have to live with that. I didn't come here to seek your help, sir. To tell the truth, I don't really know why I came here today. I think I needed some familiarity. Men go back to their families on leave. Odd as it may seem, the medical school is my family.'

'Come back, then. Come back home to us, Cuthbert.'

'Impossible. I have ten days – eight now – and then I have to go back.'

'Not necessarily.'

Littlejohn explained to Cuthbert the recent shift in the War Office's position on senior medical students who had enlisted as regular combatants. As it had become obvious to them that the war would drag on for years, and as the death toll escalated, there was a growing concern that the country would face the real prospect of a shortage of doctors for many years to come. Their solution, Littlejohn explained, was to encourage those who had enlisted to leave the force and return to their universities to complete their studies.

'They are talking about students exactly like you, Cuthbert. One letter from me is all it would take. One recommendation for re-admittance and you could stay here in Edinburgh and complete your studies. And you could do more than that. You could assist me personally in the O.T.C. and you could make sure that what we teach these students is . . . well, *accurate* is not the word, perhaps *realistic* would be better.'

Cuthbert looked up at the Dean and did not know what to say. He simply rose from the chair and checked the shine on his boots. He held out his hand to the professor who took it in a firm grip, as if to hold onto him.

'What do you say to it, Cuthbert? Can I count on you to stay?'

Cuthbert simply nodded. He was as deeply conflicted as the first time he had sat in the Dean's office asking for advice on what to do at the outbreak of war, but the last thing he wanted now was to go back to all that.

He could hear the shells and the screams and the gurgling of men choking on their own blood. He could smell the ordnance and the mud and the men. He could still feel the rotting remains of that young German's torso clinging to his boots. And he recalled all this while he looked from the Dean's window at the late summer breeze rustling through the green trees on the Meadows. Of course, he wanted to stay, but what exactly would be the point. Something inside him was broken, and he doubted that any medicine could fix it.

Chapter 11

London: 16 April 1929

Sergeant Baker always found it difficult to believe in coincidence. But just as he was preparing to arrange a time to interview Clare Haskell again, he received a phone call, transferred from the switchboard downstairs.

'Good morning, sergeant. This is Clare Haskell. You may not remember me, but we spoke at U.C.L. a while back. In the refectory. And at the time you asked me to get in touch if there was anything else. Well, I think I might have something.'

Baker asked her this time to come to the Yard so that he could hear what she had to say and formally interview her at the same time. She arrived promptly that afternoon, and he met her in the foyer. He took her upstairs to the third-floor interview rooms, and as she climbed the stairs in front of him, he was able to take a good look at her.

She was slim with fair, almost blonde, hair, but he thought her fresh complexion was somewhat spoilt by the thick, horn-rimmed spectacles she chose to wear. Why, he wondered, would a young woman deliberately make herself unattractive like that? Could it be that she was trying to conceal her femininity in order to fit into that male-dominated world she inhabited at university? He dismissed his musings, realising he spent too long looking for motives. Perhaps she just had bad eyesight.

He seated her in the interview room and explained that he had wanted to check her statement, so it was fortuitous that she had called when she did.

'Saved me a trip across London, miss. But, first things first, what was it you wanted to tell me?'

'The thing is, I really didn't think anything of it at the time, but now I wonder if it might be important. Especially now that Freddie is dead. It's the man he was going to see that day. I really can't help thinking that the man he was meeting must have been his killer. And, of course, the whole story about the retired Home Office civil servant must have been a subterfuge. There was never anyone who was going to give Freddie the inside story, was there? That was just pie in the sky. The first time we spoke, you asked about whether I knew who his contact was, and I said I didn't know the name, and I still don't, but I now realise that I did see them together. I must have done.'

The sergeant's interest was aroused, and he stopped taking notes for a moment to study the young woman's expression. She looked drawn and much less animated than she had at their first meeting at the university, when it had only been a missing person's investigation. Now, the stakes had been raised, and she found herself at the centre of a murder enquiry, sitting in a dank interview room in Scotland Yard.

'What makes you say that, miss?'

'Not the Monday Freddie went missing, you understand. I didn't see him that day, but the Friday before. That was when Freddie met me in the courtyard before we went to the refectory. It was while we were there that he first started boasting about his contact and how great it was going to be.

The thing is, as I was waiting for him outside the refectory, I saw him talking to a man in a taxi outside the university gates. After they spoke, the taxi drove off.'

'Did you get a look at the man, miss?'

'No, not really. He was in the back of the taxi, and I suppose that was one of the odd things. It had just drawn up and the side window was only half down. Freddie didn't get in. He just spoke to him through the window. He was only there for a few moments. Perhaps they were arranging to meet later, but I think that must have been the man.'

'Why would you think that?'

'When Freddie met me immediately afterwards and we went in for coffee with the others, as I said, that's when he first started talking about "his contact". He hadn't said anything at all before. When one of the others pressed him, he said that he'd received a letter from someone but hadn't actually expected to meet the person, and now he had. I think he may even have said, "I just have." So, now I think about it, that must have been their first meeting that I witnessed. The timing of it fits, don't you think?'

'Can you tell us anything, anything at all, about this man?'

'I know it's not much to go on. He was wearing a hat and was sitting in the shadows in the taxi. I really didn't see his face. It was only the briefest of conversations, and then he tapped the driver with his cane, and they drove off.'

When Clare Haskell had started her witness statement, Baker had certainly hoped for a more substantial lead and was unsure if he was learning anything at all of value from this interview. However, he carried on and revisited the young woman's previous statement. This time, he also pressed her more on Dawson's relationships and connections at the university. Again, she kept to the story that Dawson had no romantic relationships with girls, and that he had a rather narrow group of friends, of which she regarded herself as one.

'Just a legal clique. A few of us in third year would study together sometimes and share lecture notes, that sort of thing, but we never really all sat down and had anything you would describe as deep and meaningful.'

'And just one more thing, miss. Did you ever discuss Freddie Dawson with your brother, Robert?'

'With Robbie? What do you mean? What's Robbie got to do with it?'

'It's one of our lines of enquiry, miss, so if you could answer the question, please.'

'Of course not. I don't know what you're getting at. Robbie isn't even at university any more. And he was never at U.C.L. He was up at Oxford and now he works at Quintons in the city, the merchant bank. And besides, I hardly see him to talk to him these days. He moved out to his own place about a year ago. He's quite the high-flyer now, you know. What could you possibly think he has to do with it? You must be mistaken.'

Baker watched her become as animated as before and wondered if she was protesting a little too much. The link between Robert Haskell and Dawson was always a weak one, but until they had spoken to the brother, to see what he had to say for himself, Baker was trying to keep an open mind. He concluded the interview without saying anything more and left behind a young woman who was distinctly on edge.

The whole Haskell line of enquiry was not making a pretty picture on the pinboard. If the man Dawson was to meet was his killer, it was hardly surprising that he may have written to the young man and even suggested an initial meeting to gain his confidence. But because the man in question, even if he had been the one spotted by Miss Haskell, could be no more fully described than as 'wearing a hat', Baker was pretty sure how the Pie would take it.

The best thing to do would be to arrange the interview with Robert Haskell as soon as possible. That might deflect some of the flak that would be coming his way.

*

Quintons was one of the less well known of the merchant banks in the City, but often that bore no relation to their size and importance in the eyes of financiers. Money, he had learned, had a liking for obscurity, especially money that had a past. Baker looked into everything they had on file about the bank before he called Haskell's secretary and set up the interview for the following afternoon. The boss wanted to lead on that one and would be available to join him then.

*

'Robert Haskell? I'm Detective Chief Inspector Mowbray and this is Detective Sergeant Baker. Thank you for agreeing to speak with us, sir.'

'Not at all, but what's all this about? My secretary just said it was concerning one of your investigations. Do please sit down, gentlemen.'

The chief inspector explained that Haskell's name had come up in their murder investigation, but he did not explain exactly how. The young man was in his mid-twenties but sported the traditional garb of the City – black morning coat and waistcoat with grey pinstripe trousers and a stiff wing collar. Already outdated, the outfit was perhaps designed to convince Haskell's clients that, in fact, he was not too young to look after their money.

When Mowbray mentioned the word 'murder', Haskell paled and had to be reassured that, no, he was not being interviewed as a suspect, at least not at this stage.

'You can't possibly think I had anything to do with that. I work at the bank. I don't know anyone called Freddie Dawson or Henry Melville, and to my knowledge I've never even met anyone of that name. Did you think they were clients of the bank? I can check if you like.'

'That won't be necessary for the time being, sir. What about William Galton? Does that name ring any bells with you?'

'Galton was my Latin master at St Peter's. What's it got to do with him?'

Haskell was by this point more confused than ever. He was suddenly unsure quite what he'd agreed to with this interview and was wondering if he should have a solicitor present. Until then, Mowbray had seen no reason to enlighten him, always preferring his suspects to feel a little out of their depth.

'We have reason to believe that Mr Galton and Mr Melville are one and the same and that, consequently, William Galton is dead.'

'Old Virgil. That's what the boys called him. Who'd have thought it? Dead. What happened to him?'

'That's what we are trying hard to ascertain, sir. Had you seen Mr Galton since you left school?'

'No, I don't think so. I left St Peter's and went up to Oxford in twenty-four. He was very excited at the time that I was going on to read classics, but that was it really. We didn't keep in touch or anything. It wasn't that kind of school.'

'What do you mean by that, sir?'

Haskell cleared his throat and rearranged the papers on his desk. He appeared to deliberate, carefully weighing his words, before speaking. 'Just that it wasn't a warm environment. "Tough love", isn't that what they call it these days? None of the masters believed in sparing the rod, if you get my drift.'

'Punishments?'

'Rather more than that, I'm afraid. Not everyone, of course, but some were a little heavy-handed, in my opinion. Not, I suppose, that it did me any harm. Perhaps it just prepared me for life. That's certainly what they always used to tell us.'

'And was Mr Galton one of those masters? One who was as you put it, "heavy-handed"?'

'He was. Probably the worst. I was one of his star pupils, so I didn't see the half of it, but if you didn't come up to his standards, he let you know and how.'

'With beatings?'

'Yes, but there were other things too. Some of the boys were simply terrified of him, and it must have been much more than just his cane that spooked them. I remember there was one boy in the lower fourth who had awful burns that were never explained. I'm not saying it was the master, but that was the word in the dormitory at the time.'

'Burns, sir?'

'Yes, they were small and round and looked like cigarette burns. But they must have been something else. Chickenpox or something. Look, I'm not trying to get anyone into trouble. It was a long time ago, and little boys make up all sorts of things, don't they? I've probably said too much.'

'You studied classics at university, you said. I take it you are familiar with the *Aeneid*, sir.'

'Of course, chief inspector. In fact, it was the subject of my dissertation. Book Eight to be precise. I doubt there has ever been anything more eloquent or more powerfully written.'

'And now you work in a bank, sir.'

'Indeed, but we can't live in the past, no matter how much we might want to.'

On the way out of the offices, Mowbray asked Baker for his thoughts. The sergeant was unused to such an enquiry, and he was uncertain whether he had heard correctly. The chief inspector smiled when he saw the look on Baker's face.

'Yes, hard as it is to believe, I am asking you for your opinion, sergeant. Did you buy all that from Haskell?'

'I thought he sounded as if he was being truthful, sir. I was watching him very closely when you asked about Dawson and Melville, and I don't think he was lying when he said he didn't know them. And I think he told us more than he thought was proper about – what did he call him – "Old Virgil".'

'I agree. I have to confess I was really quite keen that he might have been the one, but I just don't see it. Unless, of course, he's a far better liar than we give him credit for. And, after all, he does work in a bank. But if what he says about Galton is true, at least we have a motive for someone to want to hurt the old man, perhaps even to want him dead.'

*

There was little new to add to the pinboard back in the duty room, and Mowbray was starting to feel nervous. His strategy of raising the profile of the case with his superiors upstairs was in danger of backfiring.

As he hoped, they had developed quite an interest in the investigation, and they were now asking for regular updates, almost daily reports. But he found himself with no new leads and no suspects, and he needed something to feed the beast he himself had created. He looked around at his team working at their desks in the duty room and decided to visit Cuthbert at the hospital.

He had never been fond of mortuaries, although he had spent more time in them than most. It was not the bodies that he disliked, it was the doctors. He had never found any police surgeon or pathologist who understood what was needed by the investigative teams.

In his experience, they were too full of their own importance and adopted an air of superiority, hiding behind their Latin whenever it got tough. They never saw themselves as part of the team in any way. No, he had never found one whom he could work with as an equal. Never, that is, until now.

In truth, he was still unsure about Cuthbert, and he was quite prepared to be disappointed by him, just like all the rest. However, this case now needed everything Mowbray could throw at it, and that included any insights he could garner from the boys in the mortuary.

'Chief inspector, to what do we owe the honour? We don't often see you in the department.'

'Don't get too used to it, Cuthbert. I'm not planning on making it a habit. I just thought it would be useful to go over a few things.'

Cuthbert could see the chief inspector was more hesitant than usual and finding it a little difficult to ask for help outright. The pathologist decided to play along, and he invited him into his office on the pretext that it would be very useful to hear the latest developments from the Yard.

'I'm afraid I can't offer you a drink, chief inspector, if that's what you were hoping for. Contrary to popular belief, we Scots don't all have an open bottle of malt wherever we are. Take a seat, and now that the door's firmly closed, why don't you tell me what's worrying you?'

Mowbray explained the situation honestly and now without reserve. Cuthbert had had little dealings with those men upstairs at Scotland Yard who were now giving Mowbray such a difficult time. However, he was inclined to dislike them as he did all bureaucrats who demanded results without ever understanding how the work was done.

'How is it you think I can help you, chief inspector?'

'You have a different way of looking at things, don't you? It's almost as if that big Scottish brain of yours is wired differently from the rest of us. To be honest, sometimes it makes you into a right pain in the arse. But the rest of the time it makes you see things that no one else can see, even though we're all looking at the same sets of facts and figures. I need your brain, Cuthbert. That's how you can help.'

Cuthbert was not easily flattered, but he knew that was not Mowbray's intention. He was merely relating the facts of the situation as he saw them. Cuthbert knew he wasn't trying to make him into a friend – in fact, he doubted Mowbray had any. No, what the chief inspector wanted was an ally, and Cuthbert could work with that because that's what he needed too.

'My opinion, for what it's worth, is still that we need to find someone who knew Dawson well and who knew Galton well. As for Galton, from what we now know of his life before he metamorphosed into Henry Melville, that probably means someone connected to the school. He didn't seem to have a big social circle and he'd worked at the same place for over thirty years. As for Dawson, again because of the background picture your team has managed to assemble of his life, it looks as if it would have to be someone connected to the university. That was pretty much the boy's life and accounted for most of the people he came into contact with.'

'So where do we start looking?'

'The school is too big a problem. Over all those years, there are just too many pupils to track down and eliminate from your enquiries. Until you know more about what you're looking for, that would be a thankless task. I think it would be much more productive to look again at the university. Dawson was younger and he had only been at the university for less than three years. That gives you a much smaller pool of potential suspects, chief inspector.'

'Baker has talked to the Haskell girl, and we've both been to see the brother.'

'And you've decided he's got nothing to do with it. Am I right?'

'You said as much, if I remember, and yes, he doesn't look right for it. So who else is there?'

'There are his teachers and tutors and the other students. I know you've talked to many of them already, but perhaps it would do to revisit them. Few of them, I seem to recall, had much to say about the boy. Well, I think one of them's lying. I think one of them knows a lot more about Freddie Dawson and especially about how he died.'

Mowbray nodded and stood up to leave. As he was going out, he turned back and said, 'I don't like doctors, you know.'

Cuthbert shrugged. 'Nobody does, chief inspector, until they need them.'

*

That evening after dinner, Madame Smith noted that Cuthbert was smiling as he was drinking his coffee.

'Is my café finally meeting your approval, monsieur? Or can there be some other explanation for this miracle?'

'Can't a man show his contentment without having to explain it?'

'No. What is going on, Dr Cuthbert?'

'Just the tiniest of victories at work, that is all. Nothing that important, but a small step in the right direction, madame.'

'Any victory is a cause for celebration, as long as it is not won at the expense of another.'

'No one was hurt. I can assure you of that. Perhaps quite the contrary. Now I think I'll go up to bed and read. Have you seen my book?'

'Your Catullus, monsieur? It is most likely where you left

it, which is on the sidetable in your study. Perhaps you should purchase a second copy. That way you can have your beloved yet immodest poet with you in your study and with you in bed.'

'Good night, madame.'

'Good night, monsieur, and do not read too late.'

Chapter 12

London: 22 April 1929

Mowbray had so far largely been relying on the files that Inspector Franklin had assembled while carrying out the initial investigation into Dawson's disappearance. Apart from Clare Haskell and the few students whom Mowbray had managed to track down on the afternoon he visited Cuthbert's house, none of the other U.C.L. staff or students, or indeed Dawson's parents, had been re-interviewed since this had become a murder enquiry.

As he read over Franklin's notes again, he was struck by how half-hearted his predecessor's investigation had been. Clearly this was someone who was just going through the motions of the job and should have been put out to pasture a while ago.

Mowbray despised any of his colleagues who were not giving one hundred per cent. He worked hard and expected others to see how important it was for them to do the same. His was a job of putting those things right that had gone terribly wrong. He couldn't bring back Freddie Dawson, but he could, with hard work, put his killer away and see that justice was done. He could bring some closure to a grieving family and finally allow the boy to rest in peace.

'Right, Baker, we're starting again. We need to go back to the family first. And after that, it's the U.C.L. crowd. Get your hat.'

*

The Dawson house in Hampstead was still in mourning. After his run-in with Franklin, Cuthbert had eventually persuaded Chief Inspector Mowbray that the family could not possibly identify their son's remains. As the police pathologist, he was willing to sign off on the body's identity based on the combined fingerprint and bone studies. However, the Dawsons had still to be informed, and Sergeant Baker had drawn the short straw on that.

After nearly three months, the parents were expecting the worst, but when it was brought to their door the shock was overwhelming. Mrs Dawson had been under sedation ever since, and Mr Dawson had not returned to work.

When he opened the door to Chief Inspector Mowbray and the sergeant, he simply said, 'What can you possibly want now?'

The interview revealed nothing new. Mr Dawson was still dumbfounded as to why his son would be murdered and became irritated when he was asked about Henry Melville, William Galton and Robert Haskell.

'Is that who you think did this to my boy? You have a nerve bringing those names in here, sir. Haven't we been through enough, Maud and me? She'll never get over it, poor soul.'

Mowbray pressed him with regard to the names, assuring him that it was all to help find his son's killer, but he confirmed he knew none of them.

'Did your son ever speak about a man who was helping him with his university work? A retired gentleman from the Home Office?'

'No, that's the first I've heard of that. Was it him? Was he the one?'

'We don't know yet, sir.'

'No, you don't know much, do you? None of you do.'

*

In the car back down to the city and the university, Mowbray was quiet, and Baker knew it would be best to hold his own tongue too. At U.C.L., the chief inspector dispensed with the lodge porter. After reading Franklin's report on his interview with the man, he had concluded the porter was both unreliable as a witness and probably incompetent. Mowbray had better ways to spend the time awaiting him inside the building.

He and Baker went first to visit Dawson's tutor Dr Gossett and spent some time going over much of the same ground as before. Gossett again gave a detailed account of his own movements on the tenth of December and answered Mowbray's questions about Melville, Galton and Haskell. He said the only Haskell he knew was one of the third-year students, Clare Haskell, but he wasn't sure if there was a connection. As for Melville and Galton, he said he knew no one of those names.

He enquired more about the progress of the case and asked the chief inspector if he could be kept informed. He explained that, as the boy's tutor, he was regarded as the point of contact in the university for all communication either with the family or the press.

'As you might imagine, chief inspector, I've already had to field a lot of enquiries. The so-called gentlemen of the press are getting terribly interested in this now that it has become a murder investigation. They want to know everything about the boy. There are issues of confidentiality, but I'm also anxious that the family are protected as much as possible, and that Dawson's memory is appropriately honoured. And, of course, there is the university to think about. We in the faculty are more than concerned about how this might all play out. I'm sure you understand the position we are in, chief inspector.'

'I'm sure it must be very difficult for you and the university, sir. But perhaps not quite as hard for you as for his family, or, for that matter, young Dawson himself. We'll show ourselves out, shall we?'

Mowbray scowled at Baker as they walked from Gossett's rooms and asked, 'Are they all like that here, sergeant? Just one big happy family?'

As Baker knew their next port of call was Dr Nicholas Pemberton, he was loath to say anything.

For the second time in as many visits, Baker found Pemberton's office door ajar and the room appearing as if it had been ransacked. He registered his boss's initial thoughts and simply whispered, 'No, sir, it's always like this.'

On this occasion, Pemberton was at his desk, and as they entered, he hurriedly put away the glass he had been holding.

'Can I help you? It is customary to knock, you know.'

Mowbray, who had already used up his day's allocation of patience, was in no mood to be civil. He pulled out his warrant card, shoved a pile of papers from the chair onto the floor and sat down.

'Detective Chief Inspector Mowbray, Scotland Yard, and this is my sergeant with whom I believe you are already acquainted. We need to ask you some further questions, Dr Pemberton.'

Pemberton bristled and was clearly not happy.

'Let's begin on the day that Freddie Dawson disappeared, shall we? Tenth December last. What were your movements that day, sir?'

'This is simply not on. I see this as harassment, chief inspector. You have no grounds, no grounds whatsoever, for this line of questioning. I've already said all I have to say on that. I absolutely refuse to answer any further questions on this topic or any other, and I would thank you to leave my office forthwith.'

Pemberton stood up and expected the officers to do the same, but Mowbray simply stared Pemberton out and very slowly and deliberately said, 'Dr Pemberton, I don't like your tone. This is a murder enquiry, and, in my opinion, you are obstructing it. And that is an offence. I don't imagine, sir, I have to remind a lecturer in law like yourself of that fact.'

Pemberton shrank back into the seat. He had gone too far, and he sought to appease Mowbray. 'A thousand apologies, chief inspector. Please forgive my outburst. It's my nerves. They're shattered, shot to pieces, and I don't know what I'm saying half the time.'

'Really, sir? And does this lack of self-control manifest itself in other ways? Do you always know what you're doing, or even what you've done if, as you say, you don't know what you're saying?'

'Oh, chief inspector, I didn't mean that at all. It was just a figure of speech. Please, we've got off to such a very bad start. Shall we try again?'

'I think it's your start, sir, that's been found wanting. But be that as it may, perhaps you could begin by answering the question. What were your movements on the day Freddie Dawson disappeared?'

'As I told the other officers, I saw Freddie that afternoon in my room. He was here to discuss the progress of his dissertation. It was a regular appointment, every two weeks. And then immediately afterwards, I went to Paddington to get the four-fifty to Bristol. I was attending a conference the next day.'

'Did Dawson discuss with you a lead he was following up? A retired Home Office chap who was providing him with information for his dissertation.'

'No. I don't know where you're getting that from. Sounds very far-fetched, chief inspector. Why would anyone from the Home Office share anything with a third-year law student? Seems highly improbable.'

'Might the boy have believed it if he had been approached?'

'Who's to say? They might be third-year students, but they are often really quite green around the edges. I suppose it's possible.'

'Can anyone vouch for you, sir, that you got on that train and went to Bristol when you said you did?'

'I travelled alone, chief inspector. And I didn't meet anyone I knew until the conference started the next day at eleven o'clock. I was definitively at the conference. I was speaking at it, and at least fifty attendees can verify that.'

'But not that you travelled out of London on the previous afternoon, sir. You could have taken a morning train and still been in Bristol in plenty of time for the conference. Is that not the case, sir?'

'Yes, but I didn't. I'm telling the truth, chief inspector.'

'Do you know a Mr Henry Melville, sir, or a Mr William Galton?'

'No, I don't think so. Should I?'

'Which school did you attend, sir?'

Pemberton forgot himself and snapped, 'What on earth's that got to do with it?'

Mowbray was very still and raised his eyebrows just enough to bring Pemberton back to heel.

'I'm sorry. I went to school in France, chief inspector. You won't have heard of it. Papa was a diplomat, you see. All the other offspring were sent back to boarding school in England, but he thought it would do me good to be educated out there.'

Mowbray had disliked Pemberton from the moment they had met, but he had learned from long experience that such an opinion did not necessarily make someone guilty – more was the pity. He was not sure the tutor was out of the woods yet as far as this investigation went, but he also felt in his gut that this killer was likely to be a great deal more organised than the bumbling fool he saw before him.

*

The case conference the following morning was longer than usual as Mowbray wanted to review all the evidence and hear reports on any leads that were being followed. Baker brought the team up to date with the latest round of interviews.

'Mr Dawson senior claims no knowledge of Melville, Galton or Haskell, and he has never heard of the Home Office man that his son was supposed to be meeting. Gossett, his tutor, seems more concerned with the impact of Dawson's murder on the reputation of the university than with the poor lad himself. He does seem to be accounted for on the afternoon and evening of tenth December and says he has never heard of William Galton. Pemberton, down the hall, is a bit of a fruitcake, and he has no alibi for the time of Dawson's abduction and probable murder. He is also somewhat vague about his schooling.'

'Could he be putting on the fruitcake act to mislead us, do you think, sir?' The constable was earnest and was trying to make an impression. However, Mowbray was still in the same mood as when he had left Pemberton's office the previous day. He looked at the young officer and shook his head. 'Just sensible questions from now on, all right.'

'What about Haskell, the brother – where are we with him?' asked the other constable, trying to take the heat from his colleague.

Baker chipped in to help them both. 'Haskell is an old boy of St Peter's and admits to knowing William Galton, but he denies any knowledge of Dawson. He does raise some interesting questions about Galton's teaching methods. We're perhaps looking at assault there, and that might be a possible motive.'

'Assault, sergeant?' asked the first of the constables rather less forcibly than before, but it was Mowbray who answered. 'Looks as if he might have been stubbing out his fags on the boys.'

'Charmer, I'm sure.'

Cuthbert was seated at the back of the group, listening carefully to the reports. He was taking notes along with the others, only his were simpler, more abbreviated and often more visual. He joined names and dates with arrows, circled what he saw as key pieces of information and clustered common themes together in boxes. He drew a question mark besides Gossett's name and spoke up: 'Dr Gossett certainly seemed overly concerned with how the university's role would be perceived in it all, when he spoke with me.'

Mowbray turned from the board and leaned into Cuthbert.

'What do you mean, "when he spoke with me"? When did this happen?'

'He ambushed me outside St Thomas's one evening a few weeks ago. He said he was looking for information that he could share with the family, to make it look as if the university was doing all it could. That sort of thing.'

'And when, pray, Dr Cuthbert, were you going to share this information with us? And what right have you to speak with one of my suspects in this investigation? You are in this room at my invitation. You are here on sufferance. Never forget that and do not abuse the privilege, doctor.'

Cuthbert looked at the chief inspector as his voice became louder and more aggressive with each phrase, but the pathologist was unruffled. He was afraid of no one, and just found other men's anger faintly amusing to watch close-up.

'As I said, chief inspector, *he* approached *me*, not the other way around. I said nothing about the investigation, and he went on his way. Perhaps I should have told you, but I can't see that it has much bearing on the case.'

'Well, tell me this then. How did he know to approach you? How did he know *you* were the pathologist on the Dawson case?'

Cuthbert's expression changed, and he realised that although there had been some press coverage, his name had never been mentioned. And he had certainly not discussed his involvement in this or indeed in any one of his cases with anyone outside the Yard.

'That, chief inspector, is a troubling question. How indeed? No one outside this station or my department would know that I was the pathologist.'

'Unless you told them.'

But as he said it and watched the pathologist recoil, Mowbray realised it was a ridiculous proposal. He had never met anyone who had a higher ethical code than Cuthbert, and he hastily added, 'Or someone else here did. So who's been talking?'

The group looked at each other and back at the boss who was looking more disappointed than angry.

'Baker,' he snapped. 'Sort this out!'

*

Later the same day, Cuthbert was sitting in his office in the pathology department and Morgenthal was watching him. Cuthbert had been staring at the same file for over an hour and appeared to be brooding. His assistant was unsure whether he should disturb him, even though he needed him to sign off the purchase of some new laboratory glassware. He knocked at the door so tentatively that Cuthbert almost did not hear him, and only when Morgenthal coughed did he look up.

'What do you need?'

'Just your signature, sir. Can I help you with anything?'

'Like?'

'Well, Dr Cuthbert, I couldn't help but notice that you don't seem yourself this afternoon. I was wondering if something was worrying you, something that it might help discussing?'

Cuthbert looked at Morgenthal with a frown and made it plain that he did not regard him as his confidant. Nevertheless, he did choose to speak.

'I've made a blunder, Simon, and the problem is, I don't know how I did it.'

He explained the outcome of the case conference at the Yard and the question that arose from his meeting with Gossett.

'How could he possibly know I was on the case? We don't talk about our work outside these walls. That's the first rule and the last.'

Morgenthal was quiet and then very hesitatingly said that he had sometimes talked about Cuthbert with Sarah, his fiancée. 'Nothing about the cases, you understand. She's interested in my work. It's only natural she would ask about it.'

Cuthbert suddenly stood and rounded on his assistant. He didn't touch Morgenthal, but he didn't have to; the sheer heft of his towering presence was enough to drive his assistant back into a chair. Slowly and deliberately, Cuthbert spoke. 'What exactly did you tell her?'

'I've told her that I work with you. About how much I admire you – how I want to be like you. How much you have taught me. How difficult the cases we work on are.'

'Answer me truthfully. Did you tell her you were working on the Dawson murder?'

'I don't know, sir. I might have done.'

Cuthbert rammed his fist so hard into his desk that everything on it shook.

'Come with me. We're going over to Scotland Yard. And speak only when I tell you to, laddie.'

*

In Mowbray's office, Cuthbert explained the possible leak and throughout it all he defended his assistant. He claimed it was a foolish but hardly malicious breach of protocol that would undoubtedly be a useful lesson learned. He also tried to deflect the chief inspector's obviously rising gall by saying that this opened up a new line of enquiry. Morgenthal had not spoken with Gossett, only with his fiancée, so how did the information get to him?

It worked. The chief inspector started to pace his room, clearly thinking about his next move in the investigation. 'You,' he said, pointing at Morgenthal, 'get out of my sight and don't ever let this happen again.'

Cuthbert nodded at his assistant and then at the office door and watched him scurry away.

'You need to keep your young 'uns on a tighter leash, Cuthbert. But you're right: we need this woman in for questioning. I want to know if she spoke with Gossett, and what that one is up to. Let's take another look at his statement.'

Cuthbert had acted quickly because he did not want aspersions being wrongly cast on any of the other officers when the leak was so obviously from his own department. Baker, when he learned of it, was relieved to call a halt on his painful task of questioning the men. Morgenthal, on the other hand, would have to cope with some wounded pride but that, thought Cuthbert, was a very small price to pay for his stupidity.

Now, the Gossett file lay open on Mowbray's desk, and unusually, the chief inspector had drawn up a second chair beside his for Cuthbert.

'Look at this,' said Mowbray, pointing to the record of

Gossett's original statement to Inspector Franklin. 'He said at the time that he didn't think Dawson had run away, and then when I next interviewed him, he said, and I quote, "It's such a tragedy. A bright young man ending up naked in a ditch like that." We haven't released that to the press, have we? We've never said that the bodies were found naked. Either your assistant has been saying much more than he's letting on to the little woman, or–'

'Or Gossett's our murderer. But he has an alibi for the time of Dawson's disappearance and there is no connection with Galton. And remember we need a suspect who has a direct link with both victims.'

Mowbray leafed through the pages of the file and started comparing text on one page with another.

'Let's see about that alibi. When I interviewed him, he said he had not seen Dawson that day. At around four p.m., which, according to Miss Haskell, was a good half hour before Dawson left the university, Gossett went to a meeting of the University Senate. That lasted for two hours. He said he left that and took a taxi to his club where he met two friends for dinner and spent the night there. Both have confirmed that he met them in the bar there at six-fifteen and they were with him until close to midnight. If Dawson hurried away to meet the mystery man from the Home Office at four-thirty, it doesn't put Gossett in the picture.'

'Could he be lying about the Senate? If he didn't attend that meeting, he would have had time to meet and kill Dawson before showing up at his Club.'

'It a was large gathering, but he was listed as an attendee in the minutes.'

'And who types the minutes, chief inspector?'

A quick phone call by Sergeant Baker to the law faculty office confirmed that Gossett's secretary normally typed up the minutes based on notes supplied by one of the attending Senate officials. Gossett was in the habit of checking them over personally before they were released as he said they were too important for there to be a mistake in them. And, yes, Dr Gossett did sometimes make changes, and, no, she couldn't recall if on that occasion he had, but then again, she had been off during the first two weeks in December with appendicitis, so she didn't know who had typed up the minutes for him then.

'Oh no, I'm sure he wouldn't have done them himself. It will have been one of the other girls, sergeant.'

Mowbray's suspicions were growing but he kept them in check while he considered Cuthbert's second objection – the link with Galton.

'He could simply be lying. Perhaps he did attend St Peter's and was at the receiving end of Galton's cigarette butts.'

'No, your sergeant said himself that he had checked Gossett's story about that. He said he had attended Harlowe, and the school office there confirmed it.' Cuthbert checked his own notes and said, 'Yes, he was a pupil there from 1906 to 1913.'

'Nevertheless, I think it's time we had another chat with Dr Gossett. He's certainly got some explaining to do, even if he never knew Galton.'

*

The follow-up interview with Sarah Fielding, Morgenthal's fiancée, was kept deliberately gentle. As soon as he met her, Mowbray was inclined to believe that she had done nothing consciously untoward and had merely been an unfortunate victim of circumstance, if a rather foolish one.

It was clear from her statement that Julius Gossett was a friend of her father and had attended a number of family dinners in the past few weeks.

'More often than usual, to be fair, chief inspector. I only remember him visiting once or twice a year in the past, but since February, he's been dining with us every other week. It's becoming a little boring, actually.'

'And what did you discuss with him, Miss Fielding? Did you tell him about your fiancé?'

'Of course. Simon and I are engaged to be married and I talk about him all the time. I'm very proud of him, you know. He's done so well. I believe he's really quite senior in the department now and works alongside a Dr Cuthbert. You may have heard of him, chief inspector.'

'I believe I may have come across him. Do you recall specifically mentioning Dr Cuthbert in Dr Gossett's presence?'

'I expect so, chief inspector. I've never met him, of course, but Simon talks about him a lot. Thinks very highly of him.'

'And what about any of the details of the cases that Dr Morgenthal would be working on? Were these discussed at all?'

'Of course not! That's hardly dinner-table conversation, chief inspector. Besides, I don't want to know any of that. That's Simon's bag and from what he tells me he's really rather good at it all.'

'Indeed, miss. Thank you for your time.'

*

In the laboratory over the next few days, Morgenthal kept a low profile. He only spoke when he was spoken to and was acutely aware that he still had a job there only by the skin of his teeth. And he felt terrible because his indiscretion had caused so much embarrassment to his mentor.

Cuthbert, however, did not know how to hold a grudge and had all but forgotten how angry he had been at the time. His assistant had the makings of a fine forensic scientist, but he was still young and would make more, and possibly bigger, mistakes than the one he was now so penitent over. But he did notice it had meant that the effort Morgenthal was putting into his work had doubled, and every day there were new books on his bench. He had to hide a smile when he saw that even Locard had appeared in the pile.

Eventually, Cuthbert thought the young man should be let out of his cell, and he called him over to review a firearm killing that had come into the mortuary the day before.

'Tell me, Dr Morgenthal, what would your approach to this case be?'

The young man was still reticent and unsure if he had any right to an opinion. Tentatively, he began to describe a classic strategy for the retrieval of a bullet from a victim. He went on to outline the subsequent analyses which would be required to identify the make and model of the gun used. He concluded by proposing that through comparison with file photographs of other bullets, it might even be possible to pinpoint the exact weapon that had fired the fatal round.

Throughout his explanation, he did not smile once, and his voice was almost a monotone. This was not the Simon Morgenthal Cuthbert knew. Although he could find his usual buoyancy somewhat irritating, he missed it when it was so clearly absent.

'You know that you made a mistake, Simon. It was a stupid mistake, and it was an embarrassing one, and it was almost as stupid and embarrassing as the mistakes that I have made.'

Morgenthal looked up from his feet and was frankly incredulous that Cuthbert could ever had done anything of the sort. Cuthbert saw his disbelief and put his hand on the young man's shoulder.

'Don't put me on a pedestal, Simon. Don't do that with anyone. I only seem to know more than you because I've been doing this a lot longer. It only seems to you as if I never make a mistake because you've never seen me make one. But that's because you didn't know me when I was your age, or younger. We all make mistakes, and hopefully we all learn from them. For example, I know for a fact that you will never again mention to anyone anything that happens in this mortuary.'

'Dr Cuthbert, I am so very sorry that you had to deal with my foolishness, and you're right: it will never ever happen again here or anywhere else. I know you are just trying to be kind and to make me feel better, but you don't have to pretend that you've done anything as downright destructive as me. I know you could never have been so foolish.'

Cuthbert looked at the young man before him, who was by this time close to tears, and he wondered how Simon really saw him. Now, he was a successful forensic pathologist leading on cases for Scotland Yard, with an education behind him that was the envy of many. He was assured and refined, with a reputation for accuracy and attention to detail. When people looked at him, they saw a man in his prime. But what they could not see was what was going on inside his head. What they failed to realise was the weight of the burdens he still carried.

Chapter 13

Edinburgh: 4 October 1916

D o you remember what you said to me, Cuthie? After I died, when you were on the Crags? You said you loved me. I knew you did, you oaf. I do hope you know I loved you too, just not in the way that you wanted. But even that was beautiful. In truth, despite all the talk of girls, I never believed anyone could fall for this skinny ginger top. I'm glad it was you, and I'm only sorry I never gave you back what you wanted, what you needed, from me. I do know what you're feeling, Cuthie. I'm inside your head, you see, and it's a jolly dark place just now, but I know what's on the other side of it all.

Of course, you're doubting everything – why wouldn't you? The truth is you saw much more action than me and much more of everything else for that matter. I was too full of it and couldn't keep my head down. You know me, always gangling about. German sniper got me on the second day, but it took them weeks to let my folks know. It was quick, clean, and I'm still in France. I don't really know where, but I'm also with you too.

Look, Cuthie, the thing is, I need you to do something for me. I need you to get back to the books and the clinics and even those infernal ward rounds, and I need you to qualify for us both. You were right, I threw it all away too easily, and I need you to be a doctor – I need us to be doctors. So do get on with it, old man. Thing is, I'm positively pooped. Need to rest now . . .'

'Need to get up now, Mr Cuthbert, or you'll be late. Can't have that on your first day back. You'll be the talk of the place. Your hot water is on the landing. At least it was hot when I brought it up the first time I called you.'

Mrs Green was knocking on Cuthbert's door. He sat up in bed, rubbing his eyes, and reassured her he would be down in a jiffy. He sprang from the bed and splashed cold water on his face from the basin in his room. He collected the jug of hot water Mrs Green had left outside his door and quickly washed and shaved. Downstairs, he begged Mrs Green's pardon for having to be called more than once and for having missed breakfast.

She reached up and dusted some lint from his shoulder and stood back to look at him. 'Yes, that's the Mr Cuthbert I know. And that shine on your boots looks very smart. Can see your face in them. Here, take this.' She handed him two slices of warm toast wrapped in a napkin. 'I won't have my gentlemen leaving here without anything to eat in the morning. Now, get on with you. I'll see you at six o'clock sharp for your dinner, and don't be late. It's lamb chops and I can't wrap them in a napkin.'

It had been barely two months since Cuthbert had come home on leave and visited Littlejohn. Since then, the young man had discovered that, despite what he had said, the Dean was far from certain how the new policy would be put into practice and was using him as a test case, as it were. Littlejohn wanted to check the resolve of the War Office and force them to put their pronouncements into action.

As it turned out, the process was altogether easier than he anticipated. The Whitehall officials replied to his application by return, enclosing the student's discharge papers. Cuthbert was to re-enrol in the medical school, essentially picking up where he had left off, but they had two conditions. Should hostilities still be continuing at the time of Cuthbert's subsequent qualification, he would then be required to re-enlist as an officer in the R.A.M.C.

The second stipulation was that, despite his service, he would not be permitted to wear uniform during the remainder of his studies. Littlejohn protested over the latter, but it was a battle not worth fighting, given that his main objective had been achieved.

Cuthbert walked up Victoria Street and on to George IV Bridge. It was not the first time he had made the journey to the medical school without Troy, but he felt his absence most acutely that morning. At the archway on Teviot Place, which led through into the quad, Cuthbert stopped. He was breathing heavily, and he had no need to take his pulse for he could feel his heart racing. And he was sweating as Mackay approached him.

'Mr Cuthbert, it is an honour to welcome you back, sir.'

The old porter could see the fear on the student's face and saw his eyes fixed on the doorway that led through to the stairwell up to the main lecture room. He was frozen to the spot. Mackay had dealt with many cases of first-day nerves, although never in so senior a student. Nonetheless, he knew what to do.

'I wonder if I could trouble you, Mr Cuthbert, to assist me. It's the lumbago, you see. I need to get this mail basket up those stairs and, well, you'd be doing me a great service if you would carry it for me. And don't worry, I'll hold the doors open.'

He thrust the wicker pannier into Cuthbert's hands, and he

was jolted from his thoughts and forced to acknowledge the porter and politely accede to his request. He had been too well brought up to do anything else. Before he knew it, Cuthbert was through the door, up the stairs and outside the lecture hall. Mackay took back the basket, opened the door and gently pushed Cuthbert in.

It had been agreed with Littlejohn that Cuthbert would still need to take some of the courses which he had missed when he left in the middle of his fourth year. He would also need to complete, or even retake, those he had left unfinished and, more importantly, unexamined. That would allow him to enter his final year in September 1917 and thus complete the remainder of the course before his graduation the following summer. That said, the Dean was keen to acknowledge the time Cuthbert had spent in military medical service and therefore exempted him from any further classes or clinics in injuries or shock management. However, he did express his hope that the young man would attend his own lecture course on medical jurisprudence.

*

On his first day back in the class, it was inevitable that Cuthbert would recognise no one in the steeply raked lecture theatre. Fresh and oddly youthful faces filled the rows everywhere, and on the far side a group of around thirty women were all seated together. He took a convenient seat just off the side aisle that allowed him to stretch out his long legs.

This was the inaugural lecture for the new fourth-year class and the first in Littlejohn's medical jurisprudence class. When the Dean entered, he appeared to have dressed specially for the occasion and looked even more dapper than usual. As he surveyed the class, he spotted Cuthbert but did not embarrass him with any acknowledgement.

'Gentlemen . . . and, of course, ladies, may I extend a very cordial welcome to this, the fourth year of your studies. I am only too pleased that it falls to me to teach you by far the most important subject you will study during your residence in this venerable seat of learning.'

The class smiled, and some eager students at the front laughed out loud, but all were relaxed by this remarkable lecturer who proceeded to hold them in the palm of his hand for the next hour. He was fond of carrying out picturesque reconstructions of the violent crimes he was describing, whether they be stabbings or strangulations or deaths by poisoning, and this very much played to the imaginations of the students.

Cuthbert listened, equally enthralled, but not because of the pictures Littlejohn was painting with his words. Cuthbert had quite enough violent imagery in his head to last him a lifetime. No, what captivated him was the notion that the meticulous study of the finest details could yield the truth.

Littlejohn impressed upon him in those lectures the paramount importance of observation. This was a skill that was needed in all branches of medicine, but nowhere else in the curriculum was it given such a prime focus. Forensic medicine, Cuthbert came to realise, was an entirely objective science that ideally required complete detachment from any emotion.

'I have often heard it remarked that the specialist in forensic medicine is a detective. Let me disabuse you of that notion, ladies and gentlemen. Leave the detective work to the detectives. You are a scientist, skilled in the techniques of observation and analysis. You are not there to catch killers, nor indeed is your job to prove them innocent. You are there first and foremost to gather the facts, to arrange them so they can be understood, and to present them in as neutral a way as possible. You are neither the judge nor the jury. You must remember your role, its importance and its limitations, and never stray from it. Let the cobbler stick to his last.'

*

Cuthbert found his way back into medical school through Littlejohn's classes and began reading again. He found the forensic medicine textbooks in the library absorbing, and he read far more deeply than was required for the course. He overheard some of the students talk of how gruesome it all was, and how the photographs in the books showing crime scenes were almost too horrid to look at. He wanted to take them for five minutes to his A.D.S. behind the front lines and show them how horror really looked, sounded and smelled.

His interactions with the new fourth year were little more than perfunctory. Always polite but never warm, he engaged with the other young men when he was obliged to. There was almost no age difference between them, but Cuthbert felt he might be of a different generation. He could not join in their small talk, and when he would hear them discussing their eagerness to get out to the front, he would always walk away.

The women who had joined the university that year, after the separate Edinburgh School of Medicine for Women had finally closed its doors, were largely a mystery to him. Before the war there had been a small handful of female students at the university, but now there was such a large cohort that many of the gentlemen were intimidated. At first, they made fun of them. At one of the early lectures in the term, some wag had chalked a poem about them on the blackboard:

> *One by one they come trooping in –*
> *Tall girls, short girls, fat girls and thin!*
> *Pale girls, stale girls, burly girls bluff,*
> *Haughty girls, knutty girls – Gee! Some stuff.*

– 188 –

It was all very puerile, schoolboyish humour, and as it turned out, after the results of the first, interim exams were posted later that autumn, it was the ladies who were laughing at the men.

Perhaps it was this growing sense of equality, perhaps it was just that the young men who found themselves for the first time in a co-educational setting were finally maturing, but Cuthbert started to notice a change in the way they looked at the women. Gone were the snigger and guffaws as the women passed by: in their place, he started to see the wide-eyed lust of young men roused by the rustle of a petticoat and the heave of a bosom.

On the one hand, Cuthbert found it amusing to watch, but on the other, he was brought low by the realisation that he could not share their feelings. He badly wanted to, just to feel normal, but he knew that his eyes widened in that way when he looked at the angular jaws, the strong arms and the hard thighs of the men, but only if he let it show. And he had already learnt long ago never to allow that.

Around that time, just as he was coming out of the library in Old College one day, Cuthbert was approached by one of the medical students. She stopped in front of him, blocking his path, and made no attempt to move to either side to let him past. She simply extended her hand to shake his.

'Miss Mary Matheson. And you are Mr Cuthbert. I have heard a great deal about you, Mr Cuthbert, and would be interested in learning more. Might we take tea together? Shall we say four o'clock in Lyon's on Nicolson Street? Excellent, I shall see you then.'

Cuthbert had no recollection of agreeing to the meeting, but before he could protest, her skirts swept past him and into the library.

At just before four he found himself, against his better

judgement, standing in the street outside the tearoom intent on explaining to his fellow student that he was unable to come. Miss Matheson strode purposefully towards him and did not stop to say 'Good afternoon' or 'How lovely to see you'. She simply pushed through the tearoom door without waiting for it to be opened and said, 'Excellent, you're on time. I do appreciate punctuality.'

She took a seat at one of the nearest tables and nodded at the seat opposite her, which Cuthbert duly took. He wasn't entirely sure what was going on and had met sergeant majors with more finesse.

'Now, Mr Cuthbert, lest there be any misunderstanding, I want to reassure you that I am not trying to seduce you. I simply don't have time for that sort of thing and neither do you. I am in a predicament and I need your help. And before you get up and leave, I ask you to hear me out.'

The waitress arrived and looked at Cuthbert waiting for the order, only to be surprised by Miss Matheson's sharp cough.

'Yes, two teas, please, and two slices of the Victoria sponge, I think.' And turning back to Cuthbert, 'And please don't let's have any nonsense, I will be paying for this. After all, I'm the one who's dragged you here.'

'Miss Matheson, I do not know you. I do not know what you could possibly want from me, but I am perfectly sure I can be of no use to you whatsoever. I really must bid you a good day.'

'My brother's in the trenches, and you're the only one I know who can tell me what it's like for him.'

Cuthbert, who had half risen to leave, sat back down. 'And what makes you think I can do that?'

'Come, Mr Cuthbert, I've heard some of the talk at the school that the tall one who never smiles and who joined the class this year was at the front. Is it not true?'

'It is true, Miss Matheson. I was in France and Belgium for almost a year and a half. I spent my time in the trenches, but I also spent most of that time working with the wounded. I'm not sure, however, that anything I've got to say would be suitable for a lady's ears.'

'Oh, fiddlesticks. What do you think I am? Am I not following the same course as you? Am I not going to be a doctor, with all that entails? Surely you must realise I have a strong enough stomach for anything you can tell me.'

The waitress arrived with the teas and cake plates and tried not to concern herself with the strength of anyone's stomach.

'Tell me about your brother, Miss Matheson.'

'Usual story, I'm afraid. Young fool eager to get the head blown off his shoulders. He'd been accepted to study engineering here but joined up instead. Our mother is beside herself. I can't tell you how worried she is.'

'And you?'

'Honestly, Mr Cuthbert, I'm more angry than worried. Of course, I'm concerned about his safety, but I just want to get him back home and box his ears for him.'

'Perhaps you are of the opinion that I need my ears boxed too?'

Miss Matheson yielded her gaze for the first time since they had met outside the library, and her cheeks coloured.

'Of course not, Mr Cuthbert. Please forgive me, that's not what I meant at all. I can't sleep for worry and it's the not knowing what he's going through that is taking its toll. At least you can sleep at night now. You're home. Me, I toss and turn, not know-ing where or how he is. All the time wondering if he might be . . .'

Her voice caught in her throat and her eyes suddenly filled with tears. She was in distress, and Cuthbert decided it would be best not to tell her the truth. That almost every night since he had come home from the front, he had been hauled back there as he slept. That there were terrible nightmares, sudden awakenings from sweat-soaked sheets, and tears. More tears than he had ever been able to shed in the trenches.

But those nights, terrible though they were for him, were not the worst. That was the sudden, unexpected panic. While he was in a clinic, taking his breakfast or even just walking along the street, an overwhelming sense of fear might grip him, paralysing him, when he was least expecting it. He had tried to analyse it all as objectively as he could, but he could not identify the causes.

All that was left for him was to try to cope and to deal with it in the only way he had learned how. He looked down at the toe caps of his boots as he listened to Miss Matheson regale him with her feelings. The black leather still wore its mirror shine, and somehow it allowed him to breathe a little easier and for his racing heart to calm.

'I won't lie to you, Miss Matheson. He might indeed be dead. But it is more likely that he is not.'

She wiped her eyes, trying to regain her composure. 'I'm all bluster – you can see that – and I'm not nearly as resilient as I pretend to be. But I have to pretend in this course. We all do.'

'Yes, we do.'

'Oh, I didn't mean you. Not the men, and certainly not the men like you. I meant the women.'

'Don't flatter yourselves, Miss Matheson. Ladies do not have the monopoly on fear, on anxiety or on feelings of inadequacy. When did you last hear from your brother?'

'We last got a letter from Norman about three weeks ago. He says he's writing regularly, but the post is very erratic, I understand. Once we received two letters on the same day that he wrote a week apart. He said he was well. Talked of nothing in particular. We certainly don't know where he is or when he might be coming home. What can you tell me, Mr Cuthbert? Can you describe what he might be feeling? Can you help me understand? Anything would be better than what I'm imagining. I mean, was it really awful?'

Cuthbert looked at her face, expectant, almost pleading, and he doubted very much whether her imagination could trump his reality.

'Yes, it is awful. The war is not what they tell you it is, Miss Matheson. And it is not even the same for everyone. Your brother may not even be in the trenches on the front. Or if he was, he may not be now. There is constant movement, regular redeployment at every level. The only thing that you can be sure of is that he will be doing his very best to survive. All men do.'

'That's just it, though. He isn't a man, he's only a boy.'

'Miss Matheson, believe me when I say this: there are no boys in a war. I won't romanticise it for you. It is difficult for everyone. Many will be wounded, some will even lose their lives, but most will not, and you must remember that.'

'You came home, I suppose. I have to believe Norman will come home too.' The young woman stirred her tea more than was needed and took only a sip before pushing it away. 'I think I owe you an apology, Mr Cuthbert. I have behaved abominably. The very last thing you want to do, I'm sure, is talk about your experiences of the war. Can you forgive me?'

'Only if you let me pay for my own tea, Miss Matheson.'

*

Over the weeks, the young woman would nod in acknowledgement as she passed Cuthbert in the corridors and in the library. She said nothing more about her brother until mid-December, when she came to Cuthbert and again stopped him in his tracks.

'We've had a telegram! No, I don't mean that sort – a good one. Norman is coming home on leave. It's wonderful, isn't it?'

'Wonderful, and an opportunity for an ear-boxing. I'm happy for you. Just one thing, please be gentle with him. Not too many questions. Let him tell you what he wants to tell you. That will work best.'

'Thank you, Mr Cuthbert . . . Oh! Forensic medicine.' She noted the book Cuthbert was carrying from the library and plucked it from his hand.

'It's become something of an obsession, I'm afraid.'

'Don't apologise. I share your fascination, Mr Cuthbert. If I had my way, that's the speciality I would pursue after qualification.'

'Why don't you?'

'Don't be ridiculous! They'd never let a woman do that. No, it's general practice or obstetrics for me. Could be worse.'

*

As the year progressed, as well as studying eyes, psychiatry and completing his skins, more of Cuthbert's time was spent attached to the medical and surgical firms of the Royal Infirmary. Along with the other students, he would spend days and often evenings and increasingly weekends working on the hospital wards. One allocation had him, unusually, teamed with four of the women students, including Miss Matheson.

One day in January, Cuthbert arrived early before the surgical teaching ward round. He went as usual to his locker to change into his white coat but was stopped before he did so. Tied to his padlock with a piece of green ribbon was a long white feather. He took it and ran it through his fingers feeling how beautiful an object it was.

He walked upstairs to the ward duty room where the other

students mustered before the round. He went in and held up the feather.

'Ladies, who is responsible for this?' His voice was clear and steady and almost without emotion.

There were some gasps and muttering as each one looked at the others. Then Millicent Pollok stepped forward with her jaw set and said, 'That'll be me, Cuthbert. And what of it? Can't be the first of those you've received, I'll wager. I cannot abide cowards. I have a brother at the front and what are you doing? A man like you should be in uniform. You disgust me.'

Mary Matheson took her forcibly by the arm and physically bundled her from the room. As she went, Mary shook her head and said, 'I'm so terribly sorry, Mr Cuthbert. She doesn't know what she's saying.'

Cuthbert stood unmoved, without anger but filled with confusion. He ran the feather through his fingers again. One of the other women students who knew his story apologetically tried to take it from him, but he held it back and put it in his inside jacket pocket.

Mary returned without her colleague. 'I simply don't know what to say. That was unforgivable. Millie's mortified now she knows the truth. Poor thing. Of course, I don't mean that, not at all, not poor Millie, poor you. You must have found that all so hurtful.'

'Do you think a white feather can hurt me, Miss Matheson, or even the ignorance behind it? Shrapnel can hurt me, sniper bullets, shells, but not the ignorance of a woman. Now, we have a ward round to attend to. I suggest you get ready.'

Millicent Pollok did not appear for the ward round that day or the next and she was also absent from McIntosh's and Jackson's lectures. A rumour started that the faculty office had learned about her humiliation of Cuthbert, and the Dean himself had summoned her. Cuthbert was troubled by this and did not feel that was the way to deal with such behaviour. He was the one to stop Miss Matheson on the steps of the library the following day, and he asked about her fellow student.

'Is it true?'

'I'm sure I don't know what you mean, Mr Cuthbert.'

'Your friend – Miss Pollok, is it? – has the Dean had her over the coals?'

'Millicent is no friend of mine, Mr Cuthbert. Let me assure you of that. And, yes, it is true. Apparently, he has taken an exceedingly dim view of her prank. I think she'll be lucky to keep her place here.'

Cuthbert had never felt any animosity towards the woman, and he certainly didn't want that for her. He thanked Miss Matheson for the information and made straight to Littlejohn's rooms. Once more he found himself having to negotiate the prickly Miss Plunkett in the outer office.

'Please may I leave a message for the professor? I know he is very busy, and I do not have an appointment, so if I could just leave a note to–'

Miss Plunkett interrupted him, and although she did not exactly smile, she did soften a little. 'Mr Cuthbert, the Dean has left instructions that should you come, you are to be admitted forthwith. That is to say, he is expecting you. Please go right in.'

Cuthbert thanked the secretary and bowed just enough to tease the corners of her mouth into a smile. He knocked on the Dean's door, and Littlejohn rose to greet him as soon as he entered his office.

'Ah, Cuthbert, do take a seat.'

'I'll stand if you don't mind, sir. I really don't want to take up your time.'

'Ghastly business. Ghastly. But it won't happen again. I'm in the process of seeing to that. I simply won't tolerate that sort of behaviour amongst the students of this faculty. I won't have it, not in this university.'

'That's just it, sir. I would very much like you to forget it happened. I think she feels foolish, and I would greatly appreciate it if the matter could be dropped. I don't want her to suffer because of it.'

'Damn it, man, she humiliated you in front of the others. She called you a coward, a slacker.'

'And I am neither of those things, as you know, sir. And I think she knows that now too. So all we are left with is some name calling, which should not be the concern of a man such as yourself. You have more important matters to deal with, sir. Please do not force her from the profession because of a mistake. We all deserve second chances, do we not?'

Littlejohn had been impressed by Cuthbert ever since he first met him, and again the young man did not fail him. He knew that Cuthbert also had more important matters to deal with.

'If that's what you want, Cuthbert, I will of course bow to your judgement. You are the injured party here, and you have every right to call the shots. Consider the matter closed.'

Cuthbert thanked the Dean and turned to go, but just as he was leaving the office, Littlejohn called him back.

'How are things going with you, Cuthbert? It's been, what, about three months now.'

'Fine, sir. I'm settling back in. Everyone has been very helpful and supportive.'

'Well, not quite everyone, but I'm supposed to be forgetting that. How are you liking jurisprudence? You can be candid – I'm too old to be fishing for compliments, young man.'

'In truth, sir, it's my favourite subject. I would very much like to take it further when I qualify – after I satisfy the conditions of my temporary discharge, that is.'

'Perhaps it won't come to that. This frightful war may be over by the time you graduate.'

'I think we both know that is unlikely, sir.'

'Well, know this, Cuthbert – whatever happens, you have a place on my team when and if you want it.'

Cuthbert's jaw dropped for he had not expected this. Suddenly, the possibility of a meaningful path opened up before him. He had become absorbed in forensic medicine and science, and even at this comparatively early stage he knew he wanted to pursue it as his career without thinking how he was ever going to achieve it. Here, in a single sentence, he was being offered a route map to his destination. He did not know what to say to Littlejohn, and the Dean could see that his student was taken aback.

'Obviously, you don't have to think about that just yet, Cuthbert, but do keep me in mind. It would be an honour to have you. If, that is, you manage to get through the rest of the curriculum.'

'Of course, sir. I . . . I don't know how to thank you adequately. For your confidence in me. Nor, I have to say, can I pretend to understand it. But I promise you, I will work as hard as I am able to earn it.'

'Of that, Cuthbert, I have not the slightest doubt.'

Chapter 14

London: 29 April 1929

Their kiss when they greeted each other was hardly warm. The last time they had met, they had parted only after she had peeled herself away from his urgent embrace, but today was very different.

Simon Morgenthal was keen to talk to his fiancée about what had happened at the police station. He had seen her leaving the building after her interview with Chief Inspector Mowbray. Although she had looked rather shaken, he thought it best to let her go in case anyone saw them together.

The whole problem had arisen because of his inappropriate disclosure of information to her. The less contact they had in sight of the officers at the Yard, the better. Now, a week later, things had moved on, and Morgenthal thought it was safe to call Sarah and arrange for a walk in the park near her home. After the perfunctory kiss, she was distinctly cool towards him, and Simon began, as he had planned, with an apology.

'I am so very sorry you were put through all that, my darling. It was my fault, my fault entirely. I should have known better than to talk about my work and the case. I was simply showing off, and it was nothing but vanity.'

They walked along the circular park path, a little apart, and appeared more like friends than lovers. Sarah was dressed beautifully as always in the latest spring fashion of peach silk satin, and as she walked, she was careful where she put her new matching shoes. She kept her silence as she put up her parasol even though there was barely a sun, and Simon could see he needed to be more contrite.

'Can you forgive me for it all, my sweet? I know it's a lot to ask, but I've certainly learnt a lesson. Dr Cuthbert has made sure of that. I let him down so badly. I felt simply wretched.'

At the mention of Cuthbert's name, Sarah stopped and fixed Simon with her gaze. 'Is that why you really feel so bad – because you upset your Dr Cuthbert? And I suppose the rest is just words. Well, you should know, Papa is not best pleased with you.'

'With me?'

'Yes! His little girl is dragged down to a police station to answer a series of humiliating questions.'

'No one dragged you, Sarah. And it was because you had told Gossett about the case. I nearly lost my job over it.'

'Only because you told me. And I don't recall you saying anything about it being a secret.'

'Well, it will be the last time I tell anyone about my work.'

'And does that include me? Are we to have secrets from each other? And that's not all. Papa is really very angry about Julius Gossett. He says he was a good friend, and because of you and your Cuthbert, he's been dragged into all this.'

'No, he's been dragged into this because . . .'

Morgenthal stopped himself, remembering why they were having this conversation in the first place.

'Anyway, Simon, once you're finished with all this, we can put it behind us, can't we?'

'Finished?'

'Yes, with all this nonsense working with Scotland Yard. When you start being a proper doctor again. When you put your plaque up in Harley Street. That's what everyone expects, darling.' Sarah took his hand, smiled and pulled him gently towards her.

'I am a forensic pathologist, and for as long as I can be, that's what I want to do.'

Sarah took her hand away and started fussing with the buttons on her glove. Without looking at Simon, she said in a new tone, 'Well, that does rather change things, doesn't it? I mean, it's all very well to get a little interesting experience when one is young, but making a career of all that ghastly business . . . that's quite another.'

'What are you saying, Sarah?'

'I'm saying that I'm not so sure I want to be married to someone who spends his days cutting up corpses. And, on top of that, who can't even talk to me about it.'

'Sarah, darling, you're being unreasonable.'

'And you're being beastly!'

She walked on briskly, and Simon thought carefully before he ran to catch her up. The grey clouds parted briefly overhead, and a shaft of sunlight made its way onto the path, illuminating where they had been rather than where they were headed.

The next morning, Morgenthal knocked on Cuthbert's door and told him that a D.C. from the Yard had phoned about the release of Dawson's body.

'They're asking if the remains can be returned to the family for burial. I said I would check with you, sir.'

'Yes, the lad has told us everything he can about his end. It's time he was put to rest. Tell them we'll get the paperwork ready for his release. I expect it will be quite a funeral.'

'Sir?'

'When any young person dies, whatever the circumstances,

the turnout for the funeral is often very large. When a young man dies in such tragic circumstances as Dawson, it's likely to be standing room only.'

'Do we attend, Dr Cuthbert? I mean out of respect.'

'No, Simon, pathologists don't go to funerals. If we did, we'd do nothing else.'

When the ceremony was confirmed, Chief Inspector Mowbray told Baker to get there early for the same reason as Cuthbert had given Morgenthal. He expected there to be a mass attendance.

'And I want you to take a good look at the mourners. I wouldn't be at all surprised if the boy's killer shows up. This is a weird one, Baker, and he's just the sort that would want to enjoy the consequences of his handiwork. Take two constables with you and keep your eyes open.'

*

The church was a modest affair in Hampstead, but the chief inspector had been right about the numbers. The small church had quickly filled, and when Baker drove up, there was already a large crowd of mourners spilling from the churchyard and on to the pavements outside. There were even people lining the route of Dawson's cortege.

When the hearse arrived at the church there was a remarkable silence. It was suddenly so quiet that Baker rubbed his ears. The insignificant-looking coffin was slid from the back and lifted onto the shoulders of six rather ill-matched men. Three were fellow students, one was Dawson's cousin, and the others were his father and his paternal uncle. His father was clearly very distressed but appeared determined to do his duty by his son.

Baker noticed Clare Haskell close to the hearse outside the church. She wiped the tears from behind her glasses and gripped the hand of Michael Masters, the other student Baker had spoken with at the university. The coffin was carried into the church and all those outside simply stood while the muffled organ began to play 'Abide with Me'.

Close to Clare Haskell, Baker spotted a very stern-faced Dr Pemberton. He was chatting quietly to several others he obviously knew, people whom the sergeant took to be other staff at the university. Dr Gossett was standing apart, leaning awkwardly on his cane. Baker thought he must have regretted showing up too late to get a seat in the church. Now he could hardly turn and leave in front of all his colleagues.

Baker scanned the crowd, both there and afterwards at the cemetery when Dawson's coffin was lowered into his grave. Under his breath, one of the constables remarked that at least this time he had it to himself. When Baker heard, he scowled his disapproval. Dawson's mother was almost unable to walk and was being supported by her husband and other relatives. Baker kept well out of their eye line, for the last time he had met them it had been to bring them the worst news of their lives.

*

'It was certainly a big affair, as you said, chief inspector, and a very sad one. All the university crowd were in attendance, as were the family. There were a few new faces amongst them, an uncle, for example, whom we didn't know about. I don't know whether you think it's worth pursuing that. I did a little asking, and it turns out he lives up in Bristol. He hasn't been in the Smoke for a few years and only came back for the lad's send-off.'

'I don't suppose it's worth the shoe leather, Baker. Let's leave them to their grief for the time being. While we're on the subject of funerals, what about Galton? When's his?'

Baker looked blank, but one of the constables spoke up.

'No date's been set for that yet, sir. It appears that Mrs Galton has made no request for the return of the body.'

Baker rolled his eyes and muttered into his sleeve, 'Too busy with her bridge club, I expect.'

The chief inspector didn't catch it and just told them to make sure they went to that funeral too when it happened because he especially wanted to know of anyone who attended both.

'It might be a shot in the dark, but it's worth a try.'

*

It was Sunday just before lunch, and Cuthbert was expecting to hear Madame Smith any moment. She had every Sunday afternoon free and used it to recapture some of the world she had left behind in Belgium before the war. Dressed well but not expensively, she adjusted her cloche hat, checked her lipstick and straightened the seam of her pale silk stockings before putting her head around Cuthbert's study door.

'I am leaving now, monsieur. Your lunch is under the cloth in the kitchen as usual. Please remember to eat it.'

'Anywhere nice today, madame?'

'A concert at the Wigmore. Vivaldi's *Four Seasons*, which, with your English weather, is most appropriate, *n'est-ce pas*?'

'Enjoy yourself, madame.'

After she had closed the front door, he went to the window to watch her walk away along the street. As soon as she dressed in her Sunday clothes and left the house, she always became someone else. No longer a servant, but now a refined European lady with taste and breeding. Cuthbert knew it was not an act. The act, if there was any, was when she served him in his home, dressed as a maid.

He was ambivalent about his employment of the young woman. She had transformed his domestic arrangements from disorder to a household that ran like a well-oiled machine. She had taken away any concerns he had about all those matters he was singularly ill-equipped to deal with. And she had brought companionship into his life. But he also worried that her position was demeaning to one of her background, and he even said so on several occasions.

Her reply was always the same: 'You took me in when you did not have to. You have given me a roof and a sanctuary. I have my life again thanks to you. There is no need to feel any guilt.'

And, of course, it was guilt that he felt when he watched her clean and scrub and cook for him.

Late that evening, he heard her key in the lock and her soft footsteps as she tried to enter without disturbing the house. He was still in his study, and although she saw the light through the door, she slipped past and went up to her room, wishing neither to apologise nor explain.

*

The following morning, Cuthbert did not ask about her day or her evening. Instead, he read his morning paper in silence as she served the simple breakfast of strong coffee and bread he had come to enjoy since she arrived.

That morning, like most others when he had an early appointment at the Yard, he chose to walk the two miles. The London streets early in the morning were always alive with activity, the day starting as it meant to go on.

There was the rush of deliveries, the calls of the news boys and the clatter of horses and carts vying alongside the motor transports that had in recent years become such a feature on the roads of the capital. The sun was streaming across Russell

Square as he walked along its east side, and the daffodils that Morgenthal had been so keen to see were now almost over. Some of the late spring blossom was still hanging on the trees by way of compensation.

On the corner of High Holborn, he stopped to buy matches from the street vendor. Although he did not smoke, he still bought them every day that he passed and always from the same man sitting on the pavement, his one good leg folded under him and the stump of the other resting on a rolled-up coat. The man never spoke and never smiled, but simply nodded as he took the copper coins in exchange for his wares. He was one of the thousands who had come home from the war to a country that often found their injuries, both physical and mental, an embarrassment.

Each day the man sat there reminding everyone that it had only been just over a decade since the guns fell silent. For Cuthbert, the old soldier and the many others like him, sitting on street corners throughout the city, were a much more poignant reminder than the cenotaph that had been unveiled in Whitehall. That was merely stone and flags; these were broken flesh and blood.

Down towards the Strand the roads became even busier, and Cuthbert, who had never lived anywhere but in a city, felt at home in the flurry of one coming to life. The Strand itself had been the subject of so many roadworks in the last few years that it had become a standing joke. 'The Strand is up again!' they would shout from the open-topped buses. Today they were digging in order to widen the thoroughfare, and Cuthbert had to negotiate both the traffic and the workmen with their pickaxes to make his way across.

When he reached the Victoria Embankment, he allowed himself a few moments by the river. The great, grey Thames was high that morning and looking upriver he could make out

Waterloo Bridge and directly across the water he could see the great crescent of County Hall.

The scale of London had never ceased to amaze him, and despite all the years he had now lived in the capital, it was still with a sense of wonder that he would turn a street corner or catch the view along an unfamiliar street. London, of course, could be an unforgiving host to the poor and the destitute, but it had always held out the warmest of welcomes to him. He took a deep breath, filling his lungs with the city, and turned towards the Yard.

New Scotland Yard itself was a red-brick building banded with white stone. Turreted and with rows of small windows punctuating its grey slate roof, Cuthbert had always thought it looked more like an English boarding school than a police headquarters.

As he pushed open the glass entrance door, he recalled his first day there and the apparent difficulty his Scottish accent had caused. It had only been when a Scottish sergeant, hearing the commotion at the reception, had come out to cuff the ear of the young desk constable for being 'such a bloody Cockney' that Cuthbert had been admitted.

Baker and the chief inspector were in animated conversation as Cuthbert approached them in the second-floor duty room. Unusually for Mowbray, he was smiling and even laughing with his sergeant, and Cuthbert just caught the end of a story.

'. . . and she said, well, if you don't eat it, there won't be any afters! And so–'

'You never ate it?'

'Too bloody right, I did! It was Friday night and that's definitively the night, if you know what I mean . . . Ah, Cuthbert, we were just discussing the things a man has to do to get what he wants.'

'Wants, chief inspector?'

'The old slap and tickle, doctor. A man has his needs, doesn't he? But it looks as if you're well sorted in that department.'

Cuthbert looked suddenly indignant and said, 'I don't know what you mean, chief inspector. And now that I think about it, I'm sure it isn't a subject which gentlemen should be discussing.'

'Come on, Cuthbert. I think we both know that all gentlemen are just men when they get their trousers down. Yes, you're well sorted with your madame. Right juicy little bit you've got there and no mistake. And having her as a housekeeper – such a convenient set-up. You get your dinner made and your bed warmed and none of the nonsense us married men have to deal with. I take my hat off to you. So what's she like? Belgian, you said? I remember a few Belgian tarts during the war. Very sweet and tasty.'

Cuthbert was angry not for himself but for Madame Smith whose defence he leapt to. He would not have her spoken of in that tone, here or anywhere else for that matter. He rounded on the chief inspector and faced him off. Almost baring his teeth in rage, he spoke slowly and deliberately.

'It's nothing of the sort. Madame Smith is my housekeeper, chief inspector, and despite the thoughts which are flowing through that gutter of a mind of yours, there is absolutely no impropriety. She is a married woman.'

'A widow, I think you said. So what's wrong with her? What's wrong with you? Any hot-blooded man would want a bit of that, and when it's living in, well . . . so easy.'

Cuthbert had suddenly strayed into dangerous territory. Could he keep up the moral outrage and, at the same time, prevent the chief inspector from guessing the true nature of his feelings? He thought better than to try, and he immediately withdrew and changed the subject.

'In any case, much more important are the latest interviews. Have you had any update from your sergeant?'

*

At dinner that evening, Madame Smith served with her usual care. As she cleared away the plates, she saw that Cuthbert had eaten little. Although she was always efficient and brisk in her manner, she had relaxed into a certain familiarity with her employer and felt free to speak her mind.

'May I ask what is troubling you this evening, Dr Cuthbert?'

'What makes you think I am especially troubled, madame?'

'Because I have eyes. You have hardly eaten anything, and you have never before refused my crêpes. I conclude that you are troubled, and I think you should discuss it.'

'No other man's housekeeper speaks to him the way you do, madame.'

'That is a great pity for the other men, is it not?'

Cuthbert smiled, and Madame Smith took a seat beside him at the table.

'Tell me, what is it? Perhaps I can help. I have come to think of you as a friend as much as an employer. I do not think that is an impertinence even though others might. I think it is the natural course of events.'

Cuthbert looked at her and realised that he did regard her as a friend and companion as much as any kind of employee. In fact, when he thought of her as a servant, he found it distasteful. She had over these years become much more to him than a housekeeper, but not in the way Mowbray had implied. He decided that honesty was certainly the best policy with this woman.

'At the Yard, today, I had a meeting with Chief Inspector Mowbray. You met him when he called that day.'

She rolled her eyes at the memory of the man.

'Yes, I know. I could tell the moment you met him that you didn't like him. You have many skills, madame, but being good at hiding your true feelings is not one of them.'

'And for this I should apologise? If you English were a little more open about your feelings and a little less concerned with what everyone thinks, a lot of trouble would be saved. And before you say it, I know you are not English. But I think what I say is just as true for the Scottish.'

'Well, Mowbray was rather indelicate in his references to our domestic arrangements. As, I'm afraid, others have also been. People do talk about us, and it worries me. Not for myself, but you are a lady and must think of your reputation.'

'What is your expression? Poppycock? This is what I say to them, and what you should say too. Ours is a working relationship, Dr Cuthbert. You are a thirty-four-year-old man; I am a twenty-nine-year-old woman. Under different circumstances we would be lovers. But my reputation is quite safe as far as I am concerned. I have lost any interest I had in men, and you, we both know, have never been interested in women.'

Cuthbert looked startled.

'Oh, please save your indignation for others, monsieur. I am not telling you anything you do not already know. And what of it? Does this make you any less of a man? Certainly not. Does this make you evil, sinful? Of course not – only stupid people think that. There is enough pain in the world without adding to it by manufacturing it out of nothing. I have no time for such people, and neither should you.'

'You do not understand. How could you?'

'How could I? My brother was in love with another man in Liège, and I loved my brother. He did not enjoy a single happy day in his short life before the war finished him. What a waste of a life. And what a waste of love that people cannot allow it because it is somehow seen as less than the love between a husband and a wife. I have had that kind of love, and let me assure you, monsieur, there was nothing so wonderful about it. Nothing that made it so noble, that I could see.'

'But I am abnormal. What I am, what I feel – it is against God.'

'Are we going to talk of God, you and I? Really? We, who have been through a war and have seen what people do to one another. If there is a God, monsieur, either he is helpless to stop the pain and suffering in the world or he does not care about it. Whatever the truth of the matter, it makes him an irrelevance. I believe in friendship and honesty and trust. I believe in love, and I believe in you. I do not need to believe in God.'

She rose from her seat and finished tidying the dinner table. As she passed, he took her hand. And she stood still and allowed him to hold it. He was one of the loneliest men she had ever met, and his sadness was at times overwhelming.

He never discussed his friends because she did not think he had any. He did have colleagues, students and of course his assistants, but no one with whom he might share the burden of his past. There was no other hand to hold but hers, and she gave it freely for she knew exactly how he felt. It was how she had felt ever since she had left her home.

He began to speak, but she hushed him, knowing that no more needed to be said. She knew he wanted to apologise, to erase the feelings that had welled up in him, to ask her to forget, but she wanted none of that. She wanted him to be able to turn away from the ruins of his past and to find his life again. She wanted him to be truthful to himself.

'Tell me, have you ever been in love, monsieur? I have. Not with my husband, of course, but with a boy in Liège. He was sixteen and I was fifteen, and we never so much as kissed each other, but from the moment we met, I knew I would never be the same person again. He completed me. Have you ever had that? The feeling that without that person you will never be whole again. That unless you are together there will always be a part of you missing, perhaps even broken, which only that person can mend. That is what love was for me, and I only experienced it once, but I still feel it today. It has never left me, and I do not think it ever will. That is the nature of love. It is eternal, whether we wish it or not. Have you been in love like that?'

'Yes. And I still am, but he left and was unable to come home again. And now I am broken with no one to mend me. I carry on, I exist, but I am incomplete. I am barely even a man.'

'*Au contraire*, monsieur, you are the best man I have ever known.'

She brought his hand to the warmth of her cheek and then released it. She poured him a whisky and left him alone in the dining room.

*

The following morning at breakfast, he was sheepish and unsure of whether he should raise their discussion from after dinner the night before. He had slept badly, as he often did.

He rarely had bad nightmares any more, but his dreams were often vivid and exhausting, involving hunts through woodland where he would sometimes be the quarry, sometimes the hunter, and sometimes confusingly both at the same time. His dreams were often peopled by those from his past. He would see his father, whom he barely remembered, and students from the early days at university. Sometimes his patients would walk through his dreams, and sometimes even the dead tried to tell him their stories. And Troy would be there, always laughing and flailing his arms, his red hair catching the summer sun on the hilltop before they said goodbye.

He often woke and was relieved to find that the chase or the crowds had been nothing but a dream, but he was always saddened to remember that Troy had indeed said goodbye and would never be coming back.

Madame Smith was business-like in her morning routine and would not allow anything to disrupt the smooth running of the home. On a work day, it was her job to ensure that Cuthbert left on time, refreshed and ready for the day. But that morning, she could see he was far from either.

She served his croissant and filled his cup and took the initiative, for she did not have enough time to wait for a man.

'Last night you spoke from the heart, and that was the most healing thing you could have done. You must not regret what you said to me, and you need to know that I will always be here to listen. But I will never cause you embarrassment by repeating anything you say to me. I think you know all that without me having to say it, but sometimes it is better to say it than to imagine it has been said. Now, monsieur, please drink your coffee, eat your pâtisserie, say nothing and go to work. There are dead people who rely upon you to help them find peace.'

Chapter 15

London: 7 May 1929

The knock on Gossett's office door was more forceful than before and stopped the tutor in mid-sentence. The three students in his room had been hanging on his explanation of a subtle point of criminal law and were equally startled by the interruption.

Before their tutor could say or do anything, Mowbray marched into his room. Gossett could see from the chief inspector's stance that he had not come with any intention of leaving alone, and he pre-empted any further embarrassment by dismissing his students and telling them he would reschedule their tutorial for another time. They left quickly, pushing past the chief inspector who was still standing in the doorway.

'I would like you to come with me to the station, Dr Gossett.'

'Am I being arrested, chief inspector?'

'No, sir. You are being asked to attend the station voluntarily to help with our enquiries. There are a number of matters we need to clear up. You will, however, be interviewed under caution – that is to say, you do not have to say anything unless you wish to do so, but what you say may be given in evidence.'

'All sounds rather serious, chief inspector. Do I need a solicitor?'

'You have that right, sir, but I see it rather more as an informal chat. And, in any case, aren't you a lawyer yourself, sir?'

'All right, when do you want me? I'll warn you I'm not as mobile as I once was.'

'No problem, sir, we have a car for you. Shall we say right now?'

*

In the interview room at the Yard, Gossett took a seat with some difficulty and laid his cane on the floor at his side. Across the table sat Mowbray and beside him Sergeant Baker, who was taking notes. The room smelled of stale cigarettes and the paintwork was yellowed with age and smoke. Gossett looked around and shifted on the hard seat. Before he began, Mowbray himself lit a cigarette and retrieved a small tin ashtray from the window sill and positioned it directly in front of Gossett.

'Thank you for coming in today, Dr Gossett. For the purposes of our record, I would like to remind you that you are being interviewed under caution in relation to the disappearance and murder of Freddie Dawson. Can I begin by asking you to explain the nature of your relationship with young Dawson?'

'I would hardly describe it as a relationship, chief inspector. I was his tutor at university, and he was my student. Nothing more.'

'But surely there *was* more, Dr Gossett? Didn't you say you felt a responsibility to Dawson's family when he went missing, and later when he turned up dead? Didn't you try to get details about the case from Dr Cuthbert, our pathologist, with the intention of sharing those with Dawson's family?'

'Ah, so that's what this is about, is it? Look, I admit that I was foolish to do that. I was worried about the Dawsons, and in truth I was worried about how it was all going to play out for the faculty. The boy was killed when he was a student, for heaven's sake. We weren't to know whether his disappearance and his murder might be in any way connected to the university and its staff, or even its other students. There was almost nothing appearing in the press, and that just fuels speculation, doesn't it? I thought if I could get some facts, I could show the Dawsons that we at the university were taking it seriously – doing everything we could to help. You must believe me, chief inspector. My intentions were good.'

'And we know where *they* lead, don't we, sir?'

'The road to perdition, chief inspector? *The gates of hell are open night and day; Smooth the descent, and easy is the way: But to return, and view the cheerful skies, In this the task and mighty labour lies.* Or in other words, going down is a great deal easier than coming back up. Come now, chief inspector, if that's all, then I don't think we need to waste any more of our time.'

'It's not quite all, Dr Gossett.'

Mowbray took a mental note of how little Gossett was sweating. In his experience, most interviewees in a setting like this would already be damp with perspiration. They would be agitated, perhaps developing nervous tics, like scratching the back of their hands or a shaking leg beneath the table. But with Gossett there was none of that. He sat stock-still and appeared, if anything, to be enjoying the experience. The chief inspector decided to press him harder to see what effect it might have in breaking his composure.

'How did you know Dawson was found naked?'

'I'm sure it was in the papers. Everyone was talking about the case at the university, and I expect I picked it up there.'

'No, you didn't, sir. We did not release that information into the public domain. So I will ask you again: how did you know he was naked?'

'There is no need to raise your voice, chief inspector. If it wasn't from the press, I must have heard it from the Fielding girl. She's such a chatterbox when she gets started. Have you met her, chief inspector? Lovely girl, but she does like to talk about her darling Simon and his awfully important work. And to think a girl like that can now vote. It really doesn't bear contemplating. I expect it was her.'

'Miss Fielding denies knowing any of the forensic details of the case and further denies sharing any with you. So I shall ask you for a third time, how did you know?'

'Really, chief inspector, are you going to take her word for that? I never asked her about the case. She just started talking one evening over dinner. I admit I was interested. After all, I had been trying to find out more for the reasons I told you, but I'd certainly hit a brick wall with your department and with Dr Cuthbert. Miss Fielding was a godsend in that respect, but she really did seem to love talking about the more grisly aspects of the murder. She said the bodies were found naked. And that's how I knew.'

Mowbray couldn't discount the possibility that he was telling the truth, so he pressed further. 'If Miss Fielding told you that, what else did she tell you about the case?'

'Well, primarily that Dr Cuthbert was the lead forensic pathologist on the case. That was by far the most useful nugget. But she also mentioned the nature of the bodies and how they were positioned in the grave.'

Mowbray glanced over Gossett's shoulder at the mirrored glass behind him. Cuthbert was there in the dark, watching the proceedings through the observation window. If Morgenthal had spilled all this outside the Yard, he would be answering to

Cuthbert personally and would soon be looking for alternative employment.

'Tell me more about that, sir.'

'Surely you don't need me to tell you the details of your own case, chief inspector. But, of course, you're asking because you want to know how much I know. Well, she said it was the queerest thing, in that the two bodies seemed to have been bound together. I believe she said something about this happening when one of them was dead and the other alive. That was fascinating. Of course, it immediately evoked the *Nupta Cadavera* – the marriage with the dead, chief inspector.'

Gossett wore his condescending smile lightly, but Mowbray was not to be made less of. He leaned forward and pushed the Latin text Cuthbert had given him across the table and glanced briefly again at the mirrored glass.

'It's in Virgil, I believe. The *Aeneid*. Book Eight, if I'm not mistaken.'

'Oh no, you're not mistaken, chief inspector, but it's much older than that. Aristotle himself talked of it, but then he was always going on about something or other, wasn't he? So much less attractive a dinner companion than Socrates, I've always felt. Don't you agree? No, good old Aristotle knew it was a particular speciality of those pesky Etruscans. But, of course, he couldn't just enjoy it for what it was – he had to see it as a metaphor for the punishment of life – the soul shackled to the body, the living essence to the mortal flesh and all that.'

Gossett looked vaguely into space and appeared to the chief inspector to lose consciousness momentarily. As quickly as it had happened the reverie was broken, and he smiled again and became animated.

'You see, the important part of it all, even for Aristotle, was that every part of one body has to be positioned carefully in exact opposition to the other. Chest to chest, thighs pressing on thighs, knees touching and, of course, lips to lips. That was the best part, making them kiss. And eyes to eyes. The living looking into the eyes of death, and death enduring the horror of looking into life. A pact of putrefaction, if you like. A marriage, where the living perishes in the embrace of the dead. Held captive by death and decay, we die as we stare into the mirror of our own demise. Beautiful, don't you think? Poetic. Just, even.'

'If we could put poetry aside for a moment, perhaps you can tell me where you were on the early evening of tenth December last year. It was a Monday, if that helps jog your memory, sir. Although you previously said you were attending a Senate meeting, we now believe you might have been mistaken in that. Would you like to tell us where you really were?'

'Oh, are we playing that game, where you try to trip me up on my alibi? Where I say rather gruffly, "How can I remember exactly where I was and what I was doing four months ago?" And you say very schoolmasterly, "Come now, sir, it's a straightforward question, and I expect a straightforward answer." And I say, "I was at my Club all evening." And you say, "Can anyone corroborate that?" And I say, "Oh, chief inspector, if only they could, if only there was a lovely young thing keeping me warm in my bed at night whom you could question as to the veracity of my statement."

'Well, even though that would be so much fun, chief inspector, why don't we just save everyone some time? What do you say? After all, this is becoming just a little boring, don't you think? Where was I on the early evening of tenth December last year? I was killing Freddie Dawson, that's where. Happy now, chief inspector? Maybe you'll get home in time for tea tonight after all.'

Mowbray was not prepared for this and had expected to have to work a great deal harder to extract anything like a confession. However, he was practised and did not flinch. He simply pushed the files before him to one side, knowing he would no longer need them. Gossett watched the police officer, studying Mowbray's reaction and unable to conceal his smile. He was enjoying every moment, but if Mowbray wanted more, he would have to ask.

The chief inspector sat in silence, calculating his next move but never losing eye contact with Gossett. After a full minute, Mowbray pushed the cigarette pack across the table and simply nodded in its direction to offer one to the man. Despite his resolve, this was all the invitation Gossett needed to start talking again.

'Thank you, chief inspector. How kind, but I won't if you don't mind. So bad for one's health. Now, I expect you'll want some details.'

Mowbray nodded again but was now unsure if he could believe anything this madman might say. 'Please do explain, sir.'

Gossett brightened at the politeness being shown him and sat up just a little straighter to tell his story.

'Well, chief inspector, I knew that Dawson was writing his honours dissertation on criminal prosecution during the war, and it was the easiest thing in the world to entice him into a meeting. First of all, I wrote to him – you won't have found the letters because I asked him to bring them with him when we met. And then I tested my disguise by seeing him briefly from a taxi the Friday before we met properly. I suggested a meeting in a suitably clandestine spot that afternoon. I thought he would like that; the young always love a bit of mystery, don't they?

'I stayed in the shadows, just to make sure he wouldn't

recognise me, and the first thing I did was ask for the letters. He obliged – he was good that way. I told him in my best muffled, croaky voice that we needed to go back to my lodgings, where I would provide him with some interesting material for his work. He was keen and didn't seem to think twice about going up a dark stairwell with a stranger, even one with a limp. Again, that's youth for you – fearless and stupid.

'To tell you the truth, I hadn't really worked out how to do it at that stage. I think I was playing it by ear a little, seeing how far I could get him to come to me. I had a knife just in case, but I thought that might make a frightful mess, and strangulation seemed an altogether less sticky affair.

'Once I got him into the room, I sat him down at the table and placed some bulging folders in front of him. He was eager to read them but polite enough to await my instructions. I said something, I can't remember what, something about how it was good being able to get this off my chest after all these years. Anyway, I invited him to browse the files, and as he did so, I stood behind him.

'He was slightly built, so I didn't think he would have put up quite such a fight while I was throttling him with the tie I had taken off. And it took a little longer than I had anticipated. I don't mind telling you I was quite out of breath myself by the time he slumped. I left on the tie, just to be sure, and I noticed he'd wet himself, so I thought that was a good sign. I left him there for a good twenty minutes and then checked to see if everything was all right. Fortunately, he was gone. And so to work.'

Mowbray had interviewed countless suspects, but he had never encountered anyone quite so disconnected from his crime. This man was coherent, conscious of detail, and was very probably telling the truth, but there was another possibility. He might also merely be a fantasist, getting a thrill from telling the elaborate tale of a murder he had only committed in his dreams. Whatever the case, he betrayed no sense of right or wrong. Indeed, Mowbray wondered if the words meant anything to him at all.

'Where are these lodgings you speak of?'

'Church Street, 27A, just off Tottenham Court Road. I don't live there, of course. I wouldn't want you to think that. I just needed somewhere convenient, you understand.'

'And what next? What did you do with the body?'

'Ah, well, the next part is a little indelicate. I had to undress the young man to see what I'd got. I took off his clothes, which is harder than you might expect without any help, but he was very pretty. Very good skin and just a hint of very dark hair in all the right places, if you know what I mean. Very soft skin too.

'When he was naked, I laid him on the bed and just looked at him, really. Lovely. I did touch him. I mean, how could you not? But already he was beginning to stiffen, around the eyes and his hands. I knew that it would spread, and I only had a short window to be able to move him. I couldn't leave him there, of course. I needed to get him back home, and that's why I had the trunk.

'I burned his clothes in the grate, even his underclothes, which I did think about keeping, but then I thought better to be safe than sorry. His wallet took the longest to burn. I took out the ten-shilling note and the other few bits and pieces he had in it, but it took an age. I meant to give the money to the Salvation Army, but do you know, in all the confusion, I think I may have forgotten. That's unforgivable, isn't it? I must sort that out later.'

Mowbray needed a break from this. He turned to Sergeant Baker at his side and stated, 'Organise some tea for Dr Gossett and us, will you? I'll be outside.'

He rose without explaining further and walked past the mirror and out into the corridor. Meeting him there was Cuthbert, who had recognised that he was being summoned.

'Thoughts?'

'Clear as day, chief inspector. The man is a psychopath, without any notion of remorse for his actions. He is calmly explaining everything. He needs no prompting, and I think everything he says is likely to be the truth. It certainly fits with what we know about the murders.'

'Queer?'

Cuthbert frowned, as much in thought as in discomfort, and shrugged. 'I'm not sure. Is there a sexual motive for this killing? If there is, it's not a straightforward one. He certainly hasn't admitted to any kind of sexual violence against the young man before the murder, or after it for that matter. He's almost talking about him as a work of art rather than as a human being.'

Mowbray paced the corridor, thinking while running his hands through his hair for a few more minutes. He then walked back to Cuthbert and patted his arm.

'Right, I need to get back in there. Keep watching, will you?'

Three rather stained cups without saucers were now on the table, and Mowbray continued without any formality.

'Dr Gossett, why did you kill Freddie Dawson?'

'Oh, chief inspector, that information is not available. I am happy to tell you where and when and even how, but I will not be revealing my motives. Not to you. And why could it possibly matter, anyway? I'll hang no matter why I did it, won't I?'

The chief inspector looked up from his notes to see Gossett smiling again. It was a soft, almost indulgent smile, and suddenly Mowbray wanted to hit him hard just to wipe it from his face. He took his clenched fist in his other hand and held it under the desk and checked himself.

'Do carry on, sir. You have described burning the deceased's clothing and personal effects. What happened next?'

'Now we get to the fun part. It takes about four to six hours for rigor mortis really to take hold. If you don't believe me, do ask that lovely Dr Cuthbert. I'm sure he will corroborate. He is just on the other side of the glass, isn't he?'

Gossett smiled and waved at the mirror, but Cuthbert was unmoved.

'As I was saying, the fun part. I had to work quickly so I could still manhandle the youngster enough to fold him into the trunk. I had lined it with some tarpaulin, just in case of any leakages or the like. Can't be too careful. And I had arranged for its collection and transport back to Wimbledon. I'd already made all the preparations there. I have a big lean-to greenhouse that I'd cleared out before laying more tarpaulin on the floor. I knew it was going to get messy at some point, and no need to clean up any more than you have to, eh?

'When the trunk arrived the next day, I waited until the delivery men had left and then I got the trunk through the hall and out the back door. It's a big garden, nobody overlooking me. Just trees, so I could afford to take my time. When I opened the trunk, he was starting to smell a little. A lot of people don't like the smell of decay. I've always found it not exactly pleasant, but earthy in a slightly sensual way, like soiled linen. I admit I am unusual in that, but I think it's best to be candid at this stage of the proceedings.

'The boy was beginning to be easy to handle again and just as soft as before. Still lovely. I laid him out on his back on the floor of the greenhouse and arranged his hair. I tied his wrists and ankles together, just to make it easier to move him. And I left him. To ripen. Unfortunately, being December, it was far from warm, so I turned up the pipes a little and made sure all the vents were closed.'

'And what about William Galton?'

'You already asked me about that name at the university, and I told you I don't know who you're talking about.'

Mowbray looked him over. What kind of game was Gossett playing? Why would he confess to strangling Dawson but deny Galton when they must have been the victims of the same killer? He decided on a different tack.

'Do you still deny knowing a Mr Henry Melville?'

'Ah, you mean the other one. I was a little naughty there, chief inspector, and I did tell you a white lie. Yes, I did know Melville. He was the other half of the fun.'

'Where and when did you meet him?'

'You do like your dates, don't you, chief inspector? Let me see. It must have been in the autumn of last year, early October, most probably. That was the first time we had ever met. He needed money, and I needed instruction, amongst other things, and we came to a deal. He was really very accommodating.'

Mowbray was becoming increasingly irked by Gossett's airy tone, but he had no choice but to carry on, to get the full story. He and his team still had only a very incomplete picture of what had happened, and Gossett looked to be in a talkative mood.

'Do go on, sir. What was the nature of the arrangement?'

'Well, it was a private matter, chief inspector, but seeing as it's just us, I suppose I can tell you. I first bumped into Melville, quite by chance you understand, one day at the library. He didn't really look the part, but he did have a visitor's card for the university collection. He was in the classics section, to where, I have to confess, I escape myself from time to time. Beautifully written Latin is such a solace for the soul . . .

'Anyway, I got chatting with him because I saw him poring

over a rather interesting text. And he told me he had been a Latin teacher. Well, I was certainly interested then, and after a very pleasant and, I must say, illuminating discourse on the relative merits of Juvenal's satires versus those of Horace, I made the proposal. That is, I would meet him once a fortnight for, what shall we call it, special instruction in Latin poetry, and I would pay him.

'He was obviously a little down on his luck, and he jumped at the chance. We met in the Fredsons' Café in Tower Hamlets. Not the most salubrious of locations but needs must, and it was convenient for him. However, in the New Year, I suggested we meet at my home in Wimbledon, and, of course, I would pay for his taxis there and back. In the end, I only had to pay it one way, of course.'

'Did you kill Henry Melville?'

'Certainly not, chief inspector. Whatever gave you that idea? It was Dawson who killed him. Melville was a great tea drinker, so it was very easy to slip him a little something just to quieten him down, so I could prepare him. Again, I can't emphasise enough just how difficult it is to undress a grown man when he's not offering any assistance. But we eventually got there.

'His body was not quite as lovely as the boy's, but it was fresher. With my gammy leg, everything did take rather longer than I had wanted. He was beginning to come around, but not before I had his hands and ankles well secured. He did look rather surprised to find himself lying on his back on the floor of my greenhouse, naked and just a little immobilised. He started blubbering, and it was most distracting because I was trying to manoeuvre Dawson into position. Melville even started to complain about the smell. "Wait till you taste him," I said.'

Mowbray swallowed hard and looked as if he was going to retch. Cuthbert, who was still watching through the glass, could see the effect this was having on the chief inspector, but he still could not explain it. Surely, Mowbray must have dealt with many murders just as ghastly as this without any ill-effect.

The chief inspector, who had half risen from his seat, sat back down and ordered the constable by the door to open the only window in the room. And he lit another cigarette. This time he did not offer one to Gossett.

'Stuffy in here. I'm sorry I interrupted you, sir. Please do go on.'

'I do hope you're feeling quite well, chief inspector. I have to say, you look a little pale. I'm afraid there's more to come. We haven't got to the really good part yet.'

'Then perhaps that would be a good point to take a break, sir. We are obliged to offer you some lunch since you have been with us for quite some time now. My constable will arrange it, and we will reconvene here in one hour.'

He turned to the sergeant who was still taking copious notes and said, 'Make a note of that as well, Baker.'

And with that he quickly left the room and went out into the hallway where he leaned heavily against the wall and bent over to catch his breath, bracing himself with his hands on his thighs. Cuthbert came out of the observation room at the same time, and he could see the chief inspector was quite shaken.

'Chief inspector, I think you need to sit down. Constable, a glass of water, quickly now. Come let me help you.'

Cuthbert took the chief inspector into an adjacent empty office where he seated him beside an open window. After a few moments, Mowbray shook his head and turned to Cuthbert.

'So the crust on the Pie isn't quite as thick as he makes out. That's what you're thinking, doctor?'

'Not at all, chief inspector. That's enough to turn anyone's stomach.'

'But you're still thinking I must have heard worse. After all, I've been doing this for a long time.'

'Well . . .'

'It's fine, and you're right. This *is* different. This is a little closer to home. I've never even told my wife this, Cuthbert, but we're both men and I know we've both been through it, so you deserve an explanation.

'It wasn't long after I'd been shipped out to the front. It was a fucking nightmare for a young lad. I don't have to tell you what it was like; you were there. And I don't mind telling you I was shitting myself in that trench when we were shelled at night.

'One time, the C.O. got three of us to retrieve some of the others who had been killed. There was a lull in the action and they had been lying in no-man's-land for a while. I don't know, it might even have been a bit of an unofficial truce, a gentleman's agreement to allow us and them to get back our dead. So I went out, keeping my head down, and the one I was carrying home was well gone. Stank to high heaven, poor sod. I had him over my shoulder and was making my way back when, out of nowhere, the sniper starting firing. Suddenly, our side returned fire, and there I am in the middle of it, getting sprayed by both bloody sides.

'I started running back to the trench and I tripped. The body fell in front of me, and I fell on top of it. My face right into his. Only there wasn't much of his face left after the crows had been at it for a week. I couldn't get up because of the bullets and I had to lie there, and I could taste him . . . I can still taste him.'

Cuthbert had listened in silence and could see that the chief inspector was reliving the whole experience rather than merely remembering it. He was shaking and sweating and in no fit state to carry on.

'Look, Mowbray, we all need to work together on this. This doesn't just have to be you. Let Baker take over now, and if you permit it, I'll sit in with him and take the notes. You've got Gossett talking, and it looks as if he's going to tell us the whole thing. Why don't you sit the rest of this one out?'

It was against Mowbray's nature to admit any kind of defeat, but in this case, he was up against too great a foe: his own mind. He agreed with Cuthbert to stand down, and after the hour was up, Baker took the lead in the interview, with the pathologist at his side.

'To what do I owe the honour, Dr Cuthbert? It's such a delight to see you again. If only the circumstances were a little more cordial.'

Baker leaned forward and explained. 'Chief Inspector Mowbray has been called away to attend to another case, sir, and I will be concluding the interview. Dr Cuthbert has been asked to join me to assist with recording your statement, given that there are likely to be numerous medical references.'

'Indeed, it does get a little "medical", as you so euphemistically put it, sergeant. Whatever the reason, it does afford me the opportunity to enjoy some more of Dr Cuthbert's company. And, of course, yours too, sergeant. Now where were we before we were interrupted by that less than delicious cheese sandwich? Oh yes, the marriage.'

Cuthbert, who had previously been viewing the interview from the next room, could now study Gossett face to face. Like the chief inspector, he was struck by the composure of the man. There was not a trace of anxiety in his voice or his expression.

'You have to be careful, don't you, doctor, when you're moving a decaying corpse? The skin does become quite fragile, and I was keen not to lose any of young Dawson. He was quite slight, so even with my leg I was able to position him lying on the floor beside Melville. The old man did become quite agitated when I did that. I think he might even have vomited a little. But when I rolled Dawson on top of him, that's when he really started to scream.

'It is a mercy that I have such a large garden. I mean, the noise would have been enough to wake the dead. But, of course, not in reality.

'Melville started writhing rather violently to shake Dawson off, which I thought was very impolite, so that's when I tightened the ropes just to make sure they were held fast. And, of course, I had to help Melville along a little, because he just wasn't kissing Dawson the way I had planned. I put my foot on the back of Dawson's head and pushed it into Melville's face. He stopped screaming then.

'Now, here's where I made my mistake. I should have put Dawson on his back, and Melville on top. That way the old Latin teacher might have enjoyed it all a little longer. It only took him a few hours before he choked on the maggots. I really must remember that for the next time.'

Everything Gossett was describing fitted exactly with Cuthbert's findings from the mortuary. It was clear to him that this was no fantasist. Rather, he was the most cold-blooded killer Cuthbert had encountered. There was much he wanted to say, but he had no role in this interview other than as the scribe, and he let Baker ask all the remaining questions.

Gossett related in meticulous detail how he had left the two, now dead, bodies roped together to allow them to enjoy each other and 'to melt into one another' as he put it. He had dug only a shallow grave on the Common, he said, partly because of the trouble anything deeper would have taken and partly because he wanted the bodies found sooner rather than later. Baker then asked his last question.

'Ah, sergeant, sergeant. As I told your charming chief

inspector – how is he, by the way? He was certainly looking a little peaky earlier. I do hope he has perked up. No, as I told Chief Inspector Mowbray, I'm more than happy to discuss the modus operandi with you, but as to my motives, they remain with me. Do you think we're done now?'

'Just one final thing, sir. Julius Gossett, I am arresting you for the abduction and murder of Alfred Dawson and for the abduction and murder of William Galton. You do not have to say anything unless you wish to do so, but what you say may be given in evidence.'

'There. That's nice and formal. But as I said, I don't know anything about any William Galton, and although I technically abducted Mr Melville, I didn't kill him. That was the boy. Otherwise, all very tidy.'

'Take him away, constable.'

Chapter 16

Edinburgh: 13 June 1918

A shaft of morning sunlight slanted through the upper windows of the circular hall and illuminated the podium on which the gowned academic stood.

'Mr Vice-Chancellor, in the name, and by the authority, of the Senatus Academicus I have the honour to present for the degrees of Bachelor of Medicine and Bachelor of Surgery with Honours, John Archibald Cuthbert.'

Cuthbert rose and walked across the stage of the graduation hall to be capped by the principal and to have his degrees conferred, and in that moment his life changed. As he walked back to his seat clutching his parchment, he couldn't help but think of Troy with whom he had started this journey seven years before.

Both of them should have been celebrating together that day, but now Dr Cuthbert would have to continue on alone. As he watched his fellow students one by one receive their degrees, including Mary Matheson and Millicent Pollok, whose brothers were still serving overseas, he took a moment to reflect on it all.

This bright summer's day was one of both endings and

beginnings, of forgiveness and expectation. The war would soon be entering its fifth year, and it had become the defining force shaping his generation.

Watching the pageantry of the graduation unfolding about him, Cuthbert saw that in some tangible way his status had just changed. He was now a qualified doctor who, along with his classmates, would serve as the next link in the chain of his profession. Many had gone before, and many would doubtless come after, but today theirs was the link that mattered. Their strength or otherwise would be all that could hold fast the profession they had now joined. That would be true at any time, but it was even more important in this time of war.

Many of the men would be leaving soon to join the Medical Corps and some, he knew, would never return. But even those who did come home would not do so unscathed by the experience. Everyone in his generation, whether their lives were short or long, would pay a heavy price for having been born at the wrong time.

*

The week after his graduation, the practicalities of re-enlisting in the Royal Army Medical Corps were eased for Cuthbert by a chance meeting with one of his final-year consultants. Cuthbert was leaving the library, after returning the last batch of his borrowed books, when Drayton hailed him from across the quad.

Dr Drayton was also a captain in the R.A.M.C. and was the Corps' points person at the university. He knew of Cuthbert's special circumstances and previous experience, and he had already been in touch with his superiors regarding what the next steps for the young man might be.

'Dr Cuthbert. A pleasure to see you, sir. I should congratulate you. It's no small feat winning honours in this faculty.

You must be very proud.'

'I owe any success to my teachers, sir.'

'Tosh! Nice of you to say, but tosh nonetheless. You worked very hard and deserve it all. So now the question of your future.'

'I am required to re-enlist, sir. That was one of the stipulations laid down when I was released from duties to come back to university.'

'Indeed, and the Corps will be lucky to have you. You will be receiving a letter soon if you haven't already. You should know I've taken the liberty of getting in touch with the brass just to oil the wheels a little, so if I were you, I'd have my bags packed.'

'Will it be the Western Front, sir? As you know I worked before at an A.D.S. in Ypres. I was wondering if I would be reposted there, or perhaps somewhere else. Maybe one of the Clearing Stations? They always seemed short of medical staff.'

'Can't help you there, Cuthbert. It's entirely up to the colonel, but I have put a word in.'

'Thank you, sir – for everything.'

*

The letter from the Corps with his commission was short and to the point. Lieutenant Cuthbert was to report the following Monday to commence training at the Queen Alexandra Military Hospital in Millbank, London. From there, he was to be posted to Colchester Military Hospital.

He was somewhat taken aback. He had fully expected that, by this time next week, he would be back on the boat to Boulogne and then on a troop train to somewhere close to the front. Now, it seemed, for the remainder of the war he would only be going as far as Essex. Either they thought that he had done his bit, or, more likely, they had come to realise that they could not afford to lose any more doctors than they already had.

He was relieved and in a small way disappointed at the same time. He had been steeling himself for a return to the front and all which that entailed. Now he was experiencing a sense of anticlimax and was feeling annoyed at himself because of it. Would he really rather be going back out there? He asked himself the question, and of course the answer was obvious.

His last days in Edinburgh gave him an opportunity to walk the length and breadth of the towns old and new. He reacquainted himself with many of his old haunts and felt he was visiting them perhaps to say farewell because he was uncertain what the future held for him. The R.A.M.C. and Colchester, of course, but after that, there was a blank.

The war could not last for ever, and there had to come a time when he would have to settle down to something. His interest in forensic medicine had not waned during his final year at university, and he was still warmed by the offer of a training position which he had received from Professor Littlejohn. Whether that would ever become a reality, and if it did, just how long it would be before he could contemplate taking it up, was what troubled him now.

In his wanderings, he found himself, as he often did, high over the city looking down on it. He had scaled the heights of Arthur's Seat once more and was, as ever, taken by the majesty of the city before him. It had not changed at all even though the world it occupied had, beyond all recognition.

Nothing was now the same as it was when he had last sat there with Troy on that hot summer afternoon when it had all begun. Now, wracked by a war of unimaginable scale and brutality, the world would take a long time to recover. And the longer the war dragged on, the more difficult and prolonged that recovery would be. In the midst of all of that, when might he be able to return to this beautiful city where so many of his fondest memories had been made?

He left Victoria Street for the last time on the Sunday evening to catch the overnight sleeper train to London. As he came downstairs for the first time in his new uniform, Mrs Green was waiting nervously in the hallway to send him on his way.

He had been required to purchase his uniform and kit from the military tailors, Kinloch Anderson. Their elegant premises in the New Town had seen many young officers before him, and their fine tailoring had ended up just as blood-soaked and mud-splattered across the Western Front and beyond as any army issue. They took his measurements with practised ease and knew exactly what he needed.

When he picked up his new uniform, he was surprised at just how comfortable it was, especially in comparison to his last. This was the first time as a soldier that he had been required to wear a shirt and tie. The jacket cuffs had his new rank insignia of two pips, and the collar bore the R.A.M.C. badges – the snake winding round a staff, encircled in laurel and surmounted by the royal crown. The same badge was on his cap. He tried on the new, knee-high brown leather boots and fitted his Sam Browne belt with its diagonal strap going over his right shoulder. He stood looking at himself in the wardrobe mirror in his room and felt as if he was a child dressing up.

'So this is it, Dr Cuthbert. You know, I can't get used to calling you that, but I've been so looking forward to it. Or should I be calling you Lieutenant Cuthbert? My, you look so fine with your pips.'

'You should call me Jack, Mrs Green. After all, haven't we been family all these years?'

'We've certainly been through it, haven't we? When I opened the door to you and lovely Mr Troy, when you first came to me, what, seven years ago, I never thought – none of us thought – what we were all in for. But look at you. A fully qualified doctor and an officer to boot. I'm so proud of you. You'll go away and forget all about me and your wee room up there at the top of the house. And that's as it should be. This part is over, and the next big adventure of your life is just starting.'

'I'll never forget you, Mrs Green. You helped me in ways that you can't even know. You held me together when I was falling apart.'

'Away with you now. You'll be starting me off, and you'll miss that blessed train.'

He bent to kiss her on the cheek. It was the tender kiss of a son, and she knew it was given with nothing short of love. He collected his bags and manoeuvred them through the door and out on to the street. He climbed the winding hill, and as he was about to head onto George IV Bridge, he turned back. Mrs Green was still standing under the glow of the gas streetlight, waving and dabbing her eyes, and whispering, 'Stay safe, Jack. Stay safe.'

*

At Waverley Station, Cuthbert walked along the platform to catch the night train. As he looked for the carriage with his berth, he passed a group of four privates in uniform standing ready to board the same train. When they saw Cuthbert, they straightened and, standing briskly to attention, saluted him. This was the first time he had been on the receiving end of such an acknowledgement. Without stopping he simply saluted back. He found the experience an odd one, but realised at once that this was something he was going to have to get used to very quickly.

Three weeks later, he had his first sight of the military

hospital in Colchester as he was driven in a taxi along its driveway. Red-brick and built twenty years or so before, it stood in leafy grounds filled with the kind of quiet that its patients needed for their recovery.

Cuthbert was placed in charge of the two receiving wards, to which were brought the newly repatriated wounded. His job was to assess and manage the men and, if possible, to move them on to the other wards for less intensive treatments.

The wards were large and bright, lit during the day by tall sash windows, and at night by gas mantles. The iron bedsteads were arranged in two facing rows down the length of the ward and above each was a luggage rack similar to those on trains. In the centre was a long, scrubbed, wooden table at the end of which sat the ward sister, keeping a watchful eye on her nurses, the orderlies and, most of all, the patients.

Cuthbert could also feel her eyes on him, and although she afforded him every courtesy, he could tell from the first moment of their meeting that she had little time for doctors, especially freshly minted ones like himself.

For the first time, Cuthbert saw the hospital blues that the wounded men were required to wear on the wards. These uniforms consisted of a bright blue, single-breasted jacket, which was worn open at the neck to reveal its white lining with a white shirt and a scarlet tie. The matching blue trousers had white turn-ups and, to complete the rigout, the men wore their own khaki service caps.

Cuthbert could not help feeling that these outfits made the men look somewhat childlike, and he noted with interest that the few wounded officers they had in the side rooms were not required to don such colourful costumes.

The work was tedious and consisted as much of paperwork as it did any kind of clinical duty. Nevertheless, he threw himself into it and worked the long hours needed to familiarise himself with the existing group of patients and the protocols and practices of the hospital.

He soon found his new rank cumbersome. It created a barrier between him and the N.C.O.s whom he had to deal with as patients. A large part of his job, he knew, was to build a trust between himself and the men, many of whom had such serious injuries that they were likely to require long-term treatment and rehabilitation.

However, forging that trust was made all the more difficult by the natural sense of otherness which existed between officers and men. Before, when he had been a lowly lance corporal at the dressings station, he had been able to speak with the men on equal terms, and they would tell him the truth about how they were feeling, whether they were in pain and what problems they had. Now, as a lieutenant, he would receive stock answers delivered by rigid men. These were men who were not necessarily intimidated by him, but nor were they minded to see him as being on their side.

Three days into his new posting, Cuthbert was in the side room early, preparing for his morning ward round, when the relative peace in the ward outside was suddenly shattered.

'Get your fucking hands off me!'

The commotion was coming from the end of the ward where one of the newly arrived patients was shouting at the orderly who was trying to wash him. The basin of water had been thrown to the floor with a loud clatter, and the orderly was busy mopping it up with the flannels he had brought.

'Get him away from me! Bloody slacker! He's a disgrace to the uniform. No gun and no balls. Get him away!'

Cuthbert strode down the centre of the ward and towered over the bed-end of the sergeant who had been shouting. The soldier had lost one leg below the knee and the other at mid-thigh, and his right arm was also heavily bandaged.

'I will not have language like that in my ward, sergeant.'

'Then, sir, get that bloody pansy away from me.'

Cuthbert looked at the orderly who was in his mid-twenties, short and slightly built. He was a corporal and was wearing a white apron over his orderly uniform. He was unaffected by the name-calling and had stopped mopping to stand to attention in front of Cuthbert.

'What's your name, corporal?'

'Griffin, sir,' said the orderly in a distinct West Country accent.

'Leave that, Griffin, and check on the patients in ward two. I need to have a word with the sergeant here.'

Corporal Griffin turned and left immediately, and Cuthbert came to the side of the sergeant's bed. The wounded man lay with his eyes closed and was breathing heavily.

'What on earth was that all about, soldier? You know very well that the orderly is only here to help you. Right now, you're unable to wash and shave yourself, and his job is to get you sorted out in the morning.'

'I don't want one of them helping me, sir.'

'One of whom?'

'They don't fight. They've had it cushy back here, while we were out there in the trenches getting it in the neck every night. And they're thieves too. Bloody R.A.M.C. – 'Rob All My Comrades' more like.'

'I'm in the R.A.M.C., sergeant. Have I earned your disapproval too?'

'Not the medics, sir. You need to be here. They don't. They're just doing women's work and they're doing it to keep themselves safe and dry back here. They're not men, they aren't even the arses of men. Sir.'

'While you're in my ward, I want no more of that language, sergeant, and that's an order. I suggest you concentrate more of your energies on trying to get well and less on abusing my staff.'

Back in the duty room, Corporal Griffin came in while Cuthbert was seated at the desk going over the case notes of those patients newly transferred to the wards.

'Nice cup of tea, sir?'

Cuthbert looked up from his files to see the orderly holding the kettle. He was smiling brightly, and the genuine warmth in his voice was cheering.

'Griffin. Why, yes, thank you. Oh, and about that nonsense earlier, I think we need to put the sergeant's poor manners down to his injuries. He seems to have had quite a time of it in France.'

'Oh, don't worry about that, sir. Happens all the time and I'm well used to it by now.'

'But you shouldn't be spoken to like that. It was disgraceful.'

'Thank you, sir, but there's others who don't think like you. We're just seen as slackers, cowards or, like he said, "no guns and no balls". Begging your pardon, sir.'

'No, it's not acceptable, and I won't have it on my watch. The R.A.M.C. rankers are part of the team. The whole machine doesn't work without you.'

The orderly prepared the tea and served Cuthbert his in a china cup, while he used mugs for himself and the other orderlies.

'How long have you been in the R.A.M.C., corporal?

'Right from the start, sir. They were the ones that would take me. It's not so much that I'm short, it's just that I like to think of everyone else as tall, you see. Didn't know what I was signing up for, to tell the truth.

'After I'd joined the Medical Corps, the sergeant shook my hand and said, "You can be proud, lad. You've joined the finest Corps in the British Army." I had no idea what I'd be doing and found out the hard way. When we were getting our kit, I remember asking, "When do I get my gun?" And they just said, "You can't fire a gun, son. Not when you're carrying a stretcher."

'That's where I started, sir, as a stretcher bearer in the trenches. At the Somme mostly, and it was bloody murder, especially that first year. None of us knew what to expect, you see. In the midst of it all, when the shells were exploding all around us, the call would go up, "Stretcher bearer! Stretcher bearer!" and we had to go running even when everyone else was keeping their heads down. I lost more than a few that way. And after I copped one myself, I ended up back here in Colchester.

'But seems to me that it's the best job I could have done these last few years. Don't think a woman could have done some of the things I've had to do for the lads or could have listened to some of the things they've told me, especially when they were dying. No woman should have to hear that. No, sir, I don't think I've done less of a job than some of those that had a rifle in their hands. Anyway, can I get you some more tea, sir?'

Cuthbert was impressed by the soldier's sense of self-worth, especially in the face of such obvious bigotry. The young man's masculinity was being called into question almost on a daily basis, but he had found the inner strength to see past the taunts and insults and cruel mockery to forge an identity – that of a man doing a job and doing it well.

As an officer and a doctor, Cuthbert faced none of these challenges, yet he found himself thinking back to that winter morning at the infirmary when Millicent Pollok had pinned the white feather to his locker door. She had been doing exactly the same, calling into question whether he was a man or not.

Cuthbert's stature had protected him from many of the taunts he might have received as an R.A.M.C. dresser when he was in Belgium, but he still had much to prove to himself with respect to his own masculinity. In that, he was far from complete and a very long way from the place that Corporal Griffin had managed to reach.

*

Each day brought new admissions and further evidence of the continuing brutality of the Western Front. In addition to the physical injuries the wounded brought home with them, there were also the psychological scars, and Cuthbert started to see signs of himself and his own feelings in many of the men.

He would spend many evenings sitting at the bedsides of some of the most severely injured, encouraging them to talk and to tell their stories. This was often the very best he could do. Even if he could offer these men nothing else, he could give them his time and his presence, and he could listen. What he heard did not shock him; it merely reinforced for him, night after night, soldier after soldier, the tremendous futility of the war.

These young men, he knew, would never fully recover from their injuries and he even found himself wondering, in some cases, if perhaps it might not have been better if they had died quickly at the front. But he tried to stop himself having such thoughts, for he also knew that with any life there was hope, and it was his role as a doctor to preserve both.

*

With the autumn came increasingly encouraging news reports from the front. There was talk everywhere that it might all be over by Christmas. But, of course, there were also those who simply said that they had been told that once before.

On a very foggy morning in November, word finally came through that the war had ended. No one who heard it believed it at first, and one of the corporals put it down to just another bit of 'cookhouse gossip'. It was only when it was said repeatedly by everyone arriving at the hospital that it started to sink in. Then the bells started to peel in the churches nearby, and in the hospital, they could hear the hooters sounding from the factories on the other side of town.

Corporal Griffin had taken the initiative to break out the brandy from the medicine store and was busy pouring a trayful of glasses for everyone. Doubtless without any sanction from the ward sister, one of the junior nurses had started tying together bandages and pillowcases to make some impromptu bunting. There was even music playing from an old phonograph in the side room.

Cuthbert wandered along the corridor between his wards and was aware of much more activity around him than usual. People had started running, there was laughter and a growing sense of almost unfettered excitement. One nurse from another ward rushed up to him, stood on her tiptoes and kissed him on the lips before laughing wildly and running off.

He found a quieter corner in the file room adjacent to one of his wards and sat there with the door closed for a moment. Outside he could hear the mounting euphoria, but in there all he could do was think about everyone he had seen die. He looked out the window of the small room and could barely see across the lawn in front of the hospital because of the fog. Nothing was clear, and beyond the edge of his vision was another no-man's-land.

The door opened, and Corporal Griffin thrust a glass of brandy into Cuthbert's hand and then took him by the arm to lead him onto the ward. There, the wounded men, some lying immobilised on beds, others sitting in their uniforms and a few standing to attention as he walked by, were all feeling much as he did. There was no cheering on the ward, no singing, no jubilation, just quiet reflection on what it had all been for.

The end of hostilities did not mean the end of new admissions to the hospital. There were thousands of casualties still being passed along the chain of evacuation from the front, and it would take weeks before the number of new cases arriving in Colchester would slow to a trickle. Cuthbert worked on, and for him and the staff, nothing had changed in any material way, although there was now much more talk of the future because people were starting to believe that there would indeed be one.

It took five more months before Cuthbert received word of his demobilisation. The process of disbanding an army of millions was never going to happen quickly or even smoothly, and Cuthbert had been realistic in his expectations. His role would be needed for some time, and he used it as an excuse not to think about what he was going to do next. When his orders finally came through, he knew it was time for him to face his own future.

In his rooms during his off-duty, he spent long hours contemplating what he wanted from his life. While he did this, he also chastised himself for such self-indulgence. He remembered all those young men whose futures had been robbed and who did not have the luxury of such thoughts.

Everything he could think of had become coloured by the war and his experiences. It hung about him like a darkness, obscuring any future he could imagine. He realised, with some alarm, that he had lost sight of hope, and if he was to carry on, he needed to find it again.

He sent off a letter to Littlejohn, although he was by now unsure if going back to Edinburgh was such a good idea. But it was the only option he could find any enthusiasm for. The R.A.M.C. had proposed that he remain at Colchester as part of the regular army, but he was certain that his military days needed to end.

A few days after he had posted the letter, he received a reply that was to shape the rest of his life.

Harvey Littlejohn, F.R.C.S.,
F.R.S.E. Dean, Faculty of Medicine,
University of Edinburgh

6th April 1919

My Dear Cuthbert,

It was with the greatest pleasure that I received your letter. That you have been working in Colchester Military Hospital this last year will, I do not doubt, have honed many of your clinical skills. Such experience will be invaluable in your future: a future which I earnestly hope will include your return to this University, to the study of forensic medicine and to my department.

A position of assistant is immediately available, which would allow you to develop your own research and ultimately to submit your doctoral thesis. This post will remain open until I receive your confirmation or otherwise in relation to it.

It only remains for me to say that your undergraduate and military careers have shown you to be of the finest of men, and I would consider it a special privilege to work with you, should you so choose.

Yours in haste.

Littlejohn

Chapter 17

London: 9 May 1929

In spite of Gossett's confession, there were still so many pieces of this puzzle that had not fallen into place. In the quiet of his office, Cuthbert was going through his notes on the case and was re-reading the pathology reports typed up by his assistant. He started to make the kind of list in his notebook that he knew Professor Littlejohn would have frowned upon.

'All right, professor, I know you don't like what I'm doing, but the chief inspector and his team need my help and it might not be such a sin to put my cobbling aside for one day.'

He wrote down his unanswered questions. First, he still did not know what Gossett's motive was. It was such an elaborate, carefully planned act, that it had to have been for a purpose. And why Dawson, why Galton?

There was apparently no connection between the two victims, just as Cuthbert had always suspected. However, he had also postulated a close connection between each of them and the killer, but nothing so far had been found to link them. Could Gossett really just have selected them at random, as convenient bodies with which to play out his twisted fantasy?

In Cuthbert's opinion, Gossett was probably a psychopath, but in his experience such individuals still had motives. And there was something about Gossett that he thought was still unexplained. Having observed him so closely during the interviews, he could see the man was at times patently mad, yet at others he appeared to be as sane as anyone.

Checking his notes and thinking more about the case, he also realised there was still no explanation for Galton's sudden departure from the school nor for his change of identity. And on top of that, Gossett was still claiming not to recognise his second victim by any name other than Melville. What on earth was going on? Cuthbert's list was beginning to appear rather daunting, but he was sure that if only one more piece of the jigsaw could be fitted into place, all the remaining questions might begin to answer themselves.

For a second time he went back over his own notes of all the case conferences at Scotland Yard, and he spotted one of his boxes of key points linked to Galton's name. Underlined three times on the page was the word 'Letters', and Cuthbert recalled the statement given by Mrs Galton regarding the troubling letters her husband had received. He picked up the phone and called Sergeant Baker at the Yard.

'No, sir, you may recall we found no letters at Melville's digs, and nothing came out of the search of his study at the big house. Maybe he destroyed them. After all, his wife did say he was upset by them. It would have been the easiest thing in the world just to throw them on the fire, especially if they contained anything incriminating.'

'Is there anywhere we haven't looked for them, sergeant? I ask because I still think they're important. They must be linked to the reason he left the school and went into hiding. If we find that out, we might be a step closer to working out what's behind all this. Gossett had his reason for doing what he did.

Of that, I'm absolutely sure. But I'm also sure he's never going to tell us unless he thinks we already know.'

'The only other possible place, sir, would be the school, but he left there eighteen months ago. I do remember the headmaster saying Galton had gone off in a hurry and there were some books and papers that he left behind. I suspect it's all been dumped by now, Dr Cuthbert, but do you think it's worth checking?'

'I do, sergeant. So much so, I'd like to come along, if I may? Two pairs of eyes might make it an easier job.'

Cuthbert was keen to be involved but he was not at all sure his input would be welcome, so he added, 'And perhaps the chief inspector doesn't need to know.'

'Of course, sir, nod's as good as a wink. I'll arrange it for this afternoon.'

*

The things Galton had left behind at St Peter's had not been thrown out as Baker feared but had instead been stored in a trunk in one of the disused rooms in the old part of the building. The janitor led Baker and Cuthbert along a rather damp passageway which joined the two wings and then unlocked the door of the storeroom. He pointed to a large wooden chest by the window.

'It's this one here, gentlemen. I'm not sure you'll find anything of value though. Mr Galton was never one for much in the way of finery. Just old papers and a few of his own books, if I remember. Take as long as you like. I'll leave the key in the door. Just lock up when you're finished and bring it back to the office. Happy hunting!'

The trunk was half-filled with papers including old exam scripts, essays from former pupils and a variety of the Latin master's personal correspondence. Cuthbert and Baker divided the piles up between them and started to read.

'What are we looking for, sir?'

'I'm not sure, sergeant, but it's likely to be a letter, or series of letters, that look a bit different from the rest. They must have contained something that frightened him enough to make him run away first from his job and then from his identity. Maybe a threat on his life?'

'Well, so far it's pretty standard stuff. Mostly from parents and regarding their sons at the school – admissions, exams and the like. Nothing that looks like a death threat.'

'Keep looking, sergeant.'

The men worked through the papers, scanning every page for a clue as to Galton's sudden disappearance but found nothing. Cuthbert had been so sure that the answer might have been here. He started to put the piles he had been reading back in the trunk when he saw that there were some Latin textbooks at the bottom. He picked them out and he could see immediately that there was a folded sheet of paper between the pages of the one on top.

'What was it you said to me once, sergeant, about people using the strangest of things as bookmarks?'

Cuthbert extracted the paper, and, sure enough, it was a handwritten page, probably the last sheet from a letter. Although incomplete, he could still read its contents.

> . . . *with some haste. I do not expect to have to tell you this again, Galton. My patience is wearing thin, and you know what will happen if you do not carry out my instructions to the letter. The time for waiting is at an end.*
>
> *Your old friend,*
>
> *Latet anguis in herba*

'Here it is, sergeant, or at least part of it.'
'What's that at the end, sir? Is that a name?'

'It's Latin, sergeant, and roughly means, "A snake hiding in the grass". And, if I'm not mistaken, it's from Virgil. Check the other books – there might be more.'

Baker found two other pages, folded in the same way, but it was unclear whether or not they were from the same letter. One page referred to Galton's position at the school and how it would no longer be possible for him to continue unless he wished his wife to learn the facts.

The other page referred to a 'Marcus' and stated that Galton had been responsible: 'And I'm sure you now believe me when I say I will never leave you alone until you pay with everything you hold dear. I will take your life, Galton, as payment for his.' It concluded as before, 'Your old friend, *Latet anguis in herba*.'

'That sounds like a death threat, sir, and no mistake. Who do you think this Marcus is?'

'I don't know. There was no one of that name who came up in any of the interviews. It's not much to go on.'

'If it's a pupil from the school, perhaps we could find him in their records. It's not that common a name, and he must have had Galton as his teacher at some point. That might narrow it down further.'

'Worth a try, sergeant. Let's see if we can find him.'

Cuthbert estimated that if Marcus was one of Galton's pupils, he must have been at the school sometime in the last thirty-four years. That still gave them over fifteen volumes of school rolls to work through. Unfortunately, there was no easy way of searching for only those who had been in Galton's class.

They started with the most recent intakes, figuring that the letters might be referring to a relatively recent event. But there was no Marcus at all in 1927 or 1926 and only one in 1925. He was a boy called Marcus Wilson, and Baker noted his details for follow-up. The years 1924 through to 1919 also drew a blank, but there were two boys with the name in 1918. These were Marcus Brown-Ackland and Marcus Smythe. When they reached 1915, that was when Cuthbert pointed at the page in the volume he was checking, and Baker smiled as he read, 'Marcus Gossett.'

*

On the way back to the Yard, Cuthbert again persuaded Baker to say it was he who had found the connection.

'You must understand, sergeant. It will keep things simple. The less said about my involvement, the better. You know how the chief inspector prefers things done by the book. Well, what I've done is not really in his book at all.'

'It doesn't sit well with me, sir. You did the hard work, and you should get the credit.'

'Nonsense. If I recall, it was you who suggested we go to the school to search Galton's things. It was you who thought Marcus might be a pupil and that we might find him in the school rolls. And it was only by chance that he happened to be in the volume which *I* was reading. No, sergeant, don't belittle your contribution this time. We don't have all the answers yet, but, thanks to you, it's starting to look a little clearer.'

At the Yard, Mowbray stood before the duty-room pin-board. He moved the photograph of Julius Gossett from the gallery of persons of interest to the centre spot. He added a new red string linking that photograph to William Galton with a note 'via Marcus Gossett?' And another from Gossett to Dawson with a note 'via university'. He had the connections between the killer and his victims now, but what he still didn't understand was why.

There was no Marcus Gossett in the police files, and if he was connected to the man in their cells, they still did not know how. Based on when he enrolled at St Peter's he would be around 26 or 27 years old, so he was too old to be Gossett's son. Perhaps a brother or a cousin, but when Gossett had been asked about him, he refused to say anything, neither confirming nor denying that he'd ever even heard of him.

Mowbray was beginning to become exasperated. He needed to bring charges against Gossett, but he was anxious to extract the whole story before he was taken out of their hands. He decided to try his old methods, and before he left the board, he took a pin and put it through the face in Gossett's picture.

The duty constable was surprised to see the chief inspector in the basement and was even more so when he asked him to wait outside Gossett's cell while he spoke to the prisoner alone. The young officer knew it was highly irregular and that he was expected always to be with the prisoner, but he could hardly refuse the Pie.

When he heard the thud, he went to look through the spyhole in the door, but all he could see was the back of the chief inspector's jacket. There was another dull thud followed by a loud slap and what sounded like a sack of potatoes being dropped. The cell door opened, and the chief inspector came out, smoothing his hair back.

'I think you'd better check on Gossett, lad. It looks as if he's had a nasty fall.'

The constable found Gossett doubled up in a heap in the corner of the cell, with blood streaming from a cut on his cheek and his left eye already starting to close from the swelling.

Despite Mowbray's attempts to loosen Gossett's tongue, he had resolutely refused to say any more about his involvement in the case. The chief inspector called on Cuthbert again to ask his advice in case he had any medical insight that might prove useful.

'How can I crack him, Cuthbert? I need to get him to talk.'

'You've tried the stick, as I understand it, chief inspector.

Why not try the carrot now? Why not offer him something he wants?'

'But what have I got that he could possibly want? I'm sure he'd like to be let go, but I'm afraid that's not on the table.'

'He's a conceited intellectual. He wants to be admired for how clever, how erudite, he is, so play to that. Flatter him – what have you got to lose?'

Mowbray grudgingly agreed on this new tactic and undertook to arrange a fresh interview with Gossett. When the chief inspector entered the room, he saw the results of his handiwork under the stark electric light. Gossett's face was puffy and red. His left eye was completely closed and blackening, and the cut on his cheek had now been stitched closed. However, he was still smiling, and he greeted the chief inspector warmly.

Mowbray acted as if their last meeting had never taken place and returned Gossett's smile. 'It's good to see you again, doctor. I was only saying to my sergeant, just now, that we don't get enough of your class in here. As you can imagine, we have to deal on a daily basis with the rougher, baser end of the social spectrum. Scum, not to put too fine a point on it.

'It's such a pleasant change to have someone here we can actually have an intelligent conversation with. I'm only sorry we won't have the pleasure of your company for much longer. You'll be missed, sir. Before you go though, do tell me: why did you kill them? Was it just for fun? Surely not just that? A man of your qualities and education, a man with a mind as agile as yours – I can't believe it could have been just for that.'

'Chief inspector, I do know what you're doing. Brutality didn't work, so let's try flattery – some honey instead of the vinegar to catch the flies. I'm so tired of your constant badgering, and we need to get this over with. So, all right, I'm willing to share my little secrets . . . but not with you. I'll only speak to the good doctor, alone. Take it or leave it, as they say.'

Mowbray left the interview room and paced the corridor outside. He ordered one of the constables to fetch Cuthbert right away. While he was waiting for him to arrive, he considered the next move. Within the hour, Cuthbert was striding along the corridor outside the interview rooms, eager to know what had happened.

'Ah, Cuthbert, thanks for coming. He says you're the only one he'll speak to about his motives. I think you should do it.'

'But, chief inspector, surely that's highly irregular? It's one thing to take notes of a medical nature during the interview of a murder suspect, but quite another for me to lead the interrogation.'

'I'll be right on the other side of that glass. You won't need to do much leading. I think he's ready to tell us everything – and I need that motive. I can't have him going to trial looking as if he's away with the fairies. I've seen that happen before. And then all we'll get is a diagnosis of criminally insane and he'll spend the rest of his days living it up on the Isle of Wight. No, sir, I want his neck stretched, and the only way I'm going to get that is if I get the whole premeditated nightmare. Will you do it, Cuthbert?'

The pathologist nodded, seeing no other way of keeping the chief inspector from going in and hanging Gossett with his own hands. This time Baker would be taking notes from the observation room, and when Gossett realised that he would be alone with Cuthbert, he brightened considerably. 'The things we have to do, doctor, just to get a little peace.'

Cuthbert was appalled at Gossett's appearance, but the man himself was almost oblivious to it all, just acknowledging what had happened with the merest of sighs and saying, 'I'm not sure your chief inspector really likes me, Dr Cuthbert. I hope you're not going to hit me, as well. But, no, I don't think that's quite your style.'

'Dr Gossett, why did you kill Freddie Dawson and Henry Melville?'

'Oh, let's stop calling him by that silly name, shall we? Galton was a monster, and he couldn't hide behind any other name then and he certainly can't hide now.'

For the first time, there was anger in his eyes, but Gossett quickly pulled himself back. 'But where are my manners? You asked me a question, and I didn't answer you. It was the oldest reason in the world, doctor: I wanted revenge. And they might tell you differently, but, trust me, it is true. It is sweet. Very sweet.'

'So you did meet and abduct William Galton?'

'No, I was telling the truth when I said I had never met Galton. I knew of him for some time, of course, but the man I finally met was calling himself Melville. I knew he was Galton, but it seemed impolite to bring it up.'

'Were you blackmailing Galton?'

'Oh, you do use such ugly words, Dr Cuthbert. I expect it's an occupational weakness. I was in communication, shall we say, with Mr Galton over a period of some weeks, during which I acquainted him with my plans for his death. I was also very keen that he should resign from his post at the school. I really felt that career had run its course and it was time for him to enjoy a well-earned, if brief, retirement.'

'How did you manage that? How did you force him to leave the school?'

'That was easy. I just told him if he didn't do what I asked, I would be telling his darling wife, who I think we might also refer to as his meal ticket, a thing or two about her husband's past. And, of course, there would be the press coverage of it all, which I promised to ensure. So he went rather sharply but then decided to do a bunk, as they say. He wasn't difficult to track down, and when I found out he was still using our library with his old card, well, I mean, it was too easy. Of course, he'd never met me, so when I got talking to him in the library, he didn't know I was his snake.'

'*Latet anguis in herba.*'

'Yes, Dr Cuthbert. Did you like that touch? I thought you might. He really was a pathetic soul when I met him. He was frightened of his own shadow. I think he thought his correspondent would be waiting for him behind the book stacks, ready to strike. Little did he know he was teaching his snake in the grass some Latin poetry.'

'Tell me about Marcus.'

'Ah, Dr Cuthbert, you found him. Good for you. Such a sweet boy, but he always had trouble with his irregular verbs. His Latin, you know. Made a terrible hash of his translations. I helped whenever I could, but there was the time I was away in France, and after I got back, I was still out of action for longer than I expected. It was around that time that the worst of it happened.

'Galton was his master at St Peter's. Our mother had sent Marcus there rather than to Harlowe; I think because she'd had words with my old house master and had fallen out with him. It would have been so much better if he had been able to join me at my school.

'He used to talk about the Latin master in his letters home and about how beastly it all was, but no one took any real notice. That's what all boys at boarding school say. No, they only realised something was wrong when he was getting washed one day during the long vacation and one of the maids saw his back. Between the stripes from the canings, he was pockmarked with burns, many of them old but a lot of them still healing and some infected.

'Mother only decided at that point not to send him back, but she somehow seemed to blame Marcus for it all. He became so withdrawn, and when I saw him again while I was recuperating, he was a changed boy. I quizzed him, of course, but he wouldn't talk to me either.

'I knew it was the school, and I thought something should be done, but with one thing and another it got rather forgotten. But then things changed. On his seventeenth birthday, Marcus went swimming in the lake at home. They recorded it as an accident, but there were those who said it was suicide. I knew it was something in between. It wasn't until a few years later that I found his diaries and discovered just how bad it had been for him.

'He described everything, every detail. And, of course, there was much more than the scars which Galton had left behind. That teacher systematically tortured and terrorised my little brother for a year. And all because of irregular verbs. I couldn't have that, now, could I? Our family had let poor Marcus down so badly. I needed to act.'

'So it was then that you decided to murder Galton?'

'No. At first, I thought just to terrorise him a little and see how it worked out. I thought he deserved a taste of his own medicine. It was only once I met the man in the flesh that I resolved to finish it.'

'Why such an elaborate affair? Wouldn't it have been easier simply to strangle him? Stab him, even?'

'He made Marcus suffer, so I wanted him to suffer too. That's not unreasonable, is it? An eye for an eye, a tooth for a tooth. The *lex talionis* is one of the oldest precepts of justice there is, Dr Cuthbert. And I wanted something appropriate for him. He had tortured Marcus and God alone knows how many others because of their Latin, so it seemed only right that he himself should die because of his Latin. He saw himself very much as a scholar of Virgil, especially the *Aeneid*. So it didn't take long to decide how it should be done.'

'And Dawson?'

'Dr Cuthbert, haven't you worked it out yet? Freddie Dawson was nothing; he was just the murder weapon.'

Once again Cuthbert saw the complete lack of remorse in Gossett's eyes. He had been willing, almost eager, to share the details of it all, and was clearly proud of himself. Cuthbert still wondered, however, if Gossett had any insight whatsoever into the crimes he had committed, and he needed to know the answer.

'Do you understand how wrong your actions have been, Dr Gossett?'

He stared back at Cuthbert with a bewildered expression. It was as if he had been asked a question in a foreign language. 'It was justice.'

'And what about Freddie Dawson? Where was the justice for him?'

'I needed him.'

Cuthbert could see in Gossett's bruised and cut face the expression of one who could never understand the full consequences of his actions. He was consumed by his need for revenge after the suicide of his brother, a death which he laid squarely at the door of Galton. But Cuthbert still wondered about the macabre manner of it all.

The desire for some form of justice in such a case was almost understandable, but to re-enact a horror from the distant past and to use a completely innocent boy to carry it out was beyond comprehension. This was pure evil, and Cuthbert knew that Gossett had not only committed the murders but enjoyed them.

They had everything now, or as much of an explanation as would ever be forthcoming from the kind of man they were dealing with. To close the interview, he asked Gossett if there was anything else he wanted to say. He looked back across the table at Cuthbert and said, 'Will we have a chance to chat again? I do hope so.'

The pathologist gathered his notes and called for the constable, leaving the question hanging in the air.

Chapter 18

London: 9 December 1929

The nine-inch, black silk square was placed over the judge's full wig, and he put on the black gloves handed to him by the court attendant. Safeguarded behind this cloak of judicial officialdom, he was no longer a person but an instrument of the state.

'Julius Anthony Gossett, you will be taken hence to a lawful prison and from there to a place of execution where you will be hanged by the neck until you are dead and thereafter your body buried within the precincts of the prison. And may the Lord have mercy upon your soul.'

As was always the case, the courtroom was silent before and after the sentence of death had been pronounced. The enormity of the moment was underlined by the ceremony of it all, but as Gossett stood in the dock to hear his fate, he was unmoved. He stifled a yawn.

The judge had felt strongly about the accused throughout the trial, but only now could he allow his distaste for the man to find its way into his expression. He would have liked to have added to his pronouncement, 'But I personally hope you rot in damnation for eternity,' and his eyes said as much as he stared at the condemned man smiling in the dock.

Mowbray, who was in the court to hear the verdict, was smiling too. This was a successful outcome and would be noted by his superiors. Every detail of the trial over the last three weeks had been followed by Fleet Street. The week before, the *Daily Mirror* had even published a court artist's likeness of Mowbray giving evidence. That sketch was now hanging proudly on the chief inspector's office wall.

The same artist, who had been sitting in the well of the court during the sentencing, was now outside. She was busily sketching from memory the last expressions of 'the smiling killer', as Gossett had been dubbed by the papers, before he was taken down.

Despite the cold, there was a throng of people waiting outside the Old Bailey to hear the verdict. Just after the judge had pronounced the sentence, one of the reporters covering the story rushed from the court to make his way to file his report for the early edition. As he was leaving the building, a woman grabbed him by the arm and asked what was happening. The reporter just took his hand and hoisted his neck by an imaginary noose and a great cheer broke out in the street.

*

'When will it happen?'

Cuthbert was in the chief inspector's office, and although he dealt in murder on an almost daily basis, he still found the thought of execution to be chilling. Mowbray took two glasses from his filing cabinet drawer and a bottle of single malt. He showed the glasses to Cuthbert, who nodded his appreciation and took the proffered whisky.

'I thought it might be too early for you, doctor.'

'Normally it would be, but this is far from a normal day.'

'In answer to your question, Gossett has waived his right of appeal. It's as if the bastard wants to hang. So, he'll get his wish within the week. They're not messing about at Wandsworth these days. Why keep feeding and watering them any longer than they need to?'

Cuthbert looked at the half-inch of whisky in his glass and took a slow sip, savouring its heat as it hit the back of his throat. Despite the reputation of his countrymen, Cuthbert drank very little and was never quite sure whether he liked the taste of his national drink or loathed it. But it always made him pensive and just a little dour.

'Do you agree with hanging, chief inspector? Isn't it just killing by another name?'

'What's to agree or disagree with? I *do* think hanging is too good and too quick for that evil monster. If I had my way, the punishment would fit the crime a little better. Might be a much better deterrent.'

'An eye for an eye? That's what Gossett said, wasn't it? But it just becomes a cycle of endless violence. Might not there be a better way to deal with it? After all, you interrogated him, you watched him in the courtroom – he was sick in the mind. Should we really be hanging madmen, no matter what they've done?'

'Yes, we should. It gets rid of them. He might have been mad, but he was also evil. And if you think we shouldn't, perhaps you'd like to tell that to Freddie Dawson's parents, to Galton's family? No, I didn't think so. Drink up, you look as if you're going to need another to get your head straight on this one.'

Cuthbert put his hand over the glass and shook his head.

'Thank you, but, no, chief inspector. I've still got work to do.'

'And I suspect you will – indeed, we all will – for a while to come. Have you been following in the papers everything that's happening in America? The world's going to hell. They say this financial crash will hit us just as hard here. We're already skint as a country, what with that bloody war – this looks like all we need. They're talking poverty and unemployment the likes of which we haven't seen in years. And that means more work for us. Make men poor and hungry, take away their jobs and what do you get? Crime, and lots of it. And that'll mean more customers for you and your mortuary.'

*

When Cuthbert arrived back at the pathology department at St Thomas's, Morgenthal was busy preparing sections of tissue for examination under the microscope. He thought his mentor would have been happy with the outcome of the trial, but Cuthbert was looking far from jubilant.

Word of the verdict had spread around the hospital, and Morgenthal had learned of it in the canteen. Someone in the queue for sandwiches had recognised him as one of the pathology team and had shouted along the line that he should be pleased. He had said that Gossett was going to hang for what he had done to 'that poor lad that has been on your slab'. Morgenthal had said nothing, for he no longer ever even acknowledged any reference to the victims or the cases he dealt with in the mortuary. But, inside, he felt a sense of quiet achievement. He had played a small, but he hoped a significant, part in it all, even though he knew he had almost ruined it for Dr Cuthbert.

Now, he thought he should say something to his mentor, but he was unsure if congratulations were the right thing. Should indeed there be any kind of celebration about an execution? Before he had a chance to think any more about it, Cuthbert spoke to him.

'Have you spoken with Sarah yet?'

'I have.'

'And?'

'And I'm sure everything will work itself out. She's rather upset about it all and so is her family. But it's given us a chance to clear the air a little. That's never a bad thing, is it?'

Cuthbert could tell from Morgenthal's demeanour that all was far from well between them but thought better of probing any further. He had watched his assistant mature in recent months. Could it be that he had possibly outgrown the girl? It was not, however, a question he was about to ask. As such, he merely looked over at his assistant at the bench and gave a weary smile before going into his office and closing the door.

*

The following day, Cuthbert received a phone call from the chief inspector.

'I know you thought you were done with this, but something rather unusual has just come in. Gossett has requested to speak with you before the execution. You're under no obligation whatsoever to see him, and, like as not, he's just chancing his arm to stay in the spotlight a little longer. That's what these buggers do. But he says he has something important to say, and he'll only say it to you.'

Cuthbert was somewhat startled by the request. And it was true: he had already moved on. New corpses were already lying on his slabs awaiting forensic examination, but his interest was piqued.

'What do you think he wants, chief inspector?'

'Beats me, but as I said, he's probably just trying to feel he's still in control. It's up to you, Cuthbert. What do you want to do?'

'Tell him I'll see him this afternoon.'

*

Gossett was being held in E wing of H.M.P. Wandsworth. Cuthbert had never had call to visit the prison before, and it was a grim experience. Everything about the place reeked of stale urine and cheap disinfectant. The glazed white tiles were chipped, the floors were scuffed and the room where he was to meet with Gossett was small and airless.

Only once Cuthbert was seated on one side of a wide table, was Gossett led in. He was wearing his own clothes, as condemned criminals were permitted to do, but he was handcuffed and escorted by two burly gaolers. He did not sit down as much as he was put in the seat, and his handcuffs were opened and then relocked around a bar under the table that Cuthbert had not noticed. The table was itself bolted firmly to the floor. One gaoler left, while the other positioned himself against the wall near the door and made it clear from his stance that he would not be leaving the room.

'Alone at last, Dr Cuthbert ... well, as alone as can be expected under the circumstances, I suppose. Tell me, how have you been?'

'I am perfectly well, Gossett. Shall we get to it? What did you want to say that was so urgent?'

'Only urgent in the sense that we won't have another opportunity to have a chat, you and I. It's tomorrow, you see. That's when I go below to the shadows, to enter the silent house of sleep, if you will.'

'Still quoting your beloved Virgil, I see.'

'Well, that's one of the reasons I wanted to see you, Dr Cuthbert. You see, no one else understands me here. "Philistines" – that's the word we must whisper. But you share my love of the ancient world and everything they held dear, don't you? Their language, their stories, their glorious poetry.'

'Indeed. But you haven't answered my question. What did you want to say to me?'

'Well, just that. I wanted to tell you that you were the only one who understood. I was so anxious not to leave without saying how much that meant to me. To thank you, really.'

'I think you should perhaps be spending what little time you have left in more meaningful ways. I'm afraid I must go now.'

'So soon! I was looking forward to a little chat. Ever since I stopped you outside the hospital that rainy day, all I've wanted was to spend some more time with you. To get to know you even better.'

'You don't know me at all, Gossett. And that's one of the things I never fully understood. How did you recognise me? That day in the rain when I came out of the hospital, how did you know it was me? You knew of me, from everything you had learned about the investigation from Simon Morgenthal's fiancée who was feeding you the information, but we had never met. You didn't know what I looked like, so how did you know to approach me?'

'Oh, but, Dr Cuthbert, we did meet before, and I have to say I'm a little saddened that you don't remember. They were difficult circumstances, I grant you. Not the most auspicious start to a relationship. But, yes, we met, and you set my leg. I was that second lieutenant in the trench. I got stung by some shrapnel, and you put me over your shoulder. Quite the hero, I must say. Got my limp because of you, but I also got my life, so the very least I can do is thank you.

'I've thought of you often over the years. I'll never forget the way you looked at me in the dugout when you had me on the table. Before you gave me the morphine, I was already getting woozy, I can tell you. You were so big, so powerful and so completely overwhelming. I would have done anything you wanted. You said we had to work together, and I thought, yes, let's do just that. I don't remember much about the next days. Ended up back at the Clearing Station, and then I was shipped back to Southampton. I was over almost before I'd started. Not much of a war, but I did get to meet you, Jack.'

As Gossett was speaking, Cuthbert was reliving that night. He began to sweat as the noise started to fill his head again and the smell of the trench his nostrils. And to make it all worse, he realised that if he had not reacted as he did, if he had simply left that second lieutenant on the floor of the trench to bleed out and die, Dawson and Galton would still be alive.

He also began to see that if it had not been for Gossett, he might not have been transferred to the A.D.S and in all probability might not have made it back home alive. In some twisted form of fate, he probably owed his life to this man.

'Of course, I already knew all about the murders, for obvious reasons, but it was such a delight to watch you and that plodder Mowbray work it all out. But, *entre nous*, we both know, it was really you who solved it. As soon as I found out it was you on the case, I think I hoped that you would. I so much wanted to see you again, to see what you had become after all these years. When I saw you walk out of the hospital, I swear you took my breath away. You were even more striking than I remembered. I'm really not sure you know just how magnificent a man you are, Jack. I can call you that, can't I? I mean, we've been through so much together, you and I.'

Cuthbert's nostrils were beginning to flare, and he was breathing heavily. Beneath the table, his fingers dug deep into his thighs as he tried to control his rage. He knew he wanted to silence Gossett. But the obvious anger rising within him was doing nothing except further exciting Gossett and encouraging him on.

'I think we are alike, you and I. Yes, I would go so far as to say we might even be soulmates. I think I knew from the start, from that night in the dugout. We know, don't we? We know when we find each other. I think we could be happy together, you and I. Once you admit it to yourself, that is. Of course, I can help you with that, Jack. Would you like me to help you? I could help you now. I could take away the pain. I'm very good at taking away pain.'

Cuthbert unclenched his hands and felt his breathing slow and return to normal. He remembered where he was and what he was doing there. He looked at Gossett, who now appeared so much smaller and less significant than at any time in the past. Here was a man who, in twenty-four hours, would be dead at the end of a rope in a room not far away from this one.

Cuthbert simply rose from his seat without answering Gossett and indicated to the gaoler that he was done.

*

The next day, Mowbray's team were standing in silence as they watched the minute hand click over and the duty room clock chimed the hour. It was exactly nine o'clock in the morning, and on the other side of London, Gossett had just been dropped the carefully calculated seven feet and two inches required to break the neck of a man his weight.

His dangling, trussed and hooded body would still be twitching, and a stream of urine would be staining his trousers. His heart would continue beating for a couple of minutes, although his pulse would quickly weaken. He would be left hanging for an hour before being taken down, undressed, washed and prepared for the formal autopsy in the adjacent room.

The chief inspector assembled his team and included Cuthbert so that he could hear what he had to say.

'That's it done, men. The final act of something that began on a December night just over twelve months ago. Freddie Dawson was an innocent lad who didn't deserve to die. William Galton, we learned, was probably a cruel, sadistic man, but even he didn't deserve to die the way he did either.

'Your hard work brought their killer to justice, and moments ago he paid for his crimes with his life. The world is a considerably better place without the likes of Julius Gossett in it, and it was you who got rid of him. So give yourselves a pat on the back, have a drink on me tonight and then get back to work because, unfortunately, there are more Gossetts out there, and we need to be their worst enemy.'

As the meeting broke up, two of the newer constables were discussing the case at the duty-room reception desk.

'Who is Cuthbert anyway?' one asked.

'Oh,' said the other, 'he's a big Scotch doctor.'

Mowbray had overheard and suddenly came up behind them. From a distance, Cuthbert watched them both stiffen in fear of what the Pie might say.

'No, son. Dr Cuthbert is a big Scottish doctor or, if you prefer, a big Scotsman, but I think you will find that a big Scotch is a double whisky. Which, by a strange coincidence, is what I'm about to have with the gentleman in question.'

He looked across at Cuthbert and gave a faint smile and the merest of nods. It was all that was needed, and Cuthbert returned the gesture before joining him in his office.

'Here's to a successful outcome, chief inspector.'

'Indeed, Cuthbert. And here's to the end of this decade. What do they call it in the picture houses – "the Roaring Twenties"? I haven't seen much roaring on my patch, and I'll be glad to see the back of it.'

They clinked glasses, and after they had shared a drink, Cuthbert left to go back to the hospital. There, he went straight to his office and relaxed for the first time in weeks. He sat down and unlaced his boots.

He opened his bottom desk drawer and took out his box. After he had prepared the tin of polish and the cloth, he also took out an envelope that was tucked in the inside lid. From this he removed a small sepia photograph. The young man in khaki was standing tall as he always did.

'Well, Troy, still the conquering hero. Another one over, and it was harder than usual. So much of the past this time, old man.'

He stroked the image in the photograph the way he had done a thousand times before.

'But that's just it, isn't it, Joe? You'll never be an old man. Looks like I'll have to do that for both of us too. You rest now. You rest.'

*

He wrapped the soft cloth over his index finger and dipped it into the polish and started making small swirling motions on the toe cap of his boot. As soon as he began, he was overcome with a silence barely interrupted by birdsong on a late summer's day. Now, there were no shells, no bullets, no mire. There was just a silence that started to fill with thoughts of a life he had longed for, but which would remain forever unlived.

Author's Note

While this is a work of fiction, set in a past that is now mostly beyond living memory, I have made every effort to recreate a world for the characters to inhabit that is as accurate as possible. To this end, I owe a great debt of gratitude to those witnesses who have left behind vivid accounts of their lives through the primary sources of their letters, reports and oral histories. They tell what it was like to be a medical student in Edinburgh at the start of the twentieth century, to be a young infantry man on the Western Front during the First World War, to work with the Royal Army Medical Corps in the chain of evacuation during that conflict, to return home from the war on leave, to train in forensic medicine, and to work with Scotland Yard in the 1920s.

Although my characters are invented, they are animated by hard facts, and the circumstances they find themselves in are as plausible as I have been able to make them. Nevertheless, I have doubtless taken some liberties with history, and my only defence is that I have not done so consciously.

Specifically, I would like to acknowledge the following:

John Glaister's 1915 third edition of his *A Text-book of Medical Jurisprudence and Toxicology*.

The Imperial War Museum, for making its extensive archives of personal histories of the First World War freely available online.

The Royal Army Medical Corps (R.A.M.C.), for the history sections in its online collections which provided essential details.

Luci Gosling, who has written engagingly about the history of station buffets in World War One.

Eileen Crofton, for her invaluable 1997 article in the *Proceedings of the Royal College of Physicians of Edinburgh* on the experiences of University of Edinburgh Medical Students during the First World War.

Reza Negarestani, for his insightful 2008 article 'The Corpse Bride', in which he outlines the history and philosophical significance of the murder method used in this work.

Sir Sydney Smith, whose memoir *Mostly Murder*, published in 1959, is a vivid and engaging account of his life in forensic medicine.

Jessica Meyer, whose 2019 book *An Equal Burden* explores in great detail the roles of the men of the R.A.M.C. during the First World War.

Jack Dorgon, Adam Collins, Hawtin Mundy, Charles Quinnell, Emily Rumbold, J. Reid, Clifford Lane, Fred Dixon, Thomas Baker, Walter Hare, Walter Spencer, Arthur Dease, Arthur A. Martin, Philip Gosse, Noel Garrod, Clifford Lane, Ruby Ord, William Chapman and Basil Farrer, all of whom served in the First World War and left their testimonies behind.

THE DR JACK CUTHBERT
MYSTERY SERIES

BOOK 1 *The Silent House of Sleep* (January 2025)

Death is a lonely business . . .

No one who meets Dr Jack Cuthbert forgets him. Tall, urbane, brilliant but damaged, the Scottish pathologist is the best that D.C.I. Mowbray of Scotland Yard has seen. But Cuthbert is a man who lives with secrets, and he is still haunted by demons from the trenches in Ypres. When not one but two corpses are discovered in a London park in 1929, Cuthbert must use every tool at his disposal to solve the mystery of their deaths. In the end, the horrifying truth is more shocking than even he could have imagined.

BOOK 2 *The Moon's More Feeble Fire* (spring 2025)

She was someone's daughter . . .

In 1930, the killing of a Soho prostitute is hardly a priority for Scotland Yard. But when a second, similar murder comes to light, and then a third, everything changes. Cuthbert and his team find themselves in a nightmarish world of people-trafficking, prostitution and drug use amongst the upper classes. Using all his forensic skills, Cuthbert sets out to solve one of the most baffling cases of his career. One final question remains unanswered until a faded photograph reveals its tragic secret.

BOOK 3   *To the Shades Descend* (summer 2025)

Giving them back their names is one thing; giving them justice is quite another.

A visit to Glasgow for a job interview in 1931 unexpectedly places Cuthbert at the centre of a devastating crime. Unwittingly, he finds himself working at the intersection between rising British fascism, anti-Semitism and the infamous Glasgow razor gangs. To solve the case, Cuthbert needs to rely on all the expertise he can gather from those around him. But who can he trust?

BOOK 4   *The Shadows and the Dust* (autumn 2025)

You may call it a sin; I say it was an act of desperation.

Like all pathologists, Cuthbert finds dealing with dead children the hardest part of his job. However, when the body of a young boy is found in the grounds of a church orphanage, Cuthbert not only has to steel himself for the task ahead, he is also forced to revisit his own childhood grief. The boy in his shallow grave has been interred with some ritual, but just how did he die? And why was he killed? Working closely with his assistant and the team at Scotland Yard, Cuthbert slowly and painstakingly reveals the terrible truth.

Acknowledgements

A lot of people helped and encouraged me to publish this work. In particular, I want to thank my earliest readers: Ellen, Anne, Fiona, Valerie, Alex, S.J., Stephen and Alec as well as my many friends at Strathkelvin Writers' Group and beyond. Without their belief, and their almost constant nagging, the novel would likely have remained a half-forgotten file on my hard drive. But Jack Cuthbert always deserved better than that.

Special thanks must also go to the team at my publisher, Polygon, and especially my remarkable editor there, Alison Rae. She has championed the publication of this book, and without her hard work, I am sure you would not be reading it now.

Finally, I want to thank the one person who has made this and everything else I have done possible, my wife Moira.